Tracer, Inc.

A Mystery
Introducing the Tracer Family

Jeff Andrus

CHARLES SCRIBNER'S SONS
New York London Toronto Sydney Tokyo Singapore

CHARLES SCRIBNER'S SONS
Rockefeller Center
1230 Avenue of the Americas
New York, NY 10020

SCRIBNERS and design are registered trademarks of Macmillan, Inc.

Designed by Songhee Kim

Manufactured in the United States of America

1 3 5 7 9 10 8 6 4 2

Library of Congress Cataloging-in-Publication Data

Andrus, Jeff.
Tracer, Inc. / Jeff Andrus
p. cm..
1. Family—California—Fiction. I. Title. II. Title: Tracer, Incorporated.
PS3551.N4564T73 1994
813'54—dc20 94–21115
CIP

ISBN 0-684-19705-7

Tracer, Inc.

They ran out of the darkness, a man pulling a girl by the hand. They paused in light cast by sodium vapor yellowing an intersection of an access road and a four-lane divided highway. A sign to the on ramp indicated that US 101 stretched six more miles before it bypassed San Lucas and 289 when it finally dumped into LA.

The man's free hand cupped a bulge of weight stuffed under his windbreaker. He was in his early twenties, a few pimples yet, hair stringy with sweat and grime. "A male caucasian," the sheriff's deputies might say.

Because the light jaundiced her features, it was hard to tell whether the girl was old enough to be a teenager. Possibly she was Mexican. "Please. Let me rest."

Her answer was a yank.

Their labored breathing and the pad of their running feet moved down the access road into the darkness. Intermittent headlights and the sound of light traffic ricocheted from the highway embankment. On the other side of the access road a field of row crops stretched into the night; beyond loomed the black shapes of mountains.

About a hundred yards from the intersection the man and the girl took shape again. He veered suddenly and pulled her toward the brightness.

The sign for the Wild Horse Cafe & Truck Stop stood high above them as they dashed across an expanse of decomposed granite. The sign overlooked three long cement aprons bearing diesel pumps. A bordering coffee and souvenir shop were lit, but most of the lights were out in the adjacent motel. Two rows of hulking metal—tractors and their semi-rigs—were parked back-to-back in the fueling yard. Gravel crunched as the man led the girl between the trucks.

She staggered after him while he tested the locks of loading doors. He skipped a refer unit and a bottom dumper. Suddenly he crouched down behind the rear mud guard of an eighteen-wheeler, one of the dirtiest trucks in the yard. Pitted chrome silhouettes of reclining nude women glinted through the grime on both mud guards. The driver was heaving his weight out of the cab. He was big, very big, and very sloppy-looking, the kind of guy who would crush you very dead if he accidentally sat on you.

The man held a warning finger to his lips, but the girl, bent over to regain her wind, was paying as little attention to the driver as he was to them. The man watched the driver waddle quickly toward the coffee shop. His head tilted back to take in the company logo emblazoned across the trailer door—SoCalXpress. The bolt was padlocked, but the lock's closing pin dangled free. The man levered the bolt, and the door rolled upward. He vaulted inside the trailer, then reached for the girl.

She shook her head in weak defiance. He grabbed her shoulder and jerked hard. Her arm flew upward as she grappled his forearm to maintain balance.

Crude tattoos were penned over three knuckles of her hand. Three numbers. Two smeary letters—"KC"—stained the flesh between her thumb and first finger. The skin around each knuckle whitened, and she winced as she stumbled to regain her footing on the bed of the trailer.

They let go of each other. A grin cut his mouth into a mechanical, "Have-A-Nice-Day" smile. He yanked the door closed.

Soon the door moved again. This time the whole truck with it, rolling into the darkness.

Dawn broke as the truck sped past oak-dotted hillsides. Within an hour the truck encountered light freeway traffic. There was nothing remarkable about the eighteen-wheeler. The logo wouldn't win any graphics prizes, and the chrome nudes on the mud guards were manufactured with hundreds of others just like them every single day of the year. The driver was as memorable as Baby Huey, but there were no residents to spot him when he turned off into an industrial area, and workers had yet to arrive at the warehouses and manufacturing plants. The truck rolled to a stop at the rear of a low-slung, prefab building that covered a couple of football fields' worth of square feet.

The driver wheezed out of the cab, hitched up his jeans and lumbered to the rear of the trailer. The padlock was missing, but he had trouble remembering whether he had actually bothered with one for this run. Anyway, he figured, anybody who wanted to steal sixteen tons of zinc ingots was welcome to them. He tiredly threw the door partially open and squinted into the shadowy interior.

"What the—"

He didn't get a chance to finish because a .22 pistol poked into the sunlight. To the driver, stepping delicately backwards, the muzzle of the tiny gun looked as big as a dice cup. It was followed by a face that split into a Smile Button grin.

2

The Saturday night when the girl was taken hitch-hiking, Hartnell Community College of Salinas and Monterey Peninsula Community College were taking a long time to settle a rivalry that went back more than sixty years. Penalties and injuries pushed the clock toward 10:15; the fourth quarter was only half over; and the game was tied. Then a pass play exploded. The hometown crowd went wild as a Hartnell Panther rushed toward the end zone. Children swarmed across the track and formed an impromptu welcoming committee.

John Tracer trotted across the grass at the end of the field to head the kids off. Arms spread wide, he stood nearly 6'2". His reddening face hadn't yet registered all the lines of middle age; but in any given season he settled for weighing twenty to thirty pounds more than insurance actuary tables calculated as ideal because who in his right mind wanted to live a long life in a world where every victory hurt? He wore the padded blue jacket of the Salinas Police Department. Tracer was an auxiliary officer—not exactly a career track in law enforcement—but being a rent-a-cop meant he had a job. Like any other working stiff, Tracer wished he were someplace else. "C'm'on," he shouted, "the field's for football, the stands are for watching! How many times do I have to tell you?"

Most of the children skulked back, but two boys stood their ground. Tracer kept advancing.

"Don't you have parents you have to answer to?"

One of the adolescents flipped him off.

"What's that, your IQ? Get out of here before I shoot you."

"With what? Your walkie-talkie?"

Tracer roared and ran at the kid, whose eyes saucered wide. The boy whirled and, seeing the other boy already running hard, churned his little legs as fast as he could to catch up.

A full-time, fully-armed sergeant watched his auxiliary officer lose ground in the chase, either from giving up or getting winded. "John!" he yelled.

Tracer veered toward his boss and tried to read the sergeant's features.

"What are you doing?"

Tracer thought that what he had been doing was running. Running without a breather from being blindsided by his fortieth birthday, and all too soon it felt like he was about to wade into a gang tackle called forty-five. He thought that he had never wanted an RV with "John & Chris Welcome You" lettered on the door; would have preferred a condo in Hawaii, a trip to Rome, money in a Swiss bank, a full professorship at his alma mater with eager coeds hanging on his every word, a statue in the Capitol. But lately, the idea of swapping shock over the high price of butane with Lamar from Dubuque at the sewage drop-off station in some national park was beginning to sound good. An RV would at least prove he was substantial, Tracer thought. What he said was, "Crowd control."

"You call running down kids crowd control?"

"I call it doing crap for minimum wage."

"You're the one trying to make 6,000 practical hours. No one forced you to hire on part-time with us. But now that you're here, our job is to serve and protect the public."

"No fun in that."

"You want fun? Then go back to serving subpoenas for shysters. I don't need you scaring the bejesus out of people."

Tracer seemed to drop his guard and look contrite. "He called your mother a dirty name. I went crazy. Sorry."

Tracer ambled off, leaving the sergeant briefly flummoxed. "Why?"

Tracer turned with a puzzled look.

"Wha'd you make before? Forty grand a year? What are you doin' out here? I mean, really."

"Marching to a different drum."

"What the hell does that mean?"

"Waiting for my examination results."

"The State would have to be crazy to give you a PI license."

"It's a gift, isn't it? The way you're so encouraging."

"I like you better than you think. You'd be crazy to take a license. Sheesh. License for trouble."

About twenty-five yards ahead of Tracer, a boy and a girl walked along the track, away from a snack bar where Swiss sausages sizzled on a barbecue pit attached to a pickup. The girl was a thirteen-year-old orbiting puberty. Her name was Shorty; no apparent reason, just a nickname that stuck. She

couldn't lose her younger brother, either. Age ten, Brad was
all elbows and knees and wild schemes, and like the rest of
her family, a total embarrassment to Shorty. Nothing personal. Just their proximity.

The law waylaid them. "Wrong way," Tracer said. "The
home stands are back there."

"I'm just walking because I'm cold," grumbled Shorty.
"Tell him to find his own friends."

Brad frowned. Sneaking him a wink, Tracer took off his
padded jacket and draped it around the girl's shoulders. In
spite of herself, Shorty enjoyed the attention.

"It's a man's job to look after a lady," Tracer said to the boy.

"Don't encourage him," Shorty said.

"Where's Mom?"

Without answering, Shorty bolted. "Gloria!"

Momentarily confused, Tracer turned to see Shorty running toward a babyfat friend. He looked at his son.

"Mom?"

Brad pointed back to the snack bar. "Not having a good
time."

Tracer saw Christine warming her hands over the barbecue fire. The average ambient temperature difference between night and day in the Salinas Valley was thirty-five
degrees, so even the balmiest day of Indian Summer could
turn into a cold fall night. While Chris appeared cuddly
enough to warm any night, what turned men's heads were
qualities you couldn't put your finger on at first—no non-
sense in the eyes and a loyal heart with a quirky appreciation
for disloyalty. What knotted Tracer's gut was that she
seemed to be having a good time chatting to Eddie Durand,
Gloria's father, a slick community booster playing the hearty
chef.

"I asked for a Coke . . . ," Brad was saying.

Tracer brought his son into immediate focus.

". . . but Mom said we can't afford it."

"Naw." Tracer picked Brad up. "But when you get a free pass to the game . . ." He dropped Brad on his shoulders and started walking toward Chris. ". . . how much fun can you stand? You'd just rot your teeth out with all that sugar."

Tracer rolled his gaze upward, wondering how that went down, and then looked pensively toward his wife.

Chris noticed him, but she wanted him to notice her smiling at Durand. Eddie glanced at Tracer approaching, then shook his head in sympathy for Chris.

"He's not going to give up, is he?"

"He thinks he passed the exam. Two years of working for a boyhood dream is a long time to give up."

"Boyhood dream? I got the idea it's a mid-life crisis."

"I didn't say that."

"We're all friends here. I know it's been rough for you. What you need is to feel like you're in charge of your own life. I've been thinking—I mean, I can't pay much, you already know that—but there's an opening in my office. Permanent this time. With benefits."

"Benefits?"

"Great benefits."

Chris blushed. Before she had to answer, Durand abruptly thrust out his hand to shake her husband's.

"Hey, Sherlock, I was just asking the little lady if she wanted to come and put my business back on track."

Tracer plucked a sausage off of Durand's turning fork and mimicked the familiarity. "Little lady?" His eyes flicked toward his wife. "Wha'd you say?"

Chris had been saying it various ways for three years, and on Monday afternoon, walking across what was left of her dining room, she said it again with the classified section of *The Salinas Californian.*

"College degree required, experienced preferred."

Her husband sat in the living room's only chair, dialing the phone. It was an old black rotary-dial phone with an extension cord that could snake across the threadbare carpet to the kitchen, into the family room or halfway up the stairs. The living room was devoid of other furniture, and the only thing of value in the echoing house was a massive antique sideboard behind Chris.

"But they really want someone who's willing to be trained."

"He just wants you to bend down and put files in low drawers."

"I'm not talking about Eddie."

"Good. 'Cause I'm the only one who can look up your skirt."

He slipped his hand up her dress. She stepped back.

"I'm talking about you as an administrative assistant."

He rattled off, "Too old, too young, too qualified, not enough experience. Too bad you're not black, not Latino, not Asian. But how would you like to help us sell another billion burgers in Braindead, Arkansas?"

"John, I know it hasn't been easy. And no one likes rejection, but you weren't singled out. Vulcan had to lay off everyone."

"Shh." He spoke into the phone. "Mr. Matron? John Tracer here."

"One thousand two hundred people have had to go through the same things you have," Chris continued in an urgent whisper. "Some of them have found good jobs. It just takes time."

He put his hand over the mouthpiece. "Why don't you go run a bath? We'll play submarine."

She frowned with exasperation, but he kept his hand over the mouthpiece, beetling his eyebrows a la Groucho Marx, so she was forced to answer, "The kids will be home any minute."

"Yeah," he said into the phone, "that's right. The gate leg table. Well, when you were here for the table, you said how . . . 'marvelous,' is what you said . . . how marvelous that antique sideboard looks."

Chris threw a panicked look toward the dining room. "You can't sell that!"

"Just a sec." Tracer clamped the phone to his chest and spoke calmly to his wife. "We've decided to do whatever it takes."

"It's been in my family for *three generations!*"

Three generations to a Californian was like landing with the Mayflower to a New Englander. Chris's ancestral roots went even deeper into the Golden State's history, back to the Spanish explorers on her mother's side. Genetically it was a watered-down claim to superiority, but socially it put one firmly in the old guard of a state known for attracting more than its share of huddled and howling masses. Tracer's native-born status might have put him in the old guard, too, but Tracer's people came to California only in 1931—newcomers compared to Chris's family. Coming from Montana, they weren't out of *The Grapes of Wrath*, but given the circumstances of the Great Depression, with militia on the borders turning back job seekers from every state, not just Okies, they made Chris's Land Grant family look like absolute royalty. The three-generation crack was subtle, but it hit a sore spot. Tracer avoided acknowledgment . . . if you're not to the manor born, what can you say? . . . pulling a spiral notebook from between his thigh and the armrest of the chair.

"I need to attract clients, huh?" He waved the notebook, encouraging her to look at what he'd been doodling on it. "Huh?"

Chris worried her brow at a so-so rectangle containing a printed scrawl: "Tracer, Inc. Discrete Inquiries. Phone Number here." She gave him a dumbfounded look.

Enthusiastically he explained, "That's a business card *and* a space ad. Nothing more, just that. Huh?"

"You're going to sell my heritage for . . . for *business cards?*"

"We have bills, too. When we had to buy groceries that time, you didn't talk about the table like it was the Rosetta Stone."

"Because it was only a stupid wedding present!" Chris swatted him with the notebook, then dropping it, fled toward the hall.

He craned a look over his shoulder to see her running up the stairs sobbing. A dog began barking upstairs. Tracer cleared his throat before speaking into the phone.

"Uh, anyway, I was wondering whether you'd like to come out and make an offer on the sideboard. " After listening a moment, he said, "End of the week? Business is that good, huh?" Tracer put some laughter behind the little joke and frowned when the speaker didn't seem to get it. He hung up with a "Sure, okay, next Saturday morning."

With growing guilt, he picked up the notebook and looked at it. He'd just have to convince the printer to bill him. Advertising as a detective was a far cry from being Director of Personnel for Vulcan Tire & Rubber Company, but the guilt felt better than the helpless anger and gut-wrenching fear that had attended his first year of unemployment. He'd applied for jobs at 242 companies, interviewed at seventy-seven and listened to every excuse in the book to put his resume on file "for future consideration." He'd considered a future with Amway, a future with Nu Skin, a future that felt more and more like it would shape up to be one long Tupperware Party in hell.

Finally he decided it wasn't supposed to be that way for a Stanford grad who'd already been bored nearly senseless climbing Vulcan's management ladder. Marriage and mortgages kept him on it until the economy disintegrated the rungs. The book on Vietnam vets would have had him slobbering off Hoover Tower with a deer rifle and a sniper scope, but Tracer also decided that a decorated officer and gentleman had a right to go nuts any way he chose, and right now he was following through on the boyhood dream. Too bad Chris didn't understand like Brad did.

It wasn't as if Tracer had been sitting on his duff, either. For the past two years he'd been going to night school and juggling part-time jobs to get the practical hours for his private investigator's license; and, yeah, okay, he'd been feeling sorry for himself, watching the hair in his ears grow faster than anywhere else.

Frowning, he got up from the chair and moved into the hall. As he started up the stairs, a whirlwind of mongrel shag came barking onto the mid-landing.

"Stop."

It did.

"Don't even think it."

But it did. Tracer caught the leaping dog, nearly stumbling backwards as it licked his face. He tossed the animal aside. With a yelp it skidded into a corner, then cocked its head, puzzled. "You're lucky I'm not Jack Palance in the opening scene of *Shane*." Wiping his face, he started again upstairs.

Slinking after him, the dog followed Tracer's march down the hall, then stopped indecisively before he entered the largest bedroom.

In the master bathroom, Chris was splashing cold water on her face. She caught John's reflection in the mirror as he angled toward her past their bed. It was a soft sanctuary of eiderdown quilt piled with pillows. She watched him reach the doorway, his features sheepish with apology. She felt like a fool for crying, for their financial problems that kept them in the same senseless circle of her blaming him and his having to apologize. Even though she was furious at the sacrifices she always seemed to have to make for his sake, her heart did go out to him. She just didn't want him to know it right now, partly because, damn it, she was right, and partly because it might lead to another kind of circling dance in their relationship, equally senseless because it was three o'clock in the afternoon; and she felt more the fool knowing she was desperate for passionate comfort.

"Upset?" he asked.

Chris let out a snort of air, as if to say that was the stupidest thing she had ever heard, and snatched a towel to dry her face.

The dog braved entry into the bedroom, quietly dropping to its belly to watch superior beings.

"Look," Tracer said, "I know you're an old-fashioned gal who hired on for a cottage with a white picket fence overlooking the sea."

"I don't care about overlooking the sea. I do care about tottering on a third mortgage."

"I know, I know. This temp sec business must feel like a permanent career by now."

"I've never complained about working. I just don't want Shorty and Brad to become latch-key kids."

"Exactly." He paused. "Which is why we're selling the sideboard. So you don't have to take a full-time job with Eddie. Unless you want to."

"Part-time was bad enough." She moved into the bedroom. "What's wrong with *you* taking a full-time job?"

"Finding clients is a full-time job. Get out of here!"

The dog gave a start, rising to its haunches, and nervously watched Tracer turn to his mate.

Chris said, "You don't even have a license yet."

Tenderly, he held her shoulders. "Honey, you gotta face the fact that this is my career. Look at all the criminology and jurisprudence classes I took."

"Why can't you study TV repair?"

"The study part's over. The license is coming. I know it. There's a client out there. Someplace. I know it. And where there's one, there's more. Because this is it. I'm it. For better or for worse."

"I didn't marry Sam Spade."

"And I didn't marry a temp sec. But I like it when you bend over, and you're kind of cute when you're angry." He quickly cocked an elbow and ducked his head under as if expecting to be punched.

"Oh, Jeez," she said, but she was holding back a laugh. Resistance down, she allowed him to slip his arms around her and draw her closer.

"Now," he said, "tell me you don't think I'm as cute as I was at the Junior Prom when they played 'The Twelfth Of Never' and you got all gooey-eyed dancing close."

"You're the one who got flustered." But once again she felt her breath catching.

Watching them kiss, the dog began to bark.

"Get out of here!"

The dog settled into a whimper and walked in fast circles, totally forgotten, as the humans found the bed, grappling and grasping and peeling off clothing. In the midst of it, Chris tried to steel herself for a final gamble.

"You have to agree to something."

"Name it," Tracer said quickly.

"A time period."

"You want it slow, you want it fast—you got it, babe."

The dog stopped skittering around the room as she pulled away and held her husband off.

"I mean this detective business. It has to work. No license: it didn't work. No clients: it didn't work. And you have to find other work if it doesn't work."

He tried to kiss her.

"No, I mean it."

"What do you take me for? This whole struggle's been so that I can finally provide for you again."

"Promise," she insisted.

Outside, a Spreckles School bus was chugging down a street that wound past the ranch style homes of Creekside Estates. It stopped at a corner, and Shorty and Brad were among the children who got off.

After small talk and good-byes, they peeled away from the other neighborhood kids, walked passed Mr. Riley's "Jungle House" and came to a rusting, wrought-iron mailbox with tarnished letters that spelled "Tracer." From inside their house they could hear muffled howls coming from Dog. "Dog" was the dog's name because neither Shorty nor Brad would cave in to the other on Bingo or Fang. Shorty opened the mailbox while Brad started across a lawn that he was supposed to mow and whose high grass was mined with his skateboard and an arsenal of toy guns.

As she sorted through the mail, Shorty's breath suddenly caught. Without thinking, she opened an envelope as if it were her own report card. "Oh, my God!"

Brad whirled, the surprise in his face blooming into joy as he looked at the seal of the Department of Consumer Affairs,

State of California, the bureaucracy that gave barbers, chiropractors and private eyes their bonafides. "He got it!" Brad yelled.

A muted bellow came from the house: "Go on! Off!"

Shorty exchanged a glance with her brother. Together they looked toward the upper window where California's newest private investigator could be heard yelling, "Get off the bed or I'll kill you!"

Brad proclaimed happily, "Now he just has to get a permit so he can carry a gun!"

John and Chris heard Brad pounding upstairs, shouting, "Dad! Dad! You got it!" with Shorty right behind screaming, "Gimme that! I saw it first!"

Tracer forgot that Dog was trying to nuzzle its head into his armpit as his wife's whole body froze. "Did you lock the door?" she whispered in horror.

They rolled in opposite directions, each desperately trying to take the quilt. As Chris dropped beside the bed, grabbing for pillows and wondering whether she had time to dive back in, Tracer stumbled for the door. It was partially open, and he got behind it just as his son hit the threshold.

Chris had read plenty of child psychology books. She knew she was supposed to act natural. She knew that her children knew about biological reproduction, social responsibility and God's ordaining Man and Woman to enjoy their marriage bed. But, "Don't come in!" sounded like something unholy was going on.

Brad and Shorty looked up at their father, whose red face and naked shoulders appeared behind the door. Lower down, Dog's tail wagged.

"Sure hot out, isn't it? Dog needs to be taken for a walk. Your mother and I— A nice run on the highway maybe. We were just taking a shower."

Brad's anxious eyes couldn't see nipples but picked up quite a bit of his mother's cleavage and the crease where thighs met hips. Mortified, he handed his father the envelope.

Shorty looked accusingly at their mother. "He got the license."

"That's wonderful, honey." Crouching, Chris hugged herself more tightly into a pillow. She watched her husband grab for the envelope, then for the door, then for Dog's ear, and pulling the animal away from trying to sniff his privates, he propelled it toward the children. Amazing, Chris thought. He still has an erection.

Tracer slammed the door. This moment of licensing wasn't at all what he had imagined. The bless-you-my-son from officialdom was supposed to approach the first time he held and set eyes on his firstborn. Now *that* had been magic.

After eighteen hours of labor, the obstetrician decreed that Chris would need a caesarian section; and thus Tracer was absolved from having to stick out the Lamaze Method of natural childbirth to an unseemly end that promised to have Mr. Farwell, Chris's father, hovering in the delivery room with a Super 8 movie camera and absolutely no shame about showing the birth film to everyone. If life had followed its natural course, Chris's mother would have butted in on Tracer's coaching while Tracer's own mom, a widow holed up in the Sierras with his sister, would goad her: "Just keep calling the hospital and tell them you're a physician. You have a *right* to know about my grandchild!" But it was his brother in Fullerton who was the physician. Meanwhile Uncle Mike, his father's brother, would have continued his vigil on the homefront and possibly succeeded in picking up the buxom hospital auxiliary volunteer working in the gift shop of Salinas Valley Memorial. But with Chris under the knife, it was with unbounded relief that Tracer was able to preempt Uncle Mike, avoid long distance phone calls, duck away from Chris's mother and dive into a masculine haven across the street. The Oasis Bar & Grill.

For a brief time in the stormy relationship between the two families, there was at least some male bonding. Tracer called Mr. Farwell "Dad" once or twice. Dad had managed to say "Son." Uncle Mike remembered each of his ex-wives fondly, and Tracer even got all of his aunts' names in chronological order. They returned like The Three Musketeers. A disapproving nurse pressed a newborn swaddled in blankets into Tracer's arms.

"A girl," she said.

But Tracer didn't see a girl. He saw puffy eyes in a small red wet face, a delicate fist worming its way up from the blanket into the infant's cheek. Life! So fragile. He pitied his daughter's helplessness, felt awe that he was meant to protect her, knew joy that couldn't be touched by words and had never been so grateful to be alive.

"She's beautiful," said Mr. Farwell in a hushed voice.

Uncle Mike's rough finger gently prodded the tiny hand. "On the short side, but she's gonna be a heartbreaker. Too bad your pop's not here."

Tracer fought the tears in his eyes. "Yeah."

Holding Brad for the first time of course was also wonderful, but it couldn't come close to that moment with Shorty thirteen years ago. And today, only seconds ago, that same girl had looked at her father like he was some kind of brute rapist. Now her mother was convulsed with laughter.

Tracer turned with the license. "Don't we have any champagne?"

"Not unless you get a client. We can't afford it."

3

The following Saturday morning, Anne Walker opened her Mercedes convertible to the sun. Except during October, sunlight was rare in Carmel-by-the-Sea, a town populated by people who had chosen to live there and frequented by tourists who had to live other places. When the tourists came in spring and summer, the air was usually misty with fog or the sky gray with high clouds. But whatever the weather, visitors were seldom disappointed by Carmel's sights or its citizens, an impressive number of whom looked like they just stepped out of the club house, the tanning bed or the health spa. Carmelites included savvy real estate developers turned environmentalists; distinguished-looking military men retired at high rank and pension; a few famous actors on the lam from Hollywood's tinsel but still within an hour's flying time of it; artists, both rich and half-starved, whose works filled Carmel's many galleries; lawyers, lots and lots of lawyers; and thin beauties who appeared tailored to hang on to the arms of men with fat wallets. Carmel's wealthy ranged from the very conservative to the very laid-back and Rolfed, but politically they had all agreed to make it impossible to do three things within their city limits—cut down a tree, put up a parking lot and build a McDonald's.

With sunlight playing on her blond hair, Anne Walker scooted up Ocean Avenue, away from the beach, past cypress and tall pine, expensive eateries and quaint, half-timbered shops. She was a woman in her early thirties who looked as fresh as a baby, a very pretty baby, and she took the only available parking space in front of El Camino Drug Store as if she deserved it.

Anne stepped purposefully to the magazine racks flanking the store's sidewalk alcove. The racks displayed *Vanity Fair* and the Paris edition of *Vogue*. She concentrated on northern California newspapers, plucking out two dailies from San Francisco, the *Tribune* from Oakland, two dailies from Sacramento and two covering the central coast region closer to home: the *Salinas Californian* and the *Monterey Peninsula Herald*.

When Anne Walker plopped the papers on the counter near the pharmacist's register, she didn't give him more than a cursory look. She rifled her purse for two bills. With only a glance at the papers, he was already ringing up $1.50 as if they had done this before. But this time he couldn't take her money without comment.

"Do you mind if I ask why, Miss Walker?"

Her cool features broke with a start, but she recovered almost immediately.

"Three days now," he added.

Her voice laughed over the words: "Oh, you know Dick. He's so modest. When someone interviews him, he can't remember who, when, where . . . or which paper."

"I'll keep an eye out," said the pharmacist.

She scooped up her purchase and turned away.

"Your change!" he called out.

She didn't turn back.

The pharmacist pocketed the two coins, wondering whether fifty cents was worth anyone's thoughts, even in preoccupied Carmel.

A man named Reuben Bustamonte looked at Anne's newspapers. They lay on the passenger's bucket seat of her empty car. Bustamonte's eyes prowled from the newspapers to the flag and blue mailbox in front of the post office where the Mercedes convertible was parked. Bustamonte wore his hair in a razor-cut pompadour. A skin-tight black tank top showed off his muscles and an intricate shoulder tattoo of roses. His baggy pants had more pleats than a kilt. If Anne had noticed him, she would not have recognized him, but she would have known at a glance that Reuben Bustamonte was not listed in the Carmel Social Register.

Inside the Post Office, Bustamonte approached Anne with the slow ease of thick grease. She stood on tiptoes before a wall of brass boxes peering anxiously into one whose antique scroll work numbered the window 1143. No mail could be seen behind the glass; however, a letter could have been pressed flush to the wall, so Anne hastily fiddled with the combination. As she thrust her hand inside the box, Bustamonte passed behind her, close enough to draw static from her skirt. But Anne felt only that the box was empty.

When Anne Walker returned to her apartment, she tore open the newspapers to their respective classified sections. She spread them on the chrome and glass table in the dining nook. Light from outside flooded the personals as she

inspected them for the third day in a row to make sure that
her ads had been placed letter perfect.

```
JENNIFER M. call  Mom,
write  this  paper  or
P.O. Box 1143, Carmel.
Please.    No   strings.
I  love  you.   SC-394
```

Anne didn't find what she was looking for—a hint of why she
could do her best for people while they just didn't care and
made life complicated—and at first she didn't see the hope of
an answer. In two of the papers, in the same quadrants as
her personals, stood black-bordered notices, simple and con-
cise:

```
     TRACER, INC.
   Discrete Inquiries
       804-3960
```

When Anne caught sight of one of the notices, she felt a burst
of adrenaline, but it was followed by a sinking sensation as
she realized that the notice was in the *Salinas Californian*.
Carmel was the jewel community of the Monterey Bay area.
Twenty miles to the east, the city of Salinas stood guard at
the mouth of the river and broad valley for which it was
named. Salinas was an agricultural and industrial center. As
the administrative capital of Monterey County it was linked
to Carmel, and most of the year the two municipalities
shared the same Pacific overcast. But weather patterns usually kept the intervening mountains sun-baked, symbolizing
the worlds that separated them. Not that there wasn't wealth
in Salinas, but to Anne Walker it was simply a choice

between basics—to associate with those who got the best tickets to the Monterey Jazz Festival or those who got invited to the Big Hat Barbecue that kicked off the California Rodeo. She perceived Salinas as crawling with cowboys, farmers and Mexicans who, when they wanted to have a high time, invaded the boutiques and restaurants surrounding the ocean. They might come her way, but she could not imagine herself going back to theirs.

Anne looked as if she spent too much time in aerobics to indulge in tobacco, but she pulled a ladies' brand cigarette with the frenzy of a woman capable of de-activating the smoke alarm and lighting up in the toilet of a US airliner. It tasted awful, so she snapped off the filter for a deep drag of unadulterated nicotine. As she calmed, she noticed the second black border. She considered the notice for a moment, then flipped the paper to its front page. It was the *Monterey Peninsula Herald*. Whatever else Tracer, Inc. might have been, it was becoming acceptable.

Anne picked up the *Herald* and walked into the kitchen. She passed her Cuisinart and took her Slimline off the wall. Another pull from the cigarette for composure, then she tossed it into the sink, freeing her index finger to do a tap dance on the Touchtones.

The phone rang long enough for Anne Walker to impatiently start to think that she should drop the idea of a discrete inquiry. Finally a boy answered. She could hear a dog barking. The boy shouted either at her or the dog. Then a man's voice yelled, and a girl, more distant, said something back.

Anne knew she had the wrong number and felt her face flush because she spoke anyway: "Tracer, Inc.?" Why she used the short form for "Incorporated" Anne didn't know. She was about to hang up when the boy responded.

"Ink? Huh?" From the background the man said something again, and the boy continued, "There's just me here and my sister Shorty and my—"

The phone was obviously snatched from his hand, and the girl said brightly, "Wrong number!"

Anne heard the line go dead. She hung up, feeling strangely embarrassed, then angry. The unexpected emotions reminded Anne of being a teenager. It took several moments to collect her thoughts, to remind herself that she was not a kid. She was not out of control of her life. She was not at the mercy of circumstances. She had grown up. She was somebody. She had every right to contact a detective if she wanted, and she could hire him to do whatever she pleased.

Not quite sure what she pleased, Anne concentrated on checking the phone number in the paper and then carefully dialed again.

Simultaneously, all hell was breaking lose in the Tracer living room.

"Shut that dog up! Good God Almighty, that had to be a client!"

Close to tears, Shorty protested, "I was just trying to save you from that lep."

"I'm not a lep!" yelled Brad.

"Okay, then dork!"

"Don't you kids understand that's my business phone?!" Tracer spread his arms to the ceiling. "Oh, God, oh, God."

Shorty and Brad looked at each other when the phone rang again almost immediately.

Tracer thrust a straight arm toward his children. "Don't touch that!"

"But I'm expecting a call from Gloria!"

Ignoring his daughter, Tracer yelled, "Chris! Get in here and for Christ's sake act secretarial!"

"No need to swear," Chris said, crossing through the dining room from the kitchen. "Or to shout."

The phone was still ringing. Tracer dragged his hands through his hair and choked back a yelp as his wife seemed to take forever to pick up the handset.

Anne Walker heard a woman's sure, secretarial voice answer, "Tracer, Inc." The woman also abbreviated "Incorporated," and Anne was instantly gratified to have been right all along.

"I want to talk to someone about a missing person."

Chris turned her back on the renewed sounds of barking to buffer them from the caller. "I think you'd better talk to Mr. Tracer."

Enraged, Mr. Tracer was advancing on Dog, sure that this time he would be able to strangle the beast in front of his children and even they would understand. "Act like a pro," he hissed at his wife. "I'm in a conference, I'm on a case, I'll be back in an hour!"

Chris indignantly held the handset close to her chest. "That's a wonderful example you're setting. Starting a business by *lying*."

Tracer looked from his daughter, who was holding Dog protectively and whispering anxiously into its ear, "Shh, shh," to his son, who said with wide-eyed anticipation, "Maybe you'll get to use your gun."

"Great," Chris gritted. "Father knows best with a Colt Commander."

Tracer took the phone, cleared his throat, spoke huskily. "John Tracer here."

"My name is Anne Walker."

"How may I help you, Ms. Walker?"

"I think I want to hire a detective."

"Good. That's what I'm here for."

"But I'm not sure," Anne said petulantly.

"I see. Do you want to talk about it?"

"I don't think I should talk about this on the phone."

"I understand."

"Where's your office? The paper just had a phone number."

"Actually, I'm just stepping out . . ." Tracer looked at his family ". . . to check on some of my operatives." Chris shook her head as he continued, "Where are you now? Maybe I can find a moment to swing by."

After Anne gave her address and they set a time to meet, Tracer hung up.

"Who's the missing person?" Chris asked.

"What missing person?"

"She told me she wanted to talk to you about a missing person."

"She told me she couldn't talk."

"She's not hiring you?"

"Chris, I've got an hour before I have to get over there. I need a contract typed up that says whatever money she pays me is non-refundable."

"She's hiring you!" Brad said.

"Of course she is. So why don't you guys pray for a miracle while your mother types the contract?"

Chris asked, "What amount should I put in?"

"Better leave that blank. Give me a chance to negotiate up from the standard rates."

"What standard rates? You don't have standard rates."

"There is a standard for the industry, Chris. What's wrong with you?"

"I don't think pretending is the way to start out."

Tracer ground his palms into his eye sockets. "Oh, Lord, *why?*"

• • •

A gnarled hand worried a business card. Another grappled for a pair of glasses with thick lenses. These were passed briefly in front of rheumy eyes and brought the print on the card into focus—"Tracer, Inc." The heavy glasses were discarded like a nuisance on a horseshoe-shaped desk implanted with television monitors. A uniform hung on the withered frame of the old man seated behind the desk. He looked as if he had been called "Pop" since he was twenty-five. He dropped the business card next to the glasses, then blinked upward, straining to remember.

"Don't I know you?"

Tracer flicked the backside of his right index finger across his forehead, swiping away perspiration from the rush to get there. "Could be. But I'm not here for a reunion, Pop. Now does Anne Walker live here or not?"

The old man looked confused but nodded toward the elevators across the lobby of the apartment building. "Top floor." To Tracer's back he added, "End of hall." As the guard watched Tracer push the elevator button, his old face suddenly brightened. "Torpedoes!"

Tracer turned. At constant war with his brusque manner and a firm sense of life's betrayals, a core of innate gentleness kept trying to leave him wide open to the infirm and delirious. He used a handkerchief to wipe his face, wondering how he was going to respond this time. The elevator hadn't arrived yet.

"One night you were dropped off by a broad with great . . ." Pop cupped his hands to indicate his fixation with enormous mammaries, real or imagined. "Drove a clunker, but she looked slicker than snot. Legs that wouldn't quit, ass that wiggled like Jell-O. You still got her sniffing around?"

"Can't get rid of her."

Pop sucked in air for a sly, greasy laugh. "You private eyes are all alike."

The elevator rang into position, sounding to Tracer like the Bells of St. Mary's.

On the way up, though, he had an attack of nerves: he felt the butterflies breaking formation in his belly, like Huey 1Bs skittering all over the patch to drop troops on a hot LZ.

Anne Walker opened her front door to a tight, constrained, "Ms. Walker?"

Her eyes started with Tracer's head, moved down to his feet, then crawled up again. It took a while because he was a big man. He was dressed like an ex-flatfoot, off the rack. Not quite to type, he nervously held his card at her. Anne figured it was her effect on him.

What he saw was blond hair pulled back severely into a black bow and a finely boned face with soft blue eyes that revealed nothing, unlike her blouse which was open just enough to make a man notice. Her skirt, if it had been a bit shorter and a bit tighter, hinted that he could forget everything. But Tracer kept seeing those guarded eyes.

She took the card and stepped back.

"Come in, Mr. Tracer."

She gestured toward the living room. He looked around. The apartment was spacious and starkly designed, accented sparely with mostly modern furniture.

"Nice apartment."

"Thank you."

"Great view, too."

"Yes."

"Lived here long?"

"A year or so."

"Are you from Carmel originally?"

"I moved here—Is this important, or are you just making small talk?"

"I hoped I was getting some background, Ms. Walker."

"I don't mean to sound rude. I just have so many things to do and so much on my mind. And, God, I hate that feminist shit."

"I beg your pardon?"

"Sorry for the 's' word. Just call me *Miss* Walker. I guess I'm old-fashioned."

But except for the hair, she didn't look old-fashioned at all, and she gave Tracer a look that made him imagine her hair fanned out with abandon on a pillow.

"I can't imagine my background being important in this matter," she said.

"But it might be."

"I should be asking about *your* background."

Tracer hoped he was grinning confidently, like Jack Nicholson playing the wiseass detective in *Chinatown*, but it felt as fake as The Joker's painted-on smile in *Batman*. "Fire away."

"I will. But first I need your promise that whatever I say, whether I hire you or not, will be held in the strictest confidence."

"Of course."

"I don't want you talking to anyone about this."

"Conducting an investigation without talking to anyone might prove difficult."

"I don't mean the little people Jenny might hang around with."

"Jenny?"

"Do I have your assurance that this is confidential?"

"There's a pretty standard contract that could put that in

writing." Tracer patted his jacket, the inside pocket of which held the contract Chris had typed. "I have my own version of it right here. But there's a qualifier: confidentiality doesn't apply to criminal acts. If authorities need to be contacted . . ." He let the thought imply its own conclusion and hoped they could move on to signing on the dotted line.

But Anne was momentarily lost in her own world. "There should be a law against it."

"Against what?"

"People shouldn't be allowed to be selfish and hurt other people."

Tracer nodded, wondering where that came from, then returned to explaining the ground rules. "Now, if you do decide to contract for my services, you should know that I have some record-keeping responsibilities. They don't have to contain lurid details. I'd give your case a file number." Tracer brought a hand to his mouth to clear his throat. "Two thousand and one. I could code the names, and—"

"Oh, I don't care about names or numbers. People can change their names anytime they want. I just don't want this talked about all over town."

"You mentioned to my secretary this is about a missing person."

"I'm sure your secretary's fine."

Tracer smiled. Finer yet was talk like Miss Walker's, which implied he had a chance of closing a deal with her.

Anne impatiently brought up the reason she had telephoned. "For the past several days I've placed ads in various northern California newspapers, hoping to get a reply from a girl I'm looking for."

"Could we go back to the beginning? Who she is to you, etc.?"

"Going back to beginning won't help. Aren't you listening?"

Tracer rubbed his chest, a little constriction over the ol' heart, and the contract felt so light it might fly away. "I thought I was listening, Miss Walker. Please go on."

Anne moved to the room's antique counterpoint, a delicately carved secretary. She picked up a snapshot that she had ready for his arrival. "This is Jennifer."

"The girl you want me to find?"

"You or someone else." Anne handed the snapshot to Tracer, whom she was glad to see look so unsettled. "This was taken last year on her fourteenth birthday." Anne smiled as if apologizing. "For some reason I noticed your ad. I thought, 'Nothing good could come out of Salinas.'"

"I was born there."

The direct answer took her aback, and she sounded less certain asking, "Was that a dog I heard when I called your office?"

"Part of the K-9 unit."

"Oh."

"We're going to have to put the poor fellow to sleep."

"Sorry. I'm an animal lover myself. I just wish I had more room."

Tracer put on a sad face and glanced at the snapshot. Then he squinted at the glass doors at the end of the living room. They let in a view of the ocean and too much light for his eyes to adjust to the darker contrast of the picture.

Anne Walker was also breaking his concentration. "Actually, I called two numbers. I thought the first was a mistake, but I heard a dog then, too. And a child answered."

Tracer wondered whether she had heard him bellowing. "Child?"

"First a boy, then a girl."

"Oh. Well, that could have been . . . you know how the phone company has this—calls to your office can get rolled over to your home?" He rolled a finger in the air. "And vice versa?"

Anne nodded. Tracer could feel water dripping from his armpits. She clearly expected more, but what his brain was dredging up was a taunt from childhood: "Liar, liar, pants on fire!"

"Uh, maybe that explains it. I had just opened up the office when we got—I guess your second call."

She sounded triumphant: "So you're a family man from Salinas who has two children and loves dogs?"

He made his sweaty face look like The Joker's again. "You should be the detective."

"But you're the one who advertised in the Monterey paper. Which means you have clients on the peninsula?"

"Wherever I can get 'em." She's nailing me to the wall, Tracer thought, and I don't know anything about her. He turned to bring his shadow over the snapshot so that he could see it better. "Excuse me."

The dog-eared photo was of a girl, possibly a teenager, probably with Latino blood. She had large, dark, sad-looking eyes, and the smooth, pale skin of someone who hadn't seen much sun.

Confused, Tracer thought Anne Walker was too young to have a teenage daughter, and there wasn't any family resemblance between the blue-eyed Miss Walker and the girl with lustrous dark hair and beautiful brown eyes. So what was Miss Walker's interest? He forced himself to breathe evenly, preparing to re-take the interview. Interviewing people, he reminded himself, was ground he was supposed to have won during his first career.

"What's the girl's relationship to you?"

"Do you have references?"

"If I did, I wouldn't give them out. This is a very confidential business. The way you want it, remember?"

"It's my cleaning lady's kid. We think she ran away."

"Ah, that explains it."

"Explains what?"

"What's Jennifer's last name?"

"The same as her mother's. Mendoza."

"Jennifer Mendoza." Tracer nodded, committing the name to memory. "Does she have a boyfriend?"

"Why?"

"Sometimes girls run off with their boyfriends."

"I should hope Jennifer would be smarter than that."

"How do you know she ran away?"

"She's that kind of kid."

"So it's possible she's not so smart after all."

Anne Walker only shrugged, forcing Tracer to continue.

"Maybe I should talk to the mother."

"You haven't been hired yet."

"That's why I said 'maybe'."

"But this has torn Mrs. Mendoza apart. I had to send her to relatives in Mexico."

"Mexico's a big place."

Anne sounded piqued. "No one needs to find the mother, just the daughter."

"What about the father?"

"Oh, hell, Felix was—I'm sorry. I think that's his name. Mrs. Mendoza doesn't like talking about him."

"But his name is Felix Mendoza?"

"Filipe, maybe. Or Francisco." Anne pulled a face. "I must be stuck on 'F's. None of them sound right. It could be Sammy or Jorge or Al." She gave a fluttery, soft laugh. "All I really know is that my cleaning lady wishes she'd never met him."

"But she must have felt some affection for him. At first, anyway."

"People can make mistakes."

"Yes, but what happened?"

"I understand he chased after other women when Mrs. Mendoza was pregnant, and he finally ran off when Jenny was still in diapers. They were just trophies to him."

"Trophies?"

"You know how some men are. Mendoza was nobody from nowhere. To get someone good-looking and young and better than he, that was a big deal."

"He's never seen his daughter since he left?"

"I don't know," sighed Anne. "I said Mrs. Mendoza doesn't like to talk about it. She's very Old World. You can't blame her."

"But if I could talk to Mrs. Mendoza, even by phone, she might be able to help with the search. I'm sure she'd want to, being Jennifer's mother."

"I told you, Mrs. Mendoza is very upset. She doesn't want to contacted. Except through me, and frankly, I don't have a phone number for her in Mexico."

"Do you know exactly where she is?"

"Yes. And exactly when she's coming home. Look, for a servant she's almost . . . I don't know. We've gotten close over the years, but we're not buddy-buddies. I just think it's my duty to do her a favor. Because I know she's a wonderful mother. It's the daughter who's the bitch. I mean, if you only knew what she put that woman through."

"I'd like to."

"I guess a lot of teenagers are wild. I've done quite a bit of work lately with foster children. The Children's Home Assistance League. The point is, I don't have to take Mrs. Mendoza's word for it to know that being a mother is very

tough these days. She shouldn't really care about what happens to Jenny at all, but she does. With all her heart. Because
she's a good mother. And that's not really the point, either."
Anne's eyes hardened. "Can you find Jennifer?"

Tracer felt his heart fibrillating at the use of the personal
pronoun. She was going to hire him! He managed keep his
question restrained: "Would Jennifer have gone to Mexico?"

Anne answered quickly, as if by rote: "She was born in
Sacramento, is totally Americanized and wouldn't dream of
speaking Spanish."

"But does she? Speak it, I mean?"

"No more than you or I."

"*Hablo un poquito. Y usted?*"

"Taco salad and a margarita." It sounded like Anne was
definitely fed up with the direction he was taking, but Tracer
was too nervous to discern whether she was trying to hide
something. He needed to push her a bit more to see what
came up. If he ticked her off, he'd blow the job. But so far the
job sounded like it didn't have a starting place, and all
searches needed one of those.

"Where do Jennifer and her mother live when they're
here? With you?"

Anne Walker emitted a short, ironic laugh, then explained
it. "They don't live together. Or with me. I told you Jenny was
trouble. She had to be put in a foster home."

"So Mrs. Mendoza lives . . . ?"

"You can't get ahold of her now, anyway. Besides, she
doesn't know I'm doing so much to help her. I'd like to surprise her. If someone can do something useful. If not, why
bother her and get her hopes up?"

"Was she actually married to Mendoza?"

"What do you mean? I just said she was."

"Because she said so, right?"

"I think Mrs. Mendoza knows who she was married to, and her word is good enough for me."

"Well, I've got this innocent young woman pictured in my mind, and she gets hustled by some sleazebag. Maybe she's so ashamed of falling for him, she just says she's married."

"Maybe, Mr. Tracer, you're so fixated on the parents, you won't ever be able to focus on the daughter. Believe me, they won't be able to help you, and Jennifer is the one who needs finding."

"I'm just looking for a starting place."

"Then why don't I give you the address of the foster family? You can ask all your questions to people who might know something."

Tracer could have kissed her. "That would help."

Anne opened the drawer under the desk telephone. A phone book for Monterey and San Benito counties provided nesting for a more personal volume of leather-bound addresses. Anne retrieved the address book, found a piece of paper with high rag content and a pen with real gold in the casing. She began transcribing the address.

"They're the Grissom family. They actually live in Carmel."

Anne glanced over her shoulder. Tracer was gone.

He had moved into the dining alcove to allow the butterflies in his stomach to join the Air Force, play like Phantoms and do a victory roll. He felt for the contract Chris had typed while examining the apartment's one touch of crass—the clutter of newspapers.

"Who does the cleaning while Mrs. Mendoza's gone?"

"The building supplies help."

"Why those papers?"

There was no response. When Mr. Tracer moved to get Miss Walker back into view, he was surprised to see her giving him a sour look. The landing zone *was* hot. The butterflies were helicopters again, back in the damned Army.

"I mean, why those and not others? Do you have some idea of where she might have run?"

"None. Those are just papers I know. Look, if I knew anything else, I wouldn't need a detective. If I had time, I'd even go to the damned Grissoms myself. I'm just doing a good deed for the sake of my cleaning lady. The poor woman only asked me to put ads in the newspaper for her. Well, they haven't worked. So just find Jenny. She doesn't even have to come home. Just let us know where she is and give us peace of mind."

Anne Walker handed Tracer the address, which he crammed into his side pocket. "How much is this going to cost?" she asked.

He whipped the contract out. "Forty dollars an hour, no overtime charges, plus expenses."

Anne turned immediately to her desk and quickly tapped several times on an electronic calculator. "That's three hundred and twenty dollars for an eight-hour day!"

"If you want a daily rate, I could knock it down a bit." He unfolded Chris's handiwork and turned the page toward Anne's eyes. "See? I left the prices blank."

Anne took what was essentially a letter of agreement that said the client had to pay in advance for the services of John Tracer, who in good faith would do whatever was within the law to assist the client, but the client agreed not to sue him if he didn't. Indeed, one line said that he wasn't responsible for the outcome of the investigation, just for a report of what he had done and an accounting of out-of-pocket expenses. As a binding legal document, it had about the same worth as a handshake.

Anne's response was, "In the movies it's a hundred dollars a day."

"You're watching old movies."

She gave him a hard look, and he relented.

"Make it two-fifty. That's fifty bucks lower than the least expensive agency in LA."

"I'm not in LA. My God, I'm only trying to do a favor. I had no idea. *John*, you can see I'm not a rich woman. I'm sorry. Do you mind if I call you John?" She moved closer.

"Okay, first-time client. If you want a bargain, guarantee me a month's work in advance. Then it's five thousand."

"A *month* to find one little girl? You look like the kind of man who could do much better than that."

"Well . . ."

"Don't be modest." She settled her hand lightly on his chest.

"I just assume that you or Mrs. Mendoza—"

"Call me Anne."

"Or the Grissoms went to the police."

Her hand darted off his chest. "The police?"

"Yeah. And what have they done?"

Her fingers worried pouty lips.

Tracer tried to allay her fears. "No need to think the worst. You're probably right that Jennifer just ran away. Regardless, the police haven't been able to do anything because finding a missing kid isn't easy. I mean, if it were easy, she would have answered your ads, right?"

Anne gave him a sideways look, like a hurt child.

"Anne, believe me. You're getting a real bargain at five thousand for a whole month."

She surprised him with, "What makes you so special? There must be a hundred investigators in the bay area."

His forehead once again glistened with sweat, but his voice came out as an even growl: "Try the Yellow Pages. They're crawling with 'em." He watched her pull the phone book

from the desk drawer, but she didn't open the book right
away.

"You didn't answer my question."

"I spent fifteen years uncovering everything there is to
know about people. What Miss Opera in Third Grade
thought of them. How they did or didn't do on their Army
physical. What they owe on their washer and dryer and
alimony, and therefore what their motive might be when
they start dipping into your petty cash. Whether they really
left their last job, or got caught with a secretary or a bottle or
giving blueprints to the competition."

"That doesn't sound like an ex-cop."

"Lady, I've been freelance since Day One."

John Tracer stepped out of the apartment, holding his
breath. When the door closed, he held a check for $3,500 in
front of his eyes to make sure it was real. It wasn't the five
thousand he had wanted for a month's work, but they had
split the difference. He had two weeks to find Jennifer
Mendoza, but however that went, the money was non-
refundable. His feet suddenly danced like a scatback's after
a touchdown. He suppressed the urge to shout and strolled
calmly toward the elevator.

While Tracer descended to the lobby, Anne Walker tried to
figure out if it had been a smart move to hire him. On the one
hand, he wasn't like other men who usually wanted to drool
all over her, and she felt threatened when she couldn't
manipulate a guy so easily with sex. On the other hand, he
was somewhat as she imagined a private investigator would
be, cocksure and twitchy at the same time, just the right
qualities needed to take photographs of spouses cheating
on—

Anne suddenly remembered that she had heard a man's

voice in the background during her first phone call. When her detective was supposed to be opening his office. Perhaps Johnny-boy didn't know that his kiddies had an "uncle" at home when he was working weekends to make sure the little woman could buy whatever she wanted at K-Mart. Maybe it wasn't that way at all, but the thought of it made Tracer seem more like most men, a good choice all around. Anne Walker smiled.

"Dumb bastard."

4

Tracer emerged from the elevator, threw a salute to Pop and exited the building. He strutted from the canopied entrance to the parking lot where a 1978 Dodge Dart four-door sedan bled oil. The Tracers were once a two-car family, but both had been sold and replaced by the secondhand Dart.

The Dodge was the clunker Pop had remembered. Tracer hadn't thought of Chris as having a knock-'em-dead figure, but then, he was used to it after seventeen years. Tracer suddenly saw her sleeping face at night, could almost feel her cold feet in his back as she tried to get warm and he was glad just to be there. With a start, he wondered if she would always be there. He shook that thought as fast as it arose and contemplated what Pop hadn't quite remembered—that Tracer had recently worn a security uniform like his.

They had bumped into each other once or twice at the main office where Tracer would get assignments as a sub. What Tracer was really doing was collecting evidence on a timekeeper who fixed paid overtime for friends who stayed home. Tracer had moments when he looked back at this as "undercover work," but the state looked at it much less romantically as part of the 6,000 supervised hours that any would-be private investigator needed to rack up for his license. Tracer also did records searches for local attorneys who, by reason of being officers of the court, were authorized to count his searches as investigative in nature. He even cajoled a friend in the Salinas Police Department to include his stints as a rent-a-cop at football games. It all added up to accreditation, and if Anne Walker wanted to believe that made Tracer an ex-flatfoot, that was fine by him.

Tracer climbed into the Dodge muttering, "References!" and ground the engine to a coughing start.

His first freelance case was too important to start right away, so a cloud of exhaust trailed him to the bank on which Anne Walker's check was drawn. A teller who seemed as impressed by the amount as she was by the bearer verified Ms. Walker's ability to pay and after consulting with several supervisors complied with Tracer's demand to make an immediate transfer of funds to his bank.

His urgency was not only inspired by his constantly being pressed for cash of late but also by a lesson his first boss at Vulcan had taught him. After Tracer's stint for Uncle Sam, the company recruited him under a corporate policy that didn't care if you were Audie Murphy and Albert Einstein rolled into one: executive prospects had to work through the ranks, starting on the production line. The policy had been abandoned in the late seventies when Vulcan had trouble attracting young MBAs who thought they were too smart and too valuable to waste the first couple of years of their careers getting their hands dirty. Tracer protested the change, partly because he had only a BA in history, and partly because he was old-fashioned enough to believe that (1) you really only learn by doing; (2) a corporation like Vulcan could get too trendy, thinking it needed bright boys who knew how to shuffle funds into faster-growing enterprises, skirt a few laws in the process, gladhand the unions, and get jazzed about how the company defined its "corporate culture" during retreats led by motivational psychologists; because (3) it needed most of all to produce and sell quality tires. Hence Tracer learned how to wield an extrusion knife as fast as anyone on the floor, and he continued to stick fast to his Mexican foreman's definition of a deal.

"A *real* deal, it's not when you agree to something. It's not when the check's bein' cut or in the mail. Not even when it's in your own bank. It's when you take it down to the convenience store at two o'clock in the morning. Ahmed doesn't speak a word of English, see? He don't know Spanish, either. What are contracts and banks to him, growin' up in the Genghis? But he sees what you got in your hand . . . the long green . . . *dinero* . . . and he gives you a six pack of Burgie for it. *That's* when you got a deal."

As Tracer negotiated the Dodge out of Carmel, he thought that the foreman should have been made chairman of the board. He also thought he probably should start his investigation; but a short delay, what difference would that make when his whole family had been waiting three years for a conquering hero?

The Dodge crested a rise that overlooked Monterey Bay, the blue water becoming green as it rolled shoreward and caught the sun, the distant waves appearing to wrap the bay in a long, thin white crescent. The hillsides of Pacific Grove and Carmel, moody with woods, were behind him; the first capital of Spanish California lay below. Monterey's homes and hotels stretched to twisting sand dunes that marked the predominately black town of Seaside and the home of the Seventh Division, Fort Ord, about to be abandoned because of cuts in defense spending. The shoreline curved to the distant cliffs of Aptos and Capitola where if you were lucky enough to have bought an overpriced seaside bungalow for $5,000 forty years ago, you were now sitting on a million bucks' worth of real estate.

Although Tracer wasn't one to stop and smell the flowers, the view of Monterey Bay gave a haunting kind of comfort that could never be broken in his heart even by his most cynical thoughts. He turned away from the ocean, onto Highway 68, driving in the direction of where his cradle had stood.

The highway's two lanes of blacktop wound through twenty miles of the rolling Santa Lucia Mountains, past Laguna Seca Race Track and Corral de Tierra Country Club, to Salinas. Tracer's Middle American home in Creekside Estates was about three miles from the Salinas city limits, on the backside of Fort Ord, two generations and a computer revolution removed from Monterey's Cannery Row. The canneries John Steinbeck knew were now selling expensive souvenirs as art and under-cooked food as *nouvel cuisine*. Less adaptable were the packing sheds and factories around Salinas, many now abandoned, the surviving ones fighting bankruptcy.

Tracer bounced the Dart to a halt in the driveway next to the mailbox with his name, a mile and a half from where he used to work, three miles from where he grew up. He got out and sternly surveyed his peeling castle. Not enough of a deal to paint it yet, but that would come. And rainy season was fast approaching: he'd have to do something about Mr. Riley's peach tree. The neighboring yard looked like Sleeping Beauty's Castle during her big sleep, a tanglewood testament to gorging Mother Nature on mulch, but the peach tree was

something on a wholly different order, twisting out of the
dense growth like a baobab on barren savannah. Its wildly
overgrown limbs were digging up the shingles of Tracer's
roof. Every spring it dropped Dumpster loads of fruit that at-
tracted flies as aggressive as vultures. But touch the tree with
pruning shears, and Crazy Riley would threaten to sue. Well,
thought Tracer, if my roof leaks this year, I'm going into The
Jungle with the ol' chain saw.

Entering the front door, Tracer brought his knee up to
block Dog as it jumped at him.

Dog rolled, still barking, and Shorty looked up from lying
on the floor with the phone, snapping: "Shut up!"

Dog did so immediately.

"The job?" asked Brad. "Did you get it?"

"The lawn? Did you mow it?"

"C'm'on, Dad, it doesn't grow this time of year."

Tracer pointed to his daughter. "Didn't it sink in? Until we
can afford another line again, that's a business phone."

Shorty muttered into the handset, "I have to hang up."

Chris couldn't hide the condemnation in her voice. "You
didn't get it."

"First I had to make sure the check wouldn't bounce."

"The what?"

Brad ran forward. "He got it! He got it!" He hugged his
father. "Are you going to pack your .45? You're not going to
wait for the sheriff to give you a permit, are you?"

"You don't use gunplay on a woman. But now that I have
a PI license, maybe he'll reconsider letting me carry a concealed weapon."

"You got the job?" Chris breathed.

"Wha'd you expect?"

"You left so depressed. You said you were a loser."

"Family talk."

Chris drew close, tugging his tie and straightening it. "I was only repeating what you said."

"Don't repeat me when I'm out of my mind with worry." To his kids he mumbled a quick addendum: "Sorry I yelled."

Chris bussed his lips.

Shorty broke the moment by calling regally over her shoulder as she mounted the stairs. "If Gloria can overcome the humiliation of getting cut off so rudely and actually calls back, I'll be in my room."

"So what's the assignment all about?" Chris asked.

"Not assignment, Mom. *Case.*"

Chris looked up at her man. "On the phone the woman said 'a missing person.' Who's missing?"

"A girl not much older than Shorty." Tracer shook the barbed thought that his daughter could someday be in the same predicament. "Look, would you do me a big favor?"

"If I can."

"The girl we're looking for is Jennifer Mendoza, age fifteen."

Brad was all ears. "Yeah?"

Tracer smiled and touched his own head like he was an idiot. "I almost forgot to ask Anne—"

"Anne?" asked Brad.

"Anne Walker, the client. Whether Mendoza was only the mother's last name or—"

"What's the client like?" Chris wanted to know.

"I don't know. Blond, good looking, lights switched on upstairs. A little moody, a little taller than you, a little younger than me. You know."

"A little?"

"A lot. Anyway, I did ask. Anne claims Jennifer's mother isn't a common-law wife, but we've all got stories, don't we? Unfortunately, Mrs. Mendoza's in Mexico with hers, and I don't have the expenses to get ahold of her. The father's last name should be Mendoza, too. Anne couldn't remember his first name. She said that Mrs. Mendoza never talked about him because he's nobody, he's nowhere, he's never seen his daughter, and he wouldn't give two cents for her if he had. Sounds pretty passionate if you ask me, so I don't want to leave that trail uncovered. Who knows? Maybe Mr. Mendoza doesn't think he's Jenny's father, or . . ." Tracer let his voice trail off.

"But if I get what your driving at—if this guy had something to do with her disappearance—wouldn't it be more likely that he *was* the father?"

"You can lead a horse to water. Sometimes it'll even drink."

"Huh?" said Brad.

"Your mother. I'm just drawing her into this." To Chris he smiled. "Yeah. It would be more likely he's ticked off that he doesn't see his daughter. So-o-o-o . . ." Tracer shrugged.

"He kidnaps her?"

"Maybe she wanted to live with him. There are a lot of reasons why missing kids get their pictures on milk cartons."

"But your switched-on client said this is a dead-end street. Even on the phone I thought Anne sounded like a woman who knew what she was talking about."

"Fine. We're just checking loose ends. So what you need to do is go to the library and check the phone books from the places where we know Jenny has lived. The only information for now is Sacramento and the Monterey Bay area. I'll try to narrow that down, but in the meantime you should get a list of addresses and phone numbers for—"

"For the Mendozas!" cut in Brad.

"Yeah," said his father with a proud nod.

"Which," Chris said, "happens to be an Hispanic surname as common as Smith or Jones."

"Not as common."

"But your foxy blond says he's nobody from nowhere, so why bother?"

Tracer kept his mouth shut and just looked at his wife.

"Okay, okay, I'm thrilled you have a case. I'm thrilled the client isn't a pig. I am sorry for Jennifer Mendoza. But I don't feel too thrilled by spending my Saturday cooped up in the library."

"Honey, I understand. But I don't think it will really take that long. If you want to go grocery shopping, that's on the way."

"I wanted to stop off at the agency to see what the job prospects are for next week."

"Think of this as the end of 'temp sec.'"

"John, I can't just stop working."

"Who said anything about that?"

"Right." She held out her hand. "Keys to the car, please."

"You can't take the car! I'm on a case!"

"And what in God's name am I doing in the library?"

A panel truck bearing the logo "Heritage Antiques, Carmel" pulled up to the curb, and the sight of it through the window froze Chris's features.

"Hey, no, hon, really. Don't worry about the sideboard. Not when we have our first big one." Tracer drew his hand across an imaginary marquee: "'The Case Of The Cleaning Lady's Missing Kid.' Already a done deal. As good as real."

As Sylvester Matron, the lanky owner of Heritage Antiques, uncoiled from the driver's side of the van, Tracer's wife and son crowded the front porch. A meaty laborer in coveralls lumbered out of the other side of the van, holding his distance while his boss confronted the steamroller will of John Tracer.

"Now what?"

"The sideboard. I'd said I'd pick it up today."

"That's been in my wife's family for three generations. What kind of man would sell his wife's heritage?"

Chris looked extremely worried.

Matron lowered his voice. "I understand. I'm willing to jack the price a bit."

Chris called out, "He has a job!"

Matron dropped his voice to a whisper. "That's great. But will it pay the mortgage?"

Tracer moved past the antique dealer. He yanked open the door to the Dodge, yelling over his shoulder to his wife:

"Kill the ads! We can't spend money like it was water!"

Matron watched the Dart begin smoking, then approached the porch.

"What kind of job?"

Chris straightened her back to make the pronouncement as dignified as possible. "He's an investigator."

"You mean he's still getting minimum wage working as a night watchman for that security agency?"

"That was practical hours for certification."

"Yeah," piped in Brad. "Now he's a real private dick."

Sylvester Matron's eyes shifted one way, then darted the other, trying to take in the information. He finally computed it for Chris.

"Just let me know when you want to sell the sideboard."

5

When John Tracer was losing the battle for a full month's retainer, Anne Walker had again insisted that she wanted no publicity. Finding Jennifer Mendoza must be between Tracer and the proverbial wall. Tracer had promised to keep his investigation "as secret as possible," and with the qualifier "possible," he felt free to dive into official channels. He had assumed that a runaway child would have been reported missing to the local police department. He hoped, without much heart behind it, that the long arm of Carmel law was close to taking Jennifer Mendoza into its protective embrace. He reasoned from criminology and law enforcement studies that it was always best to cooperate with the authorities, if only to remain bonded in the county in which one wanted to make a living. He knew that few dealings with human beings ever turned out as hoped for, assumed or promised. Thus it was as a professional, at once intrepid and intimidated, that

John Tracer appeared before the uniformed officer manning
the front desk of the Carmel PD.

At first glance the officer looked to be wearing jodhpurs,
but actually the uniform was stretched over an enormous
behind and filled with huge, pillowy thighs. An androgynous
voice halted Tracer's advance.

"Help you?"

He took out his wallet, relieved it of his investigator's ID
and showed the document to the officer.

"I'd like to talk to someone about a missing juvenile."

A thumb the size of a bratwurst thrust over the officer's
mounded shoulder. "Sergeant Amcheck. He's the one."

Tracer passed through a swinging gate into the working
area of the department and walked toward the indicated
doorway. The officer's head swung with Tracer, apprecia-
tively eyeing his backside. In spite of body tonnage and close-
cropped hair, the officer had a feminine and surprisingly
pretty face.

The Hardy of the department was surpassed only by its
Laurel, an angular, throaty, plainclothes detective whose
droopy eyes looked like they had seen everything and preferred to forget most of it. They caught the date on Tracer's
ID but picked up something newly minted in his manner
moments before that. Betraying nothing, they now studied
the snapshot of Jennifer Mendoza which Anne Walker had
given Tracer. Sergeant Amcheck pushed the snapshot back
across the desk for Tracer to re-pocket. The sergeant waited
for his visitor to get very comfortable.

"You don't know your ass from wild honey, do you?"

Anger knotted Tracer's gut and embarrassment burned his
face. Then the Sergeant startled him by lunging from his
chair with a cheerful, "Let me buy you a cup of coffee. Maybe
a doughnut."

• • •

Red tomato sauce cascaded from a spoon onto a loaf of sour-dough. Tracer watched a deli clerk slather the loaf with meatballs.

"It's not even eleven o'clock," he protested.

It still wasn't eleven o'clock when he and Amcheck carried styrofoam cups of coffee and great, gooey submarine sand-wiches through the beaded curtains of the Mediterranean Market. On the sidewalk they turned toward a small park, Davenport Plaza, and they jaywalked Junipero Avenue to get there.

"When you do the distances I do," said Amcheck, "you gotta fuel the ol' bod with carbs and pros all day long." He glowered at an approaching car and glanced toward Tracer, who skipped onto the curb. "You don't do much jogging, do you?"

Tracer followed Amcheck's lead of stretching out on the grass of the park. He didn't try to imitate the way in which the sergeant gnawed at his sandwich. A few strolling tourists and citizens gave the men wide berth. A distance away, a knot of GIs stood waiting for something to happen. Although they were dressed in civvies, their burr haircuts and teenage faces gave them away as belonging to Fort Ord and not in the arms of any of the local cutie-pies.

"California gets maybe fifty thousand runaways a year," said Amcheck. "Carmel's just small potatoes, so I get five, ten a month. That's kids missing from the bay area. I'm not talk-ing about your BOLs coming in." The policeman explained with his mouth full: "Be On The Lookout."

"I know what BOL means."

Amcheck licked sauce off his fingers, then grappled at the inside pocket of his jacket. He produced a printed flyer fea-turing a picture of a teenage girl, any girl, and the headline,

"$1,000 Reward For Information Leading To The Whereabouts Of . . ."

"A kid came by yesterday," continued Amcheck. "A kid looking for his sister. The family's from Oregon, and they're passing these out all up and down the state. The old man's a wage slave, so this is the best they can do. It's breaking them."

Tracer drew his head back as the sergeant abruptly waved the flyer.

"Hey, soldier!"

The group of GIs turned Amcheck's way, one of them pointing uncertainly at himself. He was as a good as any other.

"Yeah, yeah! You!"

The GI looked to his buddies, then edged forward as they smirked and elbowed each other. Amcheck held the flyer out and kept holding it out until the young man took it.

"Be a good soldier and tack this up at the PX." He added a sharper, "Go on, go on."

The youngster retreated with the flyer and a puzzled expression while Amcheck returned his attention to Tracer.

"I told them it was like looking for a needle in a haystack. But you never can tell. You do realize that you can't detain a juvenile without cause? It interferes with his freedom, his pursuit of happiness, his inalienable right to get taken out in the desert, raped and cut up with a chain saw. Or just get loaded, steal a car and cream your kids in the school crosswalk."

"I know the law. Running away is no longer a crime in California."

"You know what they taught you in criminology classes. Or did you get your theory by filling in the blanks on a matchbook for some fly-by-night detective school?"

"Adult ed. Hartnell."

"I suppose jc is better than nothing. If you had Professor Peg Leg, maybe you even learned something useful."

"I don't care what you think of Captain Caputo or me. What do you know about Jennifer Mendoza?"

At Tracer's show of grit, the sergeant thoughtfully nibbled more of his sandwich, then mumbled:

"You're the first to ask."

The new entrepreneur's face betrayed surprised. The seasoned bureaucrat played with the irony.

"No grieving natural mother. No angry foster parents. What were their names again?"

"Grissom."

"And who did you say hired you?"

"I didn't."

"Well, at least somebody cares about the kid."

Late that afternoon, someone else who might have cared sauntered up a residential street with small houses sprinkled among the pines. Anne Walker might not have admitted it, but waitresses, welfare mothers and wage earners barely able to make the rent also lived in Carmel-by-the-Sea, although not so close to the water; and even the best of families weren't immune from breeding a teenager who looked as if she slathered on mortician's wax for makeup. The girl's hair was the color of orange soda, but there were natural blond roots that looked something like the remnants of innocence trying to push through her anger. She threw away a half-smoked cigarette, fortunately onto the asphalt of the street because she had no intention of grinding it out. She passed a white-going-gray sedan, parked. A man was at the wheel, head back, mouth slightly open, asleep.

She crossed the street from the car and approached a

house with shabby Cinderella carpenter work. She kicked up dust veering across its dead lawn and passed tangles of ivy where others might have put in flowers. She tried the front door, but it didn't budge.

"Shit!"

The car windows were down, so John Tracer stirred to the yelp. The girl plopped on the front steps. Her forlorn features hardened almost immediately into hostility. She fished through her tote bag for another cigarette, which she lit up for anyone to see.

Tracer looked at her a while, then down at the seat where the butt end of his submarine sandwich from the Mediterranean Market stuck out of wrinkled paper, then at the dashboard digital which clicked the five into 4:15. Tracer yawned.

When he looked at the house again a moment later, the girl was standing insolently at the passenger's window.

"What do you want?" she demanded.

"Mr. or Mrs. Grissom."

"Not here."

"I know."

"Then quit gawking."

The girl sported a halter top that showed the outlines of her nipples. Tracer blushed.

"I'm waiting."

"I don't like it."

"I can't help it. Why don't you try the back door?"

"It's locked. It's always locked. Do you want that?"

The girl pointed at what was left of the meatball sandwich. He nodded that she could take it and was going to give it to her, but she had already reached through the open window and snatched it. She peeled away the paper and chewed greedily.

"Don't you have a key?" he asked.

Her mouth was full, and only a grunt worked its way out. It meant no.

"Are you the Grissoms' daughter?"

This time it was a choking grunt, a laugh that meant, "Hell, no."

"It looked like you live here."

She was still chewing, so the words weren't very articulate: "Foster home."

"You could probably help me."

Without warning she got into the car. She kept the door ajar and swallowed back what was left of the sandwich in her mouth.

"Twenty bucks. A good time. Okay?"

While he tried to find words, she used her fingertips and tongue to get rid of the sauce around her mouth, an attempt to spruce up the merchandise.

"What's the matter?" she demanded.

They weren't exactly words: "Uh . . ."

"You a fag?"

"Look—I mean—I just want some information about Jennifer Mendoza."

"Lousy cop."

She got out of the car as unexpectedly as she got into it. She trotted down the street, not exactly running away because she felt too cool to be afraid of anyone.

The dashboard clock flipped to 5:30. The car was empty.

Tracer stood leaning against the front fender to let the neighbors see him so that they would know that he was on the up-and-up. His face was set with guilt because he wasn't sure, after what had happened with the girl, that anyone would believe it.

A station wagon that pulled into the driveway across the

street brought his mind back to the house. The Grissom family spilled from the station wagon with groceries, a huge bucket from the Colonel and the incongruity of garden supplies, lots of them. The Mr. and Mrs.—Harry and Darcy— were in sun suits and burnt to a crisp. Their boys were all lobster red, too. They were named, Harry Jr., Daryl and Westmoreland, which they had shortened to Wes.

"Hurry! Hurry!" shrieked Darcy Grissom to her brood.

"She won't be here, Ma," whined the eldest.

"Not if you want seconds, she won't be!"

This shout came from the shortest child, who accompanied it with an aggressive shove into the back of a much bigger brother.

Tracer approached cautiously. "Excuse me."

The Mister stopped looking for the door key to glare at the intruder. "I'm paid up, I tell ya!"

Wes hollered with excitement, "Ma! Ma! It's the Nielsen man come to ask what we watch on the TV."

"And I'm Mother Theresa. Get in there and get the food on the table. Hurry!"

The Grissoms pushed through the front door, leaving it open, which Tracer took to be more or less of an invitation to follow them into their lair. The furnishings were bought when Lee's Bars, Stools & Dinettes was still a going concern. As the family crowded into the kitchen, the Mister snapped back over his shoulder:

"Did I say you could come in?"

Tracer had been in a few fights in his life, not to mention Tay Ninh Province, and he didn't sense any guts behind Harry Grissom's anger, so he eased further inside.

"I'm a private investigator."

The exclamations were rapid-fire:

"*Puta* Maggie!"

"Those sluts."

"Like Magnum, PI?"

Thus Junior's croak was overlapped by his mother's judgment, Westmoreland's wish and finally his father's growl, "I don't care what they say. I told you I was paid up."

"Want me to punch him in the groin?"

Darcy Grissom returned to domestic concerns, pointing to the Kentucky Fried, "Just get that on the table!" then slapping her shortest son with, "Hurry! Hurry!" With more pointings and cuffings, Mrs. Grissom supervised the distribution of chicken. Some grocery bags were dropped to the floor; others were pillaged for more food, such as Wonder Bread to augment the Colonel's biscuits; and the garden supplies obviously would find their way outside sometime in the near or distant future. There weren't enough chairs for everyone to sit at the table, and no one waited for grace. Tracer decided not to stand on formality, either.

"I want to know about Jennifer Mendoza."

"No good," said Darcy Grissom to her husband. "I told you she was no good." Darcy then got around to acknowledging Tracer: "Came from a Mexican family in Salinas. The Patronas. For beaners they was nice folks, I hear. So I asked Harry," she now taunted her husband, "'If she's so good, and they's so nice, how come we're a-gettin' her?'" Mrs. Grissom finished with a triumphant complaint to Tracer: "They don't tell you nothin' in the foster business."

"Why didn't you report her missing?"

"Who said she was missing?"

"Do we have to save some for him?" interjected the eldest boy as he stopped eating to worry a pimple on his neck. The child was referring to food. He meant for Tracer.

"You gonna join us?" asked the senior Harry. He meant, "Are you going to take something from us?" The Grissoms were the kind of people who expected that to happen all the time.

Tracer's mind had been reeling ever since he had engaged the Grissoms, but he managed to shoot off an automatic "No thanks" before pressing the attack back to the Mrs. "Isn't she missing?"

"Wasn't enough, anyway," was the Mister's reply from the flank.

"A kid comes, a kid goes," grumbled Mrs. Grissom philosophically. "Sometimes a kid comes back. In the foster business, you never can tell."

Wes gravely repeated a family adage. "It pays not to have too many expectations."

"Where did she go to school?" asked Tracer.

"The junior high," snapped a voice from below eye level. "Where else do ya think she'd go?"

Tracer's spine suddenly tingled to what sounded like Robbie the Robot:

"'Your child has an unexcused absence. Please call the administration office.'" Then Darcy Grissom's voice switched to a hoarse laugh. "If they gave a damn, why do they keep callin' you every day with a machine?"

Nearly lost for words, Tracer managed to ask, "You have another foster child. What's her name? Where does she go to school?"

"Tiffany Ericson," snarled Daryl with his head tilted back as far as it would go. "Same place."

Tracer glanced down at Daryl, then looked at his parents. "What would you recommend for killing a fruit tree real fast?"

"What?"

Tracer gestured toward the garden supplies.

The Grissoms still looked puzzled.

"Never mind." Tracer turned on his heel and exited without a good-bye.

"Freakin' weirdo," said Darcy, gnawing into a chicken breast.

Westmoreland rushed to the window. "Did you see his car? What kind of car was it?" The boy was then struck down by the family adage as he spotted Tracer aiming for the Dart.

"Damn! He said he was a detective!"

6

Live oaks and a split rail fence framed flowers and a meadow. From the meadow rose the steep roof of St. Mark's Episcopal Church. The church was situated on a ridgeline separating Creekside Estates from Corral de Tierra, a rural subdivision blessed with large homes and a country club whose members were mainly the wealthy from Salinas and Carmel Valley. The parish supposedly served all comers from Salinas to Monterey and the rolls boasted 300 families, although it was an exceptional Christmas if half that many individuals showed up.

The Reverend Charles Ryan, Th.D., the latest in a string of St. Mark's rectors, was a thick, balding man who looked more like an ex-boxer than an ex-seminary professor who avidly quoted John—Steinbeck, Milton and *Gospel of*, in that order. He was called Dr. Ryan by some, Father by others, and said he preferred plain Chuck. A self-confessed rebel, Ryan made proud and frequent mention of having marched with Berkeley radicals protesting the Vietnam War. He otherwise stood firm with the national Episcopal establishment when it came to churchly matters.

So it was that on the Sunday after Miss Anne Walker reported the disappearance of Jennifer Mendoza, a few faint voices from the congregation joined the organized choir in singing the recessional hymn which had been changed so that the sexist language of "the hope of all mankind" was now the more inclusive "the hope of all people." During the final chorus the doors opened, and into the sunlight emerged a cross, the parish banner, and flags both American and Anglican. These were borne by altar attendants, girls wearing red and white robes, followed by a lay reader and a chalice bearer, two middle-aged women in black and white. Then came priestly vestments sported by Ryan and a fresh-faced female seminary graduate beginning her career as the parish's deacon. When the hymn ended, the organ took up a Bach fugue, stately and baroque, which accompanied the congregation as they trickled past their priest, the Reverend Doctor, Father Chuck.

Inside, Christine Tracer shook her husband awake.

"I was thinking," he said.

"It sounded more like snoring."

The Tracers merged with the people edging out of their pews into the main aisle. Shorty tried to hang back from her parents, unsuccessfully looking for a peer to relieve her embarrassment, while Brad kept closer, trying to catch every word of his parents' lowered voices. They talked out of the sides of their mouths, like bad ventriloquists, and nodded greetings here and there for appearance's sake.

"I'd like you to call Carol Durand," Tracer said, "and arrange for Shorty to stay overnight. That way she can go to school with Gloria tomorrow."

"I've always liked Pacific Grove," said Chris sarcastically. "Why don't we just move into the district?"

"I just want Shorty to find out what she can about that foster sister. You know how peers say things to each other that they'd never tell an adult."

"I know it's a really stupid idea."

He arched a look at his wife before stepping up behind a parishioner shaking the priest's hand.

Chris continued undaunted, "And besides stupid, it really could be dangerous."

He leaned back to grit, "What's dangerous about putting your ear to the ground?"

"Hey!" piped up Brad. "An inside job! I could do that!"

"Shhh," hissed Tracer as he stepped outside to narrow his eyes at the rector.

Father Chuck extended his hand. "I hear that you're, aaah . . ." The priest couldn't say the word "detective," and Tracer couldn't quite finish the sentence for him.

"Uh, yeah."

"Oh, don't be so uptight," Chris said. "He's a bona fide gumshoe, like Mike Hammer and Wyatt Earp."

Ryan put on a big happy smile to say, "Interesting." He had once preached on how "interesting" was a nonword, meaning little because it covered up emotional response and therefore commitment, but he didn't have time to read behind the tension in the Tracers' faces.

Their son tugged at his father. "Dad. Really. I could get all the inside scam you need. I'll disguise myself. One lead and we'll crack the case wide open."

Tracer forced a small laugh for Ryan. "Always wants me to talk shop. Nice sermon." Out of earshot of the priest, Tracer started to mutter, "You agnostic son of a—"

"John!" Chris snapped.

Brad turned on his sister. "Man, you get all the breaks."

"We'll discuss it later," Tracer gritted under his breath to his wife.

"Good," she said.

"It gets you, doesn't it?" he continued immediately. "That I *really* got my license. That I *really* have a case. That I kept my promise, and now *you can't live up to your side of the bargain!*"

"I don't think throwing my daughter to the wolves is part of the bargain," she answered calmly.

Heading for the parish hall for coffee, Tracer abruptly stopped. A card table was set up with pictures of Israeli soldiers in riot gear and a sobbing Palestinian women holding a baby killed with a rubber bullet in Jerusalem. Manning the table, the women of the church's Peace & Justice Committee were soliciting signatures and funds in support of more Palestinian autonomy in the Holy Land.

As if bounced off track by an unseen force, Tracer found himself grumbling toward the parking lot, "Isn't it enough that they're kicking Jewish settlers out of Galilee and Samaria?"

"The West Bank?"

"Call a spade a spade! If we did that, what self-respecting Christian would support giving up Galilee and Samaria? 'Occupied Territories.' Oh, yeah, like now they're not occupied. Occupied by people who occupied their whole lives occupying frigging baby carriages with car bombs! Next, they'll want to give back the whole country to the Ottoman Empire. General Allenby would roll over in his grave."

"Who?"

"The last of the crusaders. Colonel T.E. Lawrence was under his command."

"Colonel . . . ? Like Peter O'Toole?" She gave plaintive voice to, "'Law-rence, Law-rence.' Remember when that

Arab boy was sinking deeper and deeper in quicksand, and he kept trying and trying, but he couldn't save him? So he took his friend across the desert and got him lemonade in the bar. That Lawrence?"

"Y'know, Chris, sometimes you have a way of making me wonder if we're both on the same planet."

"What's crazy to me is, why do we attend this church if you don't like it here?"

"I'm not going to be drummed out just because everyone else has gone soft." Tracer turned and walked backwards to address his daughter.

"How 'bout it, Shorty? Want to do a little undercover work for the old man?"

"Do what?"

"Harm," said Chris. "What about *harm* to her academic standing?"

"A day! She's not going to learn nuclear fusion in one lousy day!"

He yanked open the front passenger door of their Dodge, and Chris slipped past him with maddening calm.

"So just how do you think she's going to get into Gloria's school for one lousy day?"

Tracer circled to his side of the car, flailing his arms at Chris, and forcing his children to stop in their tracks so he didn't bowl them over.

"Go the Principal. Get a permission slip. It doesn't take an Act of Congress."

Chris watched her husband squeeze behind the wheel. "Where have you been for thirty years? There's no district in the world that lets kids into classes like that! Some visitor slips, they get sued for millions."

Shorty and Brad settled into the back seat, listening to their parents with troubled expressions.

"What about some other function? I *need* information."

"A dance," said Shorty.

Her mother gave her a startled look.

"Gloria's school is having a dance tonight. I could go to that, and Mr. or Mrs. Durand could probably drive me back tomorrow morning."

"There," said her father.

As the car swayed into the curves of the road winding down to the highway, Tracer looked at his wife. "A dance on a school night. And you think I'm crazy. But what's the world coming to?"

Chris couldn't resist. "The same place as you. Using women to do the dirty work."

John gave her a puzzled look as if he really didn't get it, but when they got home, he asked whether Chris needed help with the Mendoza inquiries she had started yesterday.

First, however, he tried to complete his own unfinished business, calling the Patronas' number he had looked up in the phone book after talking to the Grissoms. There was only one listing for Salinas and most likely for the foster family that had taken care of Jenny before the Grissoms started making money off of her. But once again, the phone at the other end of the connection just rang and rang. He spent the rest of the afternoon trading off tracking down Mendozas with Chris whenever the football game on television was between quarters.

From her library gleanings through the Sacramento and Monterey Bay area phone books, Chris had come up with sixty-seven Mendozas, including five Alonsos, six Carlotas and one each of Freddy, Francine, Fidel and Zinola. On Saturday Chris had been able to cross eighteen names off her neatly copied list, two of them because, "The number you have dialed is no longer in service."

With John's help she completed them all, as well as the household tasks that had accumulated during the week. The Tracers' explanations were usually to the point, if not quite precise: "We're neighbors of Mrs. Mendoza in Carmel and we're trying to contact her daughter named Jennifer. By any chance are you related to Jennifer or her father?"

Most people didn't want to know more; a few were suspicious: "Who?" . . . "Where?" . . . "Are you a bill collector?"

Backtracking through those Mendozas who hadn't answered her first call, Chris briefly thought she had hit long distance pay dirt, then had to listen to a woman in Sacramento brag at length of her Jennifer—a five-year-old enrolled as a prodigy at UC Davis' early childhood development program. The repetitive calling was much like being a homeroom mother and trying to get parents to volunteer to make cupcakes for a bake sale—a pain in the neck, boring at best.

For a while Brad hung close to the kitchen counter, asking exasperating questions about every call until his father told him to cut the grass. Brad countered that he had to go play just as the television erupted with crowd noises from Candlestick Park.

"When are you going to cut the lawn?"

"Tomorrow?"

His father grunted vague assent, moving back to the family room to see how the 49ers were doing.

Chris used the privacy to telephone Gloria's mother about the dance. She listened to Carol Durand babble about a string of subjects; then after fifteen minutes, the conversation turned to Chris's job. Carol's husband thought that Chris was the best employee he had ever hired. Eddie was in fits since she had left, and wouldn't Chris please come back to straighten out the office so that the Durand family could have peace at home?

Chris demurred and hung up, tense but flattered. She got through the rest of the day, fighting off wild imaginings she thought she had conquered. The imaginings began on the emotional roller coaster that had gone out of control when Vulcan laid off John.

He at least had been able to find some support from a group of unemployed men in the parish. Most of them had been used to giving orders and getting things done; now they had to conquer the strain of meeting once a week to encourage each other and getting little done. As an ex–vice president in the group put it, "I just wanted to hide in the house. I mean, how many excuses can you have for being home in the middle of the week? Then one Tuesday, I think it was, I spot water running all over the sidewalk and down the street from the neighbor's sprinklers. I didn't see the gardener. In fact, I hadn't seen the neighbor's gardener for months. And just when I'm wondering whether I should go over and turn off the damned sprinklers and show everybody on the block that I'm still a worthless bum who can't take charge of his own life, there's my neighbor! He's got his beak out of the doorway, like, who's gonna see *me*? And, man, that felt good, knowing that the ship was going down, and I wasn't the only one on it!"

The men paired up whenever one went on a job interview so that another was always in the car keeping vigil. They critiqued each other's resumes, pretended to be prospective employers, exchanged tips about job prospects and sometimes shared with trepidation what little spare cash they had.

Meanwhile Chris had gone through the embarrassment, then the boredom, of listening to her husband explain their finances to people who would invite them out to dinner or to a show. But she couldn't quite get over the humility when John stopped going through the motions of reaching for the

bill or saying, "The next one's on me." Someone, she wasn't
sure who, paid their Pacific Gas & Electric bill for several
months running. She wondered if it was her mom and dad.
Sometimes the Farwells would give her money, never a lot,
and always with the admonishment that she shouldn't tell
John because he might think it was okay to stay lazy and
dependent.

While Chris watched furniture she had lovingly polished
go out the door, John re-financed the house at standard
mortgage rates, supplying the family with cash out of the
equity they had built from his low interest Cal Vet loan.
Enough cash to keep them going until he had to arrange
what amounted to a third mortgage just to make payments
on the home.

They both put up with the regular inquiries about their situation from at least two acquaintances who they knew for a
fact did not wish them well, and quickly learned not to tell
them anything specific in case their gloating thoughts haunt-
ed John's next job interview. In desperation he took a number of odd jobs as a laborer, but they drained him of what
energy he had to prepare a new attack to regain his career.

He had to learn his own counsel to others: looking for
work is full-time work. A more devastating lesson was that
potential white collar employers no longer thought much of
the work ethic or of a man who recently had sweated to pay
his bills.

When John finally embarked on his new career, taking a
literal leap in the dark by starting out as a night watchman,
Chris had reached the end of her strength. She had seen him
morose, self-pitying and snappish. She learned to hide her
own depression from him. Her facade gradually got harder
for him to penetrate.

She became increasingly critical at home and looked for

affirmation in work. She had loved being a homemaker and resented having to give up. Then about a year ago, she suddenly found herself weeping in front of Carol Durand. Several days later, Carol's husband—John's friend since high school, a vigorous, successful man—said he needed help at the office a couple of days a week. Could Chris work that into the on-again, off-again assignments from her temporary manpower agency?

Eddie Durand had acted like a perfect gentleman, sympathetically soliciting tales of Chris's troubles while non-judgmentally explaining what might be going on with John. Eventually Eddie asked Chris to stay late to finish some extra work.

With everyone else gone, Eddie reached out to touch Chris's hand to compliment her on how well she worked. Then he started moving closer to her, in a natural way and completely in control, while he included his larger business worries in the problems only she had the knack of solving. He kept moving her with fleeting touches and soft talk, but she couldn't concentrate on anything he said. His lips brushed the corner of her mouth, lightly, as if testing, and she turned toward him, balanced obligingly for the next move. His hand ran down her arm, making the skin tingle, then locked around her waist. She looked up at him, lips parted, breath held, and watched his face loom closer to kiss her.

"Your eyes are open," he whispered.

So they were. She twisted free and fled like a schoolgirl. Her reaction surprised her as much as it did him. In her mind, she compared the incident to moving a grand piano: just when the positioning is exactly right, the weight inexplicably shifts and the piano falls like a rusty safe and crashes with sprung, discordant notes. She wished he hadn't spoken. He had probably wanted to ease her tension. She must have looked like a spooked doe. She might even have been ready for passion, but his breath gave off the same slightly metallic smell that John's did when they had sex, and that just made everything too real.

She wasn't particularly sorry for the incident, not then, and dare she admit it? She had been fantasizing about an affair for weeks. Her and John's lives had become so tightly compartmentalized that Chris sometimes thought she could drop dead and he wouldn't notice. As for the children . . . well, they had no business in a fantasy. The next day in the office went well enough, with Eddie apologizing obliquely and hinting that they could pick up again whenever she was ready.

Sensibly, Chris kept her thoughts from her husband. Later she worked up the courage to confess them to Father Ryan. That was awful, hearing him say that it was very understandable that she should want a little excitement and attention. Very understandable, very natural, and very, very sinful. Thoughts led to actions. The kind of actions Chris had been contemplating would destroy her marriage. Is that what she wanted?

When the next request came for a late night in the office, Chris dashed off a matter-of-fact letter of resignation and dropped it on Eddie's desk in a how-dare-you sulk, but he acted as if everything was perfectly normal between them. He asked Chris, John and their kids over for a barbecue, using the occasion to suggest that Carol invite Chris out to a "girls only" lunch the following week. My God, Chris thought, he believes I'm a neurotic: a good talk, a roll in the hay, either way I'll be fine! Then she allowed that it was more likely that Eddie was settling back to wait for however long it took until Chris seized another opportunity to act on temptation. After all, she did go to the barbecue and to the lunch;

her daughter's contact with Gloria Durand continued to throw the families together; and Chris confessed to herself that she was a little flattered that Eddie still wanted her. Curious, too, about how long it would take until he realized her flame wasn't meant to draw a moth like him. In the meantime, she settled down to await the rebirth of her husband's confidence. It was a long time coming. She wasn't yet sure that it had really arrived.

Before she drove Shorty to the Durands' home, Chris urged her husband into the back yard. He was going to call to Brad to mow the damned grass, but Chris dragged John into the garden shed. She began unbuttoning her dress with the sounds of the game between the 49ers and the Rams issuing faintly from the family room.

"Good God," John said.

He didn't need any encouraging and pulled the warped wooden door closed. He had often tried to get Chris to have sex in the car, on the beach, against the kitchen counter, anywhere was fine with him, but just as often the kids were nearby and she would insist that they wait, which usually meant that the day ended with their going straight to sleep. Now she allowed him to take her on the rough plywood floor. Grit and moldy grass clippings pressed into her back and buttocks and the soft soles of her feet, but she didn't need any warming up because she had already worked herself into a state. She sucked in the smells of oily rags and paint thinner, and watched the dust dancing in a shaft of sunlight slanting across her husband's shoulder. She closed her eyes.

When Chris drove away from the house to take Shorty to the Durands, Tracer put in another call to the Patronas, again raised no one, and then reported to Anne Walker.

"... I checked out the Grissoms yesterday after I left you."

"What did you think?"

"Nice, real nice."

Anne gave a delighted laugh. "Tell me about it."

"You've met them?"

"Just heard about them."

"Well, they didn't want to be helpful, but there's another foster kid, Tiffany Ericson, who went to school with Jennifer. I'm following up on her now."

"That's good, John, but, uh . . . my fiancé is coming by in a moment to pick me up for dinner."

That's better, Tracer thought, because he didn't want to tell Anne that he had been working on finding Jennifer's father. "I'll make this short and sweet, then," he said.

"Please. Very short, very sweet."

"I'm trying to get hold of a family called Patronas because from what I can gather they're the ones who took care of Jennifer before the Grissoms."

There was a long silence followed by, "Yes?"

"You wouldn't happen to know if they live in Salinas?"

"That does ring a little bell."

"Do you have an address?"

"I could look. But the Patronas, they were more than a year ago, weren't they?"

"I don't know."

"Do you know what my fiancé says about me?"

"What?"

"I'm too bloody efficient."

"Sounds English."

"Doesn't he? Anyway, every year I update my address book and throw the old one away."

Tracer gave a businessman's chuckle. "Around here we got a couple, three address books, two Rolodexes, nothing consolidated, nothing updated. You'll make a good wife."

"I hope so. Are you home now?"

"Yes."

"Give my regards to Mrs. Tracer. If she's there."

"Thank you."

"And I'm sorry, but I do have to go."

"I'll call tomorrow."

"If I'm not here, leave a message on my answering machine. It sounds like you're doing a good job, John. 'Bye."

Tracer hung up and went into the family room, where Brad was watching television.

"That stuff will rot your mind."

"You watch it."

"Just a few things. What's wrong with you?"

"How come you like girls better than you do guys?"

"What do you mean?"

"Shorty gets to help you. Mom gets to help you. What do I get?"

"You get to be a consultant."

"Huh?"

"Turn that thing off and tell me in your considered opinion how I could get you to run away from home."

Shored up with such real things as a couple of sore lumbar vertebrae, Chris managed to steer clear of wild imaginings and put up with an hour of chit-chat with the Durands. Carol talked about saving Brazilian rain forests and seeing Kim Novak at Quail Lodge, and Eddie said that he had run into Clint Eastwood at the Hog's Breath where Eddie had tried to convince Clint that if Dirty Harry could be Mayor of Carmel, why not a higher calling? Look at Reagan. Heck, look at Leon Paneta: their Congressman was now President Clinton's right-hand man. Now Clinton, he was a real stud. Retroactive taxes, talk about power! And Eddie kept assuring Chris that it

would be no problem to drive Shorty back tomorrow morning
before school. Would Chris be going to work early or would
she have time to make him a cup of her great coffee? Eddie's
suggestive voice didn't stir Chris's heart as much as her bile.
She left as she had when she had quit his employ, miffed by
his casual arrogance. Then she wondered why she was letting
it bother her.

After she came home, Chris tucked Brad away in his
upstairs bedroom where his father had left him to mine the
floor with pieces of a model airplane. She padded down the
hall and slipped into bed next to John, who was re-reading
The Sunday Hangman by James McClure. She wished John
would say, "I love you." That was all. Just that.

Instead, he spoke as he usually did when caught up in
detective fiction. Tracer talked about Lieutenant Trompie
Kramer of the Murder & Robbery Squad and his Bantu side-
kick, Detective Sergeant Zondi, with the intensity of a reader who wanted to believe they were real; and more than that,
friends, who lived in a neighboring town, Trekkersburg,
South Africa, just east of Santa Cruz, California. John
launched into a gossipy chronicle of Tromp's sporadic
domestic experiments with the Widow Fourie and into spec-
ulating, along with Zondi in *Blood of an Englishman*, that
Kramer's unfaithfulness to that woman among women was
because the Lieutenant didn't believe in God.

"I don't know," sighed Chris.

Chris slipped into sleep with anxiety about her daughter
niggling her, but she was too tired to probe for a reason.
Something about danger. Or was it coffee tomorrow with
Eddie?

7

A teacher who looked like Al Gore wagged a finger at a disk jockey and, for the sixth time that evening, insisted that the volume be turned down. A slow dance made it seem like the disk jockey was complying for the seventh.

The music throbbed in a junior high multi-purpose room that was roughly divided into two groups, boys on one side and girls on the other. In the no man's land between, a few couples pressed together like bivalves to a rock. Shorty and Gloria Durand kept back from cliques of girls who either stared vacantly or chattered incessantly. Shorty's chubby friend still had growing to do to stretch curves into her plumpness, and she made herself miserable by fighting nature with constant dieting. She chewed gum rapidly and pulled at the diamond stud in her ear.

"That's her."

Gloria nodded toward Tiffany Ericson, who hung out with three girls sporting babydoll makeup and kung fu slippers.

One girl had a teardrop expertly tattooed under her eye; another, scroll work over her eyebrow that said, "Whip."

"Not exactly college prep," observed Shorty.

"They can drop out this year. Legally."

"And miss high school?!"

"Why are you so interested in meeting Tiffany Ericson?" Shorty shrugged.

"Oooo, that itches." Gloria stopped tugging at her ear and turned the lobe so that Shorty could inspect it. "I'm going to have another one put in. What do you think?"

"My dad says they get infected, and then your ear will fall off."

Gloria shuddered. "How come all the questions about Jenny Mendoza?"

"Just curious."

"Sure, Nancy Drew. They live in the same foster home. Jenny's as quiet as an ant, and Tiffany's as tough as they come. Jenny hasn't been to school for a week. Is she sick? A runaway? What is it?"

Shorty watched Tiffany peel away from her friends and move toward the refreshment table.

"Now's our chance."

"You're not going to get anything out of her. But I'm your friend, and you're holding out on me."

"All I can tell you is that my folks were arguing, and I'm here because that seemed like the best way to stop it." Shorty gave Gloria a pleading look.

"Come on," relented Gloria.

Tiffany turned from getting a sugar fix from cookies. She heard something strange: someone had acknowledged that a cup of punch was poured by a human being, namely the parent chaperon behind the refreshment table. Shorty had said, "Thank you."

Now Gloria edged closer to Tiffany. "Hi."

Tiffany started back to her friends. Shorty nudged Gloria to be more aggressive.

"Wait."

Tiffany spun around.

"I mean, I want you to meet a friend of mine. This is Shorty Tracer."

Shorty gamely stretched out her free hand. "I'm visiting."

Tiffany walked away.

Gloria looked haplessly at Shorty. "Dance?"

The girls boogied to a punk rock declaration that safe sex ain't great sex but it'll do. After a while a boy two inches shorter than Gloria tapped Shorty on the back.

"Cuts?"

A surprised grin lit up Shorty's face.

"He's in my math class," protested a mortified Gloria. Chewing her gum more rapidly, she hissed at the boy, "Can't you see I'm talking?"

Shorty murmured, "Hey, no, really." Backing away, she gave her friend a teasing look. Gloria replied with one that said, "If you tell anybody, I'll kill you."

While the lad blissfully see-sawed Gloria to his own drum, Shorty looked around. She spotted Tiffany again. Shorty swallowed her fear and boldly went after her.

"Nice dance, huh?"

"It sucks."

"What classes do you like best? Study hall? Home ec?"

Tiffany gave Shorty a cold look that freeze-dried her courage but not her tongue.

"We've got those at Spreckles. That's where I go to school."

"Crawl off and die."

Shorty hurried away from the sound of snickering from

Tiffany's gang. She snatched her purse off a chair, rounded
a corner and darted through a swinging door marked
"Girls."

A girl hunched over a sink. Shorty started toward the stall
nearest the wall, but there was a pool of water on the floor
because someone had stuffed a roll of toilet paper into the
bowl and tried to flush it down. She careened into the middle stall.

Shorty locked the door and slumped against it. Tears
welled in her eyes, and she let out a heavy breath. A moment
to consolidate her defeats, then she set her purse on the floor
and pulled a paper seat cover from the dispenser on the wall.

The girl at the sink was peeling aluminum foil from a
brown Sherman cigarette. Shermans and Cools were best.
The cigarette had been saturated in a soluble solution that
had cost the girl a week's allowance. She had wrapped the
cigarette in foil and stashed it in the refrigerator at home,
both of which were supposed to enhance its potency. She
brought it to the school dance because . . . well, there was a
boy she was sleeping with and he had promised to be there
and she wanted to share with him, and since he wasn't there,
well, that was another good reason.

The girl turned her back to the outside door and edged
halfway into an open stall to light her prize. Enough kids did
it without anything really weird happening. Besides, it was
her life, wasn't it? She would be glad if something outra-
geous did happen.

Shorty's nostrils flared to the acrid odor of the smoke. She
heard the door to the far stall creak closed.

Tiffany and her friends entered the restroom. They sniffed.
"I smell an angel," said one of the new arrivals.

Another grinned, then advanced with the other two toward
the stalls.

Shorty's purse could be seen on the floor, and her door was lightly pushed and found to be locked. At almost the same time, the girl with the Sherman was discovered behind an unlocked stall door, standing in the pool of water.

The girl didn't seem to give a hoot one way or another when Tiffany made a gimme motion with her hand.

The girl with "Whip" over her eyebrow giggled, "Just say no, man."

The girl in the stall gave up her Sherman and left the restroom, the wet soles of her shoes making kissing sounds on the concrete floor.

Tiffany took a hard pull from the cigarette, then passed it to her eager friends.

They heard Shorty's toilet flush.

The gang got more eager and fanned out around the door. Tiffany watched Shorty's purse get picked up. Shorty unlocked the door, stepped out and stopped dead.

Stony faces waited to greet her.

8

A cloud of smoke enveloped the face of Shorty's father. A woman's throaty voice made swirling patterns in it: "Our records are confidential. There's no way I can give you information on Jennifer Mendoza."

More smoke came Tracer's way as he spoke: "I already know the names of two of her foster families. I've been to the one in Carmel. I have to check out the Patronas, who I think live in Salinas. Her natural mother is out of the country, but if I could get a lead on her dad . . . Maybe she went there."

Tracer sat in a cramped, paper-cluttered bureaucratic cubicle in Monterey, a mechanical pencil poised over a pocket notebook without a note in it. He had arrived at 8:30 on the dot although he had been up since six because Chris had sent him to a twenty-four-hour market in Salinas to buy coffee. She wanted coffee *beans*, for crying out loud, not a can of pre-ground coffee that could be easily found two blocks away at the convenience store. Tracer was going to wait for Eddie to arrive with Shorty and enjoy a good cup of coffee himself, but as eight approached, he became more anxious to get to the county's Family and Children's Services department as soon as it opened. So he had made his way past "No Smoking" signs and was now breathing in secondhand lungfuls in the domain of Linda Hiyata.

She was a fiftyish Japanese-American with emphasis on the American. Her accent had a twang. She looked as if she worked as hard at her job as an alcoholic did for a bottle. Tracer saw that there was no wedding band on her ring finger, yet the nameplate on her desk gave her name as "Mrs." He figured her husband had left her, most likely for someone much younger.

"You say she's missing," said the social worker. "No police report. Not a word from the family."

"Yeah, well. The Grissoms are wonderful folks. Who would doubt 'em?"

"Do you have any idea how many homeless kids there are out there? Or how few families are willing to take them in?"

"Tell you what. Let's pretend that Jennifer Mendoza is your daughter. And the guy who's hired to find your daughter goes to the county welfare people, where the nice bureaucrat says . . ." He gestured with his pencil to cue a guilty response.

"There are rules and regulations. Look. I can't."

"So don't." He set down his notebook, put the mechanical pencil on top, patted them for emphasis. "Let's drop your daughter down a well."

Linda Hiyata stubbed out an unfiltered Camel. "I suppose I could be hypothetical. I just can't give you specifics."

"Call them parameters."

"There are so many of them, we've given them a name. 'Throwaway kids.' It starts with a girl thinking she's in love or just wanting to get out of the house. She gets pregnant. There's a slight chance of marriage. But because of Aid to Families with Dependent Children, most biological fathers can't compete with Uncle Sam as a breadwinner. The girl, then, doesn't have much incentive to get married, and Romeo's usually only in it for the sex, anyway. So he gets bored. Then he splits. Now you've got a sixteen-year-old kid with a kid of her own. More than 70% of the people under the poverty line are members of single parent households."

"I thought teenage pregnancies hit the rich and famous, too."

"You wanted parameters, remember? So our poor mother goes through some more guys. If she's not totally addicted to welfare, she works a little. Regardless, she gets used to leaving her kid with relatives or some day care agency or just home, alone. Then a real white knight comes along. Prince Charming says he'll take care of the mother but not the kid. Hey, it's not his kid. He probably gives the girl some time to work it out. In about a month she's ready to leave the kid in a bar or a bus depot."

"Let's narrow the parameters."

Linda threw a sideways look at Tracer as she dug another cigarette out of a twisted pack. He tried to exude the comfort of an old shoe, which didn't fool her a bit, but after she drew tobacco smoke into her lungs, she felt better about letting it out with:

"Our mother throws the kid to relatives."

"Where?"

"Don't push it. The relatives yap and argue. They don't like the mother. They don't like the kid. Maybe it's the Sacramento climate got them down. Whatever. The kid is thrown to an orphanage. There's a good one in the Oakland area. But the orphanage can't deal with the kid even when she's cute and cuddly."

"You mean it can't find parents to adopt her?"

"I mean it never gets the chance. The mother is a mother, remember? Woman's body, child's brain, and the fantasy that it will somehow all work out. The mother doesn't give anyone permission to adopt her darling child. She just lets her get thrown around a bit."

"Where?"

"Wherever's convenient for the mother. The kid winds up in the foster care system. She lands in a place like Salinas because that's the mother's new stomping ground. The mother finds a new Romeo, who's just like the old Prince Charming. And the mother will throw the kid to hell and gone, and visit every third Christmas or so just to rip the scab off the wound. But she wouldn't think of giving up legal guardianship because, y'know, that's like a real wicked person."

Smoke got in Linda Hiyata's eyes. She flicked the back of her hand across her face. "The throwaway kid can't believe anyone would ever want to keep her. She grows up looking at relationships like Dixie cups. You just take 'em or toss 'em as needed. When she has kids of her own, she starts the cycle all over again because, hey, who wants the hindrance of a baby when you're on the way up?"

"What about an abortion?"

"I've thought about that. There must be something really deep in these girls . . ."

The Dodge Dart approached Salinas from the bridge near Spreckles. Speeding along Highway 68, Tracer glanced southward to his right, an habitual movement, like feeling if a wound is still sore. It put into his view the Salinas River's dark, loamy flood plain which was cultivated into fields of row crops. An avenue of walnut trees, their trunks painted white to ward off bore worms, led to the faded red bricks of the Spreckles sugar beet refinery, built at the turn of the Century and abandoned in the 1970s, a portent of things to come. About a quarter of a mile from the refinery and the village surrounding it lay the low-lying hulk of the Vulcan plant, looking like an aluminum exoskeleton cast off by the guts of poor management and bad economic times. The irony of the rest of Linda Hiyata's statement echoed through Tracer's mind:

". . . I mean, if a 'good' mother won't give up her kid, you can't expect her to kill the baby."

To shake the painful image of Vulcan, Tracer looked northward. It was a clear fall morning and he could see the stacks of the power station at Moss Landing rising into the fog that was beginning to lift from Monterey Bay. The station burned oil. He remembered that an environmental group was threatening to go to court to turn it off. Win, lose or draw, millions would go to lawyers.

"Just what we need," Tracer said as he passed the city limits sign.

The skyline of Salinas swallowed Tracer's Dodge. The lights on Main Street worked against him, and ten minutes passed before Tracer could get through Old Town and turn into the Mission District.

During that time he took note of two girls, one smiling naked from a poster on the adult movie theater, and the other a bit younger and wearing what looked to be a brassiere cast off by Madonna, sunning herself on the front lawn of Salinas High School. It had been ten years since the City Attorney had stopped trying to close the theater, and twenty-eight since Tracer and his classmates had had to conform to the high school's dress code. He vaguely wondered why the student wasn't in class, but the stronger stimulus was recalling his own youth, when girls with ruby lips and laughing eyes were glittering prizes and all of life, from beginning to end, was supposed to be an adventure, possibly dangerous but never life-threatening, and always close to the comforts of a quiet Salinas street. The illusion had been most effectively shattered by the *thu-thup* of Communist small arms in the soupy green heat of a Michelin plantation in Southeast Asia.

In the green darkness of Vietnam, he had sometimes worried more about getting shot in the back by some of his own men than by the enemy lurking everywhere else. But only when he returned home did he think the world had turned completely upside-down. The sights he had longed to see were more achingly beautiful than ever, but they had become populated by strangers he didn't remember. Eddie Durand wanted to take him to a special hunting spot. Back then, Eddie had long hair and a Che Guevara beard, sported love beads and tie-dyed T-shirts and believed that their generation's most worthy sacrifices were the burning of draft cards and bras. As if that could not possibly matter between ol' high school buddies, Eddie donned Army surplus combat boots to slog through manzanita and buck brush after white-tailed deer. He talked like GI Joe, comparing the merits of the AK-47 with the M-16, the M-16 with the M-14, and, man, how he'd always wanted to squeeze off a BAR clip and make it sound as rhythmical as a cobbler tapping nails. Then Eddie proudly showed off a field of cannabis that was growing in an isolated ravine of the Santa Lucias. He explained that marijuana was the most lucrative cash crop in Monterey County.

Much later Eddie had been among those of the new Lost

Generation to settle down and become respectable, occasionally experimenting with cocaine at parties when that became fashionable, then giving it up for good when the upscale yuppie dealers were all killed off by much scarier, much tougher homeboys. Someday Tracer was going to tell Chris what he really thought of the son of a bitch whose constitutional liberties he had sworn to defend. The thing was, Tracer would then have to confess that he hadn't defended anything of the kind. He understood only too well that "doing his duty" meant representing an authority that herded boys to their deaths in a land that wasn't theirs, on behalf of a people whose leaders disdained their ideals. To Tracer's mind the fanatical zeal of the enemy was worse in the long run, and he was equally certain that more important battles had taken place at home when he was far, far away.

The gutters and sidewalks of Mission Street were sprinkled with broken bottles, an abandoned shopping cart and several disposable diapers neatly wadded up. Three transients huddled in the doorway of a hotel and leered at Tracer's car as it passed. Beyond them Tracer thought he saw a refrigerator packing carton move. It was topped by a plastic trash bag and rammed against a cyclone fence. It listed forward, then vomited, a wino's portable condo, home of the brave in the land of the free.

Tracer turned up Cedros Street. Its concrete had been poured in the twenties, and the tires of the Dart rattled over the tar that was packed into the cracks like hard black icing. Small stucco houses and duplexes with flat roofs were set far back from the street. Most were ill-kept, but Tracer parked in front of one that had been freshly painted. Royal blue. He got out of the Dodge and approached the house, squinting.

Inside, cheap wood veneer paneled the walls which were

decorated with airbrushed paintings on velvet of the Apollo Astronauts superimposed above the moon, President Kennedy over the White House, and Jesus descending from heaven and ascending thereto. Seated on a couch with a serape blanket for a slip cover, Tracer balanced a hand-painted coffee cup and waved off sticky pink confections offered on a tiered platter. Abriola Patronas set the platter down and gestured to a television set that was nearly as big as the couch.

"Gill, he's the one who got us into this."

The giant screen flickered with a soap opera although the volume had been turned down for hospitality's sake. Framed photos of children of all ages and races adorned the top of the TV. Among them were two color photos of young men in uniform, a Marine and an airman. Late the previous night, Mrs. Patronas had returned from San Diego where the Marine had just gotten married. There was also a recognizable picture of Jennifer when she was much younger than in the snapshot Tracer carried.

"When the doctor said I couldn't have children, Gill wouldn't listen. *Machismo*. Nobody tells Gilbert Patronas no. Some other man? Maybe he would go, but my Gilly, he stayed. And we adopted four."

Tracer's eyes scanned the small quarters, and Mrs. Patronas caught his unspoken question.

"Not all at once. And they're all grown. We just have one boy with us now."

Mrs. Patronas struggled to rise. With a wheezing reach, she plucked the picture of Jennifer from the TV.

"We tried to adopt her. We always try to adopt the Latinos."

"Mrs. Patronas, I'm sure you and your husband provided a loving home. What I don't understand is, what made Jennifer leave?"

"Three years ago . . . a little more maybe . . . her father came back."

Tracer leaned forward but tried not to sound too excited. "You've met him, then?"

"I saw him in the doorway. Just once. In the shadows."

"You got his first name? Age? Address?"

Mrs. Patronas said that his first name was Felix, which was what had first popped into Anne's mind before she came up with others and then said that she didn't really remember. Mrs. Patronas added only a few more details:

"Jenny knew who he was. I took her word for it. Later that night, when she comes back, she was crying." Mrs. Patronas rubbed the knuckles of her right hand. "He had marked her like the *pachucos* used to do."

"I haven't heard that word since high school."

"He put a tack on her."

"Tack?"

"Tattoo. The old way. With a sewing needle and India ink."

"Were they signs? I remember there was a special mark for when a guy got his first piece of—" Tracer caught himself. "One for when you stole. A couple of guys said they had one for killing their first man. Not that we believed them. Stars and crosses, things like that, they were supposed to mean all kinds of things."

"Jenny had numbers." Mrs. Patronas pointed between her first finger and thumb. "And the letters 'KC' right there."

"You don't remember the numbers?"

With a shake of her head, Mrs. Patronas said, "Just that there were three of them. Jenny favored her other hand because she was ashamed. The marks, they weren't pretty like tattoos today. She was going to save up all her money and have them taken off. I said I'd pay for it. Gilly said it was no problem. But for some reason Jenny goes, 'No, no, I can't do it now. But someday.'"

"Do you have any idea what the numbers or the letters meant?"

"It meant she stopped trusting."

"Do you know if her father ever contacted her again?"

"If he did, she didn't trust me enough to tell me."

"Why did she leave your home?"

The woman looked away.

"Mrs. Patronas?"

She talked in a soft voice, still not looking at Tracer; it was as if she were speaking to someone else, far away and long ago. "She was on the phone with her mother. I heard her." Mrs. Patronas's hand moved, indicating where she must have stood in the next room. "She says that she isn't happy here. I can't believe what I'm hearing. She wants to be put with another family. Afterwards I go, 'Why?'

"Jenny says she wants to be closer to Carmel, in a better school. She goes, 'I want a better life.' But this doesn't sound like Jenny. The schools here are good. I go, 'Maybe you want to be closer to your mother?' Jenny doesn't answer. 'But, honey, that's not far away. I can drive you there any time you want.' We both know that even when her mother was here she never bothered to see her. Finally Jenny goes, 'I don't want to hurt you.'"

Mrs. Patronas wiped a tear off her cheek. "'But it hurts me that you want to leave.' But Jenny just goes, 'I'll call; I'll keep in touch.'"

Mrs. Patronas looked at Tracer. "But it was only *me* who would call. I tried to keep in touch . . ." She shook her head at he futility of the effort.

"What do you know about Jenny's mother?"

"A *puta*."

Tracer gave a start. "A whore?"

"Worse, maybe. A woman spreads her legs for a man like Jenny's father, then has a daughter and doesn't even care about her. Just fills her head with ideas about a better life. A *puta* is better, I think."

They talked for a while longer. Tracer penciled into his notebook the exact dates that Jenny lived with the Patronas and where she had come from. The orphanage in Oakland, about which Mrs. Hiyata had generalized, now had the specifics of a name and an address.

After Tracer broke away from an invitation for lunch, he pulled into a gas station where the public phone booth didn't look too vandalized and put in a call to his client.

The ringing phone caught Anne Walker in the midst of directing caterers who were setting out hors d'oeuvres to feed a small gathering. She demanded that they produce another tablecloth, one without a scorch mark if that wasn't too much trouble, then answered Tracer's call in her kitchen, told him to hold for a minute while she went to the bedroom, and picked up there.

"What's going on, John? This isn't the best of times to talk."

"I need you to telegram Mrs. Mendoza."

"Good news, I hope?"

"Some questions need answering."

Anne closed her eyes. How could a man be so thick-headed? "I told you, I don't want to get her hopes up."

"Did Mrs. Mendoza ever bring Jenny by? I mean, so that you saw her in the flesh?"

Anne sighed. "Once or twice."

"Did you notice a tattoo on Jennifer's hand?"

"What kid today doesn't have tattoos?"

"It didn't strike you as unusual, then? The letters 'KC' and three numbers?"

"I didn't look that closely. But it didn't strike me as fashionable body art. I remember thinking, 'Well, girl, if you're going to get a tattoo, at least go to someone who can do it right.'"

"Did Jennifer tell you who put it there?"

"No."

"Did Mrs. Mendoza know?"

"Jenny ran with a wild crowd. Gangbangers, posers, everything in between. Why would a mother know want to know what raving they were up to? What good would it do?"

"Felix Mendoza put it there."

"Her dad?" There was fear in her voice. "But he . . ."

"But he what?"

"I'm just surprised. He hasn't been seen or heard from in years."

"You need to telegraph Mrs. Mendoza and ask if she knows where he is now. Or does she have a relative or an acquaintance who would know?"

"But so what if Jenny saw her dad, maybe? What's the connection?"

"If she saw him, she could be with him."

"Not that son of a bitch."

Like the traffic racing by the phone booth, the thought flashed through Tracer's mind that it took one to know one. He wanted to make the crack based on his firm impression that Mrs. Mendoza was a lousy mother. But she was also the housekeeper that his client thought so highly of.

"I'm sorry," said Anne. "I shouldn't swear."

"What makes you so certain that Jennifer isn't with him?"

Anne's voice sounded lighthearted. "It's a question of character, John. If a man's an SOB, why would he suddenly care
to be with a daughter he abandoned?"

"Why would he brand her with a tattoo?"

There was a long silence and no more lightheartedness.
"I'll wire Mrs. Mendoza and ask what she knows."

"Good."

"John, there's something else."

"Yes?"

Anne looked toward her closed door. "This situation is a bit
more than I bargained for. I mean, if Jenny is with her dad—
Felix, you said his name was?"

"You were right the first time."

"I'm not sure that I want you to go on with this anymore.
I mean, someone like that could be dangerous to you."

"No reason to think that. Besides, you've paid for any
inconvenience."

"But I don't know if *I* want to find Jenny now. Of course,
the money would still be yours to keep."

Tracer drew his hand across his face, rubbed for a moment.
"You're saying you want me to quit?"

"I have a position to protect."

"Uh-huh."

"It may sound snobbish to you, but my friends are not the
kind of people who would understand certain things."

"Like?"

"A Felix Mendoza, a tattooed daughter, a woman like me
getting mixed up with a detective."

"This is a private investigation, Anne. Underline private."

"So far, yes. But what if it went public?"

Tracer didn't answer.

"I sound awful, don't I?"

"A little."

"I need time to think. Maybe you should hold off until . . . Well, if Jenny's with this Felix person, we don't need to know more than that. Good riddance to both of them, I say, and I'll just tell Mrs. Mendoza we can't do anything about it."

"But we don't know where Jennifer is."

"I know where I am, and I need to keep my distance from this. It's not that I don't appreciate your efforts."

He didn't say anything. His finger traced scratch marks in the shelf below the pay phone. Someone named Ruth B. gave great head. He should call her for a good time. If he took his time, someone else would have to respond.

"Are you there?"

"Naw, I was about to walk off. With two weeks' pay for two days' work. Is that what you want, Anne?"

"I want to be protected from this. I don't want you bothering me all the time with a bunch of sordid questions."

"That's easy enough. I can go on looking, then?"

"If any of this looks like it might come back on me, just remember I can sue you for everything you have."

"I think I got it."

She hung up on him.

Figures, he thought, pushing out of the booth. A cold, self-centered bitch was bound to have a *puta* for a cleaning lady.

Tracer drove northward along US 101. The roadway rose and fell through the hills of Prunedale, an unincorporated district that jumbled together rusty buses serving as housing for fugitives from the sixties and air-conditioned stables for breeding Arabian horses. Access roads threw unexpected traffic onto the divided highway while other cars slowed abruptly to turn off to Monterey, Watsonville, San Juan, Hollister, a gas station or a pottery farm.

When the Santa Clara Valley was breached, the road

became freeway. The land was regularly subdivided for tract homes and factories, and San Jose threw an even layer of smog up into the atmosphere.

Tracer slowed to a crawl at San Tomas Road. The traffic always congealed at San Jose, and it took him fifteen minutes to nose his Dodge onto the warped blacktop of Highway 17 that swung over reclaimed wetlands toward Oakland. There he found the orphanage where Jennifer had lived and a psychologist with ebony skin as flawless as a mannequin's.

She was tall and stately, with close-cropped hair and an elegantly tailored dress. She cocked a large soft drink cup off her hip as if it were a champagne glass. She was posed before a window sealed in thick wire mesh. She stared through it with a beautifully serene expression.

Several stories below was a patch of asphalt where a cyclone fence kept little girls out of the street. They were uniformly dressed in dark jumpers and played kickball on the hard ground. To Tracer they looked like atoms being knocked around in a cloud chamber.

The psychologist swept her eyelashes in his direction. Tracer flinched. He was seated before a desk with a nameplate that read, "Fatima El Ali, Ph.D."

"It's so one-dimensional," she said, "so antithetical, so hyper-rational to try and remember one little girl," she waved grandly to the window, "out of an entire stream of humanity."

"I've given you the name and the date when she left here to move in with the Patronas family in Salinas. We've even got Show and Tell."

His finger prodded two pictures of Jenny—the snapshot that Anne Walker had given him and the younger portrait taken out of the frame at the Patronas house. Both had been placed next to the desk's nameplate, which gave Dr. Ali's other title, Administrator.

"That's the Aristotelian way of looking at . . ." The administrator rubbed her fingers together. Her Fu Manchu fingernails looked like they might pluck a word out of the air but finally gave up. "I'm more interested in karma."

"Myself? I'll settle for something on Jenny's father."

Dr. Ali slipped into her chair, appeared to think for a moment, then offered a condescending smile. "Children have levels of consciousness like everyone else. The gratifying thing about my work is the knowledge that their karma will increase. Yes, each individual has problems and regrets. But he or she has as many lifetimes as it takes to work them out. If you're in an orphanage, reincarnation can be a very freeing concept."

"I don't think I could take it again. Potty training. First date. Zits."

The good doctor smiled, and Tracer thought he was getting somewhere. "Do you happen to know Mendoza's present whereabouts?"

"Mr. Tracer, each of us is responsible for his or her own actions. How can we blame other people for what we do? Or for our own attitudes about what's happening to us?"

He put up his defenses again. "Like being gassed at Dachau?"

"True enlightenment is the long-term result for everybody."

"I've got time. Maybe you could tell me about the rest of Jenny's family."

"Have you ever been to India, Mr.—Do you mind if I call you John?"

"Not at all. I was trying to avoid a trip to Sacramento. Do you mind if I ask for a copy of her birth certificate?"

"Unlike ourselves, the east Indian is very spiritual, very advanced."

He said, "I guess that explains it."

Her eyes widened approvingly. "Yes."

"Why he has worms in his belly and his kids are starving on the streets."

Her beautiful features hardened. "I hate to say this, John, but you strike me as being very judgmental. I'd even say you've lost touch with your cosmic consciousness."

Tracer scooped up the photos.

From Oakland, Tracer worked the Dart onto Interstate 80 and his mind into an uproar about psychology, a subject he considered the soft underbelly of science. Within twenty minutes the East Bay breezes were smothered by the still, searing heat of California's Central Valley. Another twenty minutes and the freeway rose over the rice paddies and delta farms surrounding Sacramento.

A half hour had passed by the time he turned at the J Street exit and located the Sacramento County Courthouse within sight of the State Capitol dome. Tracer had difficulty finding parking near the courthouse, got lost after wandering into a graffiti-covered parking structure and walked back to the courthouse through throngs of picketers on the Capitol lawn.

Abortion activists and Pro-Lifers wielded opposing slogans regarding a bill to allow teenage girls to forego parental consent. A lone petitioner in hospital greens sought signatures for a five million dollar appropriation to update the neo-natal intensive care unit in a Los Angeles hospital. A human rights group claiming to represent the three million undocumented aliens entering California each year carried placards silkscreened with stark strands of barbed wire. These were supposed to illustrate that the couple of hundred Mexicans deported daily were being tortured in INS holding centers that were as bad as World War II extermination camps run by Nazis. A group called America For Americans argued that the US was the only country in the world that gave automatic citizenship to babies delivered on its soil by illegal aliens; by Supreme Court fiat, educational, health and welfare benefits had to be parceled blindly to applicants, citizens or not; and the result was bankrupting the state.

Tracer ducked counter-taunts of racism, skirted teachers wanting pay raises, teachers wanting new schools and teachers wanting to limit classroom enrollment. "Me, too," he mumbled, which was picked up by a teacher wanting to abolish standardized testing. Tracer took a pamphlet to avoid a lecture about patriarchal, culturally biased admission requirements for university entrance. Then, as he angled toward the nearest trash receptacle, he realized that just having the pamphlet in his hand made him a target for several sets of hungry eyes.

One carried a cardboard sign on which was penciled, "I'll work for food. Bless you." Another wanted a $200 million gasoline tax passed so that a hundred thousand acres of redwoods could be added to protected lands. Tracer kept his eyes straight ahead and his feet moving, ignoring a plea to join a protest demanding a 50% increase in MediCal entitlements, and thought he had made a break for the courthouse's wide steps when he was blindsided by petitioners outraged that a serial murderer in San Quentin was about to be executed after fifteen years of appeals. After virtually turning tail and running, Tracer entered the Sacramento County Records Department primed for attack, then had to wait five minutes for the clerk to come to the window.

Laser-blue eyes probed Tracer from the other side of the counter. They matched an electric blue half-moon pulling at an earlobe. The clerk's skin had a health spa tan, deep, evenly dark and causing slight wrinkles around the eyes and lips.

She wore a ribbed crew top to show off arms that looked as powerful as anacondas.

"And what do you want?"

"To be treated like a taxpayer. A 'sir' would help."

"You got a complaint, talk to my supervisor." The clerk started to turn away.

"Wait."

The clerk fried him again with her eyes.

"What'd I do?"

"It's been a long day. You didn't do anything." The clerk threw away, "Sir."

"I know how you feel."

"You do?"

"Okay, so I don't." Tracer tried a slight smile. "But I need a copy of the birth certificate of Mendoza, Jennifer, born this county, May '79."

"Isn't that when disco died?"

"We'll get over it. Can you help me?"

"If I want to." The clerk slid a form onto the countertop. "But first you have to fill this out, stating purpose, etcetera."

Tracer began filling in the blanks, felt he was being watched, glanced up. "What if I'm one of those guys who wants the information for a fake ID?"

The clerk's eyes moved off the wedding ring on Tracer's left hand, twinkling. "No, no, no, no. Don't put that down. It'll cause us both a hassle. Births, deaths, marriages, they're public record. Just say you're the public."

"John Q." Tracer pushed the form back.

The blue eyes took in his signature and ID number in an instant. "PI, huh?"

"Yeah."

"I once knew a PI."

Tracer wanted to leave it there, but the clerk didn't.

"Married guy. Used to hide his ring." She shrugged. "Buff, though."

"Pardon me?"

"For what?"

"'Buff'?"

"A hunk. Like, y'know, a stud. Not a 'sir'."

"Nice."

"Very. Twenty dollars and the certificate is yours, John Tracer."

It was hard being hardboiled. Tracer felt like an ordinary Joe hit with an increase in car insurance. "Jeez! Kind of steep."

"Prop 13." She watched Tracer take out his wallet and deprive it of every bill. "But I got my own proposition. It's a special deal for friends. Close friends, y'know."

Tracer put the money on the counter. "My dad used to tell me it takes a lifetime to make a friend."

"Or a clean blood test." When Tracer blushed, the clerk took the money. "You can pick up a copy of the birth certificate tomorrow. Lunch time would be good."

Tracer sounded like an irate citizen. "Tomorrow? What's wrong with right now?"

The clerk looked over her shoulder at the clock on the wall. "It's nearly quitting time."

"It's not even three o'clock."

"You gotta figure coffee breaks. Then I have to make a requisition. Then somebody has to be assigned to pull the record."

"I know the alphabet. Let me look."

"Against regulations."

Like everyone, John Tracer had dealt with the government before. In defeat he turned away with, "Mail it to me."

The clerk glanced down at the form, then called to his

back, "PO Salinas. That's a long ways from here."

Tracer made a final appeal: "Isn't there someone who can do the job today?"

"Why don't you just stay over?"

"Because I haven't got a place to stay."

"I could recommend a good motel."

"You just saw me give you every cent I have on me."

"Maybe you know someone with a couch you can camp on."

Tracer became resigned again. "Just mail it." As he turned away this time, he remembered what his mother had taught him: "Thank you."

The clerk watched him exit, then eased up to a co-worker who was filing her nails at a desk.

"Cover the counter for me, will you? I want to go up to microfilm and get a copy of something in the mail before the post office closes." The co-worker swept an oceanic wave of blonde hair from her eyes and sounded awed. "That's not your job description!" Then she suddenly understood. "It's a guy!"

The clerk sighed. "He didn't seem interested. Do you think he sensed I have Capricorn rising?"

The co-worker reassured her. "No, no, no, hon. It's guys these days. Take it from someone who knows. A person's a little assertive, and guys don't know what to do."

Tracer pulled into his driveway four hours later. He got out of the car and rolled his back to stretch out the aches. As he plodded toward the house, he saw the push mower abandoned in the half-cut lawn. Adrenalin pumped, and he started to storm his castle.

"What are you doing over there? I got slugs in my yard. You're feeding them! I know you are!"

Tracer whirled toward the side yard and the fence separating his property from the vines, foliage and undergrowth of the neighboring yard. It was known to his children as The Jungle House, and the King of the Jungle was the man Tracer called Crazy Riley.

"Feeding them? On what, you crazy doofus?!"

"Dichondra. Look at your grass. There's dichondra in it!"

The limbs of the peach tree rustled against the shingles of Tracer's roof, but no matter how hard he looked into the next yard, he couldn't see Crazy Riley.

His son, glancing over the top of a book entitled *The Criminal Mind*, saw the front door open like a falling barricade.

"Brad! I told you two days ago—"

The words caught in Tracer's throat. He saw Shorty lying on the floor with a game of Chinese checkers. She waited for a guest to make a move. The guest was Tiffany Ericson. The setting called for Father to know best, not go berserk. His voice came out again at a reasonable level.

". . . The lawn, all right?"

9

Tiffany raised her hand like a little girl waving bye-bye. "Hi," she chirped in the same quick, familiar voice she had used when she had propositioned the man of the house.

Slobbering and barking, Dog skidded into the room and made a dash for its master.

"Thanks," groused Shorty to her father. "I nearly didn't make it back to Gloria's last night. Not in one piece, anyway."

Dog leapt at Tracer, who wrestled it away and tried to comment at the same time.

"What? Get out of here!"

"Yeah," explained Tiffany. "I didn't like being spied on." She shrugged away prospective questions and contemplated a marble. "But I was feelin' kind of mellow . . ."

Shorty held out her arms for Dog. "Come." As it nestled into her, she picked up the conversation. "So it was easier for us to make friends than for her to beat me up. Tiffany's staying overnight."

Tracer's reasonable tone tightened with uncertainty. "Nice."
He saw his wife out of the corner of his eye and cut across to
the dining room. "Talk."

Chris took that as a demand for an audience, for understanding and for a host of other things that transpire between
a man and a wife that can't be contained in talk at all. She
nodded toward the kitchen and led the way.

The kitchen smelled of rising bread. Tracer's blood pressure was headed in the same direction. He'd been thinking
about the irresponsibility of Adam, the rebellion of Eve and
the malaise in America. It came out as: "You remember when
Ronald Reagan was Governor and let all of the nuts out the
mental hospitals? To cut spending, huh? But wasn't the ACLU
right behind him? How dare we hospitalize people who were
just exercising their constitutional right to piss on the streets
and talk gibberish? Right? And you know what happened at
just about the same time? Do you? Crazy Riley moved in next
door. When was the last time you ever saw him? Or dichondra? We have never had dichondra. Because we've never had
anyone in this house who cares about the damned yard."

"I thought you were trying to get information about Jennifer Mendoza."

"Don't you see? It all fits. It's all a jungle. A society that
waters down history, debases morality, wastes money, sub-
stitutes sincerity for truth and gives away citizenship is
bound to have throwaway kids. Not to mention New Math,
Nehru jackets and me. I'm a white man, I'm a taxpayer, and
now I'm the friggin' enemy!"

"What did you learn about Jenny?"

He spoke as if issuing a courtroom indictment: "Our children need you. You shouldn't work anymore."

"I'm here when they leave in the morning. I'm home when
they get out of school."

"Do you think I've lost touch with cosmic consciousness?"

"Well—"

"Half the people I met today were crazy."

"I'm sorry."

"Boy, I thought when people applied for a job and lied to you, that was crazy. But today no one lied to me—they just acted normal."

"Crazy."

"Yeah."

"John, do you know what I think is crazy?"

He shook his head.

"I think it's crazy to expect Brad to mow the lawn all by himself."

"I'm not going to get him a power mower. We can't afford it. He'd just cut his toes off."

"He's too young for the job no matter what kind of mower he has."

"Do you know what I was doing at his age?"

"You had a paper route," she said by rote, "and half the lawns on your street. And during the summer you even got a job weeding sugar beets with the *braceros*."

"Right."

"Honey, do you realize you were never in touch? You didn't even like Elvis until ten years after he died."

His head jerked back, rebounding from fallen pride. "I'm talking about serious stuff here, and you're talking . . . What's The King got to do with anything?"

"I don't know. But why don't you tell me what's really bothering you?"

"Anne Walker," he curved a first finger near his thumb, "came about this close this morning to telling me to back off the case."

"Good thing she didn't take the hourly rate."

"That's not funny. You don't want me doing this at any rate."

"I'm just stating a fact of life. She must have had a good reason."

"Sleaze factor."

Chris raised a questioning eyebrow.

"She's afraid some mud might splash back on her . . . *precious position.*"

"What's wrong with that?"

"It's too pat; it's too vague."

"How can it be both?"

"I don't like her."

"There's your reason."

"It's not just personal. I have to listen to her. I don't know what position she's talking about. Sure, I saw a great apartment, but she told me she wasn't rich. But she has a cleaning lady, you say. Who is *not* around. She mentioned that she did charity work with kids. What kids? The only kid I know about is Jennifer Mendoza. And Miss Charity acts like she'd feel wonderful if I could just tell her that Jenny is dead. Oh. And she says she's engaged. *Who* is she engaged to?"

"Why don't you ask her?"

"None of my business."

"Right. So why don't you go settle down with the evening paper while I finish dinner?"

"The way I feel, the news will just make it worse."

"Oh, I don't know." Chris kissed his cheek. "I think you might find it very soothing."

Tiffany tossed a smile over her shoulder when Tracer re-entered the living room.

Preoccupied, he settled into the room's one chair and snapped open the *Salinas Californian*. The family's subscription had nearly been allowed to lapse during the last household budget reduction, a drastic measure considered in the gruesome process of winnowing wants from needs. For over forty years Tracer had been reading the *Californian*, a tradition passed on from his father who read the paper when it was called *The Salinas Index*, a tradition that involved young John Tracer spending many an afternoon folding and tossing them in the general direction of customers on his paper route, a tradition that ended up with the adult John Tracer pounding his fist on the kitchen table and declaring he would rather sleep on a park bench under the paper than give up having it delivered daily to his porch, even if that meant on the roof or through a window.

He turned immediately to the funny pages and wished they would bring back Little Lulu and Joe Palooka. Then came national and international news, which got him talking to himself. Local items had him firing off imaginary letters to the editor. Sports was saved for dessert.

An item grabbed his attention. A picture showed a world-famous cardiologist, Dr. Richard Fencoe, wrapped around the backside of a pretty young thing whom Tracer knew as Miss Anne Walker. It was fairly clear that the good doctor knew her much better, though, and the two were listed as engaged, both to be married and in preparation for a charity golf tournament the following day in Pebble Beach. The tourney was a fundraiser for the Children's Home Assistance League.

The accompanying article briefly explained that CHAL was a nonprofit organization that worked with other volunteer groups and increasingly with local government agencies in the areas of foundling and foster care, scholarship assistance, and public awareness of child abuse and prevention. Richard Fencoe, MD, was the honorary regional chairman of CHAL.

To Tracer that meant the doctor rubber-stamped the activities for the tri-county area of Monterey, Santa Cruz and San Benito, and was on the League's California and national governing boards, which required yearly attendance at meetings in places like Hawaii and Key West. Fencoe obviously had nothing to do with CHAL administration but contributed much-appreciated money and prestige. His fiancée was co-chairperson of the entertainment committee for Tuesday's tournament and probably had to call a few caterers. Miss Walker's relationship with Dr. Fencoe explained her presence in the publicity photo. Also, it corroborated what she had said about her association with the League.

Tracer imagined that there were a number of older dowagers who held a lot more important positions in the CHAL chapter than Miss Anne Walker, but they weren't as close to Dr. Fencoe and they wouldn't have looked nearly as good in short-shorts that left the bottoms of their butts jiggling free. Tracer took the paper into his wife and flashed the picture of Fencoe helping his fiancée bone up on her backswing.

"Our client does seem to have a position to protect."

"I know."

"Judging by the doc's face, I'd say he'd like the position to be dog style."

"Set the table," commanded Chris.

Tracer obliged, pleasantly ruminating on the curves, the warmths and the cools of the female frame. So his client was a little coldhearted, a little fickle. She looked great! His eyes wandered into the living room, where Tiffany Ericson sprawled on the carpet. Her thighs and buttocks were as round as a woman's but firm and tight like a girl's. And her baby eyes were going over Tracer. Startled, he jerked back to the kitchen.

"What's wrong?"

"Nothing."

John remained edgy throughout dinner.

The rest of the Tracers didn't eat so well, either. They mainly listened. Brad with his mouth open. Shorty transfixed. Chris with tears welling in her eyes. Tiffany talked, mainly with her mouth full, as intent on getting the food in as the words out.

"I never got used to anybody's home. I wanted to. But didn't dare . . .

". . . The first couple of families, I kept hoping, Please. Let them adopt me. And I tried really hard to be good . . .

". . . But they would always put the suitcase by the front door. They can't look you in the face, so that's how they do it. Put the suitcase by the door. Then you have to have breakfast. Like nothing's gonna happen next . . .

". . . The counselor said it wasn't me. It just didn't work out, y'know . . .

". . . I'd like to find my real mom and dad. I don't care how awful they are. I mean, I don't care what they're doing. Or did.

". . . By the time you're six, if you're not adopted, there's just no way it's gonna happen. The agencies keep trying. But people keep putting your suitcase by the door." Tiffany held her plate to the man at the head of the table. "Can I have some more meat?"

Chris quickly intercepted the plate and balanced it with vegetables.

Two hours later Tiffany and Shorty lay awake in twin beds. Tiffany's face had been scrubbed of makeup, and her punk hairdo was washed and combed out. In the soft light that filtered into the bedroom from the hallway, she looked as vulnerable as Shorty and nearly as young. From across the hall and through the open doorway of another bedroom, the girls could hear a private moment between Tracer and son:

"Our Father who art in heaven, hallowed be thy name. Thy kingdom come, thy will be done, on earth as it is in heaven. Give us this day our daily bread; and forgive us our trespasses, as we forgive those who trespass against us. And lead us not into temptation, but deliver us from evil. For thine is the kingdom, the power and the glory, forever and ever. Amen."

"Does he pray every night?" Tiffany whispered.

"With Brad."

"On his knees?"

Shorty thought of her father begging and felt her face flush. She could hear footsteps approaching, so she turned toward the wall, pretending to be asleep.

"In olden times," continued Tiffany, "the knights in armor, with their swords and shields, got down on their knees."

Tracer appeared in the doorway. "Everything ship shape?"

"Huh?" Shorty grunted.

He crossed to his daughter's bed, leaned over her and bussed her cheek. She liked the attention but wasn't about to show it.

"Good night."

"Mmm."

He staightened in Tiffany's direction. "We'll see you tomorrow."

"You don't pray with girls?" Tiffany asked.

"About a month ago Shorty told me she didn't believe in God."

"I didn't say that."

"What did you say?"

"I said I didn't believe in patriarchal religions."

"Same thing."

"No, Dad, it is not."

"She wants an Earth Mother, with white witches and people like Crazy Riley getting all the benefits."

Shorty let out a deep, derisive sigh.

"Anyway," Tracer said to Tiffany, "you and I can send up a few thoughts to the Almighty if you like."

"Naw," Tiffany said, "I don't believe in that Billy Graham shit."

Tracer coughed out a "Well," and recovered with a more casual, "God bless you, anyway." He started for the door but was stopped by Tiffany's final question:

"You kissed her good-night. What about me?"

He put on an easy grin. " 'Night," he said, turning into the hall.

In the master bedroom Chris lay curled on her side, her eyes closed, her body seemingly relaxed. The bedding billowed to the small earthquake of Tracer getting in beside her. He kept space between himself and his wife and his eyes locked open toward the ceiling. After a long moment her eyes sprung open. Her statement was matter-of-fact, her tone relieved:

"You're not doing so well, either."

He shook his head. Chris could feel the movement.

"My worry's Tiffany," she said.

He nodded.

"John, we've always tabled moves to become foster parents . . ."

He held his breath.

"But you remember how serious we were about it before Brad was born."

"A couple of kids around the house, they sure tire you out, don't they? Hardly have time for anyone else."

"I think it's time we got serious again about being a foster family. We'd have to discuss it with Shorty and Brad, but I know they'd want us to act. There's a need right now in our own home. I couldn't believe what that poor kid said at the table."

"She smokes," he managed to reply.

Chris turned over and propped herself up to look at him, to reason with him and to win him. "It wouldn't be a bed of roses, I know. Of course we'd encourage her to quit. But I don't think we should force that particular issue right away. There are going to be a lot of adjustment problems."

John let his words out carefully. "I don't know how sincere she was, but she . . . kind of propositioned me."

Chris's face remained serious as she tried to compute what she just heard. "Kind of?"

"Well, it was Saturday. She didn't know who I was."

There was a pause. "So now you want to be her foster dad so we can keep it all in the family."

"You're the one who wants a foster child! I just want to go to sleep."

"That's all you have to say?"

"*I* didn't do anything."

"*Something* happened."

"You don't believe me?"

"Of course I believe you."

"Then let's table the motion."

"Good idea."

Conscience relieved, he rolled away from her with a sleepy "'Night."

She turned away, yanking the covers. After a moment she angrily swatted his cushioned body. He turned to look at her.

"Why can't you get a normal job?"

The next morning John Tracer drove Tiffany Ericson to her junior high school in Pacific Grove. The Dodge pulled up to the playing field behind the main complex of buildings as kids trickled across the grass toward the quadrangles of classrooms, but Tiffany didn't get out of the car. She looked at Mr. Tracer for a long time, sizing him up. He wasn't as bad as she had first thought, but could she trust him with a friend's life? With her own? With anything? Tiffany wasn't very good at analyzing situations, so finally she shook her head to clear it and just spoke.

"Jennifer had a boyfriend named Lloyd French. He's twenty-three. She snuck out the window at night to see him. Not that the Grissoms would ever care. I think he knocked her up. She loved him. They're going to get married. See? Nothing to worry about."

Tiffany bolted from the car. Tracer jumped, too. She was running, but he was able to stop her with a yell.

"Wait!"

He approached cautiously. She looked furtively for friends who understood her and didn't demand anything from her. He knew the best way to get information from people was for them to volunteer it, but Tiffany had volunteered as much as she was going to and he needed facts now, not some punk kid's fatuous opinions. She was shaking her head even as he spoke.

"What'd he look like? Where'd he come from?"

"I told you, he was twenty-three."

"Weight? Height? Hair color?"

"Just a guy. Kinda shrimpy, but a guy, okay?"

"From where?"

She shrugged, trying to play it cool, but her voice was more agitated. "I *don't know*. I gotta go. Will you leave me alone?"

He closed the distance between the two of them and took a chance by grabbing her arm.

"I know you're not worried about Jennifer, but other people are. What do you know about Lloyd French? Were you ever with them?"

"We did some dust together."

She squirmed. He was shocked.

"Angel dust?"

"It's not as bad as you think."

"They tranquilize elephants with that stuff. Some folks go berserk and cut their grandmothers into little pieces."

"We don't get wasted. You gotta know how to handle it. Let me go!"

"How long did she know this great guy who got her zonked and pregnant and now is going to look after her?"

"A couple of weeks. A month." Tiffany wrenched hard. "I said, let go!"

"Better do it, Mister, and do it fast."

Tracer obeyed the high pitched decree. It came from the lady cop at the Carmel PD. She had a gun on one hip and a nightstick way off on the other. She looked like she'd love to use both.

"In this burg we don't like creeps who hang around schoolyards and play with the little girls."

10

Detective Sergeant Amcheck put down his phone and looked wearily across his desk at an angry citizen.

"A rapist jumped bail, so the DA hasn't got a court commitment this morning. He'll see you in an hour."

Tracer wasn't grateful, but he repeated what his mother had taught him. "Thanks."

"Hey, it was a fluke. We try to keep her inside, but she's gotta go home, come to work." The policeman shrugged. "She drops her kid off at school, and there you are looking as suspicious as Caryl Chessman putting a red light on his car."

"She didn't even read me my rights."

"She's new at this. What's with you, Fosdick? A cop does her job, and suddenly you want to cry to the ACLU."

"I want to know what you're going to do about Jenny Mendoza and Lloyd French."

"I just did it. If the DA has any information on French, he'll give it to you. That's a big favor, y'know. And not exactly legal."

"I'll tell you what's not legal. He's twenty-three. She's fifteen. That adds up to statutory rape and misdemeanor child molestation. With charges like that you could drop the 'Be On The Lookout' and up it to an 'All Points.'"

Amcheck chuckled softly at Tracer's night-school knowledge of jurisprudence, then shook his cadaverous head philosophically.

"You're going to love the DA. He once said to me . . . it was about a dentist in Monterey who used to flash the hookers on Franklin Street . . . he said, 'No jury in the world ever let the law stand in the way of its sense of justice.'"

"Meaning?"

"Meaning did she cry, 'No! No!' when she was undergoing statutory rape and misdemeanor child molestation?"

"The law is supposed to protect kids. When you're fifteen, you don't know how to make an intelligent decision."

"A year ago her decision would have made Lloyd French guilty of felony child molestation. She's had a birthday since then, so now it's only a misdemeanor. Next year she's free to be as stupid as she wants. Teenage emancipation. Another wrinkle from the minds of our enlightened leaders. A sixteen-year-old, by petitioning the court, can emancipate herself from family, guardians, whatever. Legally she becomes like an eighteen-year-old . . ." Amcheck laughed sardonically, ". . . an adult who can live by herself and enter into contracts. When someone looks like she's in the process of becoming emancipated—and when you run away from home, that's what you look like—you got an even harder case to make that she's a victim. Technically crimes have been committed. But even if you could get a jury to convict, where are you going to find a judge in California who would put the boyfriend behind bars for a couple of years on a technicality?"

"What about the drugs?"

"Is he a pusher or a user?"

Tracer shook his head: he didn't know.

"Look, we got some info now that we can feed into the network and pass on to other departments. Maybe we'll get lucky. If they get stopped for cause—parking violation, littering, whatever—a cop someplace can run a check on the state computer. There's enough now to hold them. Overnight. This town and this county ain't spending any money to go pick 'em up."

"Overnight's long enough. I'll go wherever she is."

"You don't understand. We're still talking a million-to-one shot." Sergeant Amcheck unlimbered from his chair with a baleful expression. "C'm'on, you need a cup of coffee. Maybe a Danish or an anchovy pizza."

Tracer grinned. "Pass. I want to check in with my client."

His client peered into a little window, grew excited at what she saw and feverishly began working the combination of the postal box.

A man named Cesar Valasco kept his excitement to himself and his back to Anne Walker. He was a great blubbery fellow with a happy face and a ponytail. To pass time, Valasco stood at a table with a pen chained to it and a sign above that read, "Unauthorized removal of Federal property is a felony punishable by one year in prison and/or a $1,000 fine." He used the pen to fill in the blanks of an application for a Civil Service qualifying examination. He gave his name as Master Bates, his age as 100, his sex as faggot and his home address . . . he was working on something really good that would start with 69 when he heard Anne Walker slam her mailbox closed.

He turned casually in her direction, watched her cram an envelope into her purse, then clatter away on high heels. He watched her retreating rump and absently looped the chain around his writing hand, thinking about ripping her dress off. When she turned outside, Cesar Valasco waddled after her, flicking his wrist and yanking the pen from the table. He liked the way it wrote.

Outside, Valasco watched Anne get into her Mercedes convertible. As it pulled away, he got into a '65 Impala, chopped and raked, with red paint lacquered on in a dozen fine layers flecked with silver. His belly jiggled against a steering wheel as small a salad plate. He picked up a normal-looking $1,200 cellular phone and called his boss.

"Yo, Reuben, my man?"

"*Gordito! Que pasa?*"

"I'm all," sounded like one word. "I'm all at the post office. She got the letter."

"From the girl?"

"Who else would answer that stupid ad?"

"*Tu miras, chingaso?*"

Cesar Valasco's eye definition got lost in a frown that looked like a smile. "I'm all watchin' the bitch, man."

"And I'm all talkin' to you. Did you see an address? Do you *know* who it was from?"

"I was gonna knock her down, you know, and grab it? But like, I'm all thinking there's people—"

"Don't think. Get the letter." Reuben Bustamonte hung up on him.

But Cesar Valasco couldn't help thinking as he turned the ignition to fire up the chrome under the hood of his Impala. A real muscle car. He could feel the engine's low rumble all the way into his *cojones*, and that made him think even more. For two weeks, he and his boss and their compadre Hector had been switching on and off watching the post office, where the Walker bitch had rented a new box. It was

boring, man! One night Hector had said . . . and Hector was
so *ba-a-ad* he didn't talk much, so when he did, you had to
listen to what he said . . . why don't we tap her phone, too,
because the girl might call? The ads said she could call. But
Bustamonte told him to shut up, his brain was fried, he'd
watched too much TV in prison. What were they? The
Untouchables? As long as the Walker woman kept going to
the post office, they'd know the girl hadn't called. So they
had to hang around all day and do nothing but think. Oh,
man, the Walker bitch looked so fine! Sweet, like a Chiquita
Banana. Now that she had a letter. As he drove off, Cesar
Valasco thought about getting Anne alone in her apartment,
taking the letter from her and getting her to talk real nice to
him.

Anne Walker was disappointed. So was Tracer. The envelope
she carried bore the cellophane window of a bill, was
addressed to "Resident or Box Holder" and advertised a
chance in several million to win a cheap sweepstakes spon-
sored by second-rate magazine clearing house. Because
Anne was hoping for something from Jennifer Mendoza, she
wasn't at her apartment when Tracer rapped on the door.

He turned away and moved down the hall. He passed a
steel cart laden with cleaning supplies and linen. A white-
suited maid reached out of the open doorway of an apartment and pulled the cart inside. Tracer was pushing the
elevator button when he wheeled around and skipped up to
the doorway.

"Excuse me. I suppose you do Miss Walker's apartment,
too?"

The woman looked at him. She had high cheekbones and
a patrician nose.

"I mean, now that Mrs. Mendoza's gone. She's actually the

one I'd like to ask you about. Do you happen to know Mrs. Mendoza?"

The woman tilted her head back, veiling her eyes with her lids.

Tracer flashed his most winning smile and spoke confidently. "*Yo hablo Español solamente un poquito. Lo siento. Habla usted Ingles, Señora?*"

"*No, Señor.*"

Tracer closed his eyes and tried to remember everything else he had learned. A total of four years of high school Spanish and one in Stanford to meet the general studies requirement for his degree. Tom sits next to the window. *Tomas cerca de la ventana.* He is very tired. *Es muy consado.* Tracer opened his eyes with panic.

"Uh, *yo es . . . amigo de . . .*" He pointed toward Anne Walker's apartment. "*Usted . . .* uh . . . know . . . *hablar* with—*con*—work, I mean, *trabajo . . . Señora Mendoza?*"

The lady tilted her head back farther, like the *doña* of a *conquistador* about to order the head off one of the savages, so he pulled out a final stop:

"*Verdad*, no?"

She shut the door in his face.

In the building foyer, Pop turned his head and squinted at the opening elevator. He blinked a few times as a disgruntled Tracer emerged.

"Who's that?"

"Tracer. Miss Walker wasn't home."

The old man simultaneously grunted recognition of the voice and shook his head, confused by the words.

"But I didn't see her go out."

"I'll bet."

Tracer picked up the pair of Coke bottle spectacles on the security station counter and slipped them onto Pop's face.

"Hey." Pop adjusted the weight digging into his nose. "I don't need these."

Tracer slammed the bar that opened one of the double glass doors leading outside. His client was cranking her Mercedes into a parking space. They met under the canopied entrance. Anne was in a breathless rush to move on.

"I have a lead."

"That's great! But we'll have to discuss it later. I'm co-chairperson of the golf tournament. Children's Home Assistance League. Tee off is in an hour at Pebble Beach." She started to move past him. "And I'm not even changed!"

"Sure. I'm just goofing off on my way to the DA's office."

Anne whirled around. "I told you this had to be secret."

While they argued, a motor rumbled louder and louder, like an approaching growl.

"I didn't say the *National Enquirer.*"

"Then why the law?"

"Maybe a few have been broken. The name Lloyd French mean anything to you?"

"Never heard of him."

Behind them, a '65 Impala nosed into the parking lot. A trunkful of batteries powered hydraulic lifters that kept the chassis a whisper from the pavement. Cesar Valasco kept one arm cocked out of the cut down side window and craned his head toward Anne Walker, straining to hear what the Chiquita Banana had to say to the bozo. He cut the motor but was still too far away to hear the jerkoff speak.

"He's an older guy. Jenny probably ran off with him."

"But that's great!" exclaimed Anne. "That means she's okay. Maybe they'll get married. Maybe . . ."

A surprised reaction came from Pop. Watering, his eyes bugged toward the lenses framing them. "Damn! What's a low rider cruisin' around here for?!" The guard tore his glasses off and listed around the counter to the entrance.

Between Pop and his prey, Tracer bore down on Anne Walker. Client or not, he had a job to do.

"I need to talk to a parent. Has Mrs. Mendoza responded to your telegram?"

Anne put her hands to her ears. "Why do you keep going on about the parents? It's not them you're supposed to find! You're supposed to find Jenny!"

"Find her for what?"

"To see if she's okay."

"I already know the answer to that. She's a throwaway kid. Some real lovely people have been trying to dump her ever since she was born, but their consciences keep getting in the way and making things worse. Like the little old lady who strangles the chicken slowly because she can't stand to see it suffer from having its head cut off with a hatchet."

Pop passed them and tottered purposefully toward what he was paid to do—keep the Third World away. Having no interest in the security guard's business, Anne addressed Tracer angrily. "What makes you so self-righteous? Judging other people, looking down on them. What do you know about it?"

Tracer remembered that a career in this business meant solving cases and leaving the clients satisfied. "Not enough." He paused to put on a nearly contrite expression. "Jenny was gone for a day or two, maybe more, but the Grissoms let that slide as though it were nothing to worry about. How did the news break?"

"Jenny's mother. She calls from time to time to check up."

"What was the occasion? Leap Year?"

There was an icy silence before Anne Walker answered. "My engagement to Dr. Richard Fencoe. That may not be important to the entire world, but Mrs. Mendoza was happy for me."

"Congratulations," Tracer ventured. "So she called to tell Jenny your good news and found out she wasn't there?"

"Yes."

"But she didn't report it to the police, did she?"

"No."

"But supposedly Mrs. Mendoza was real worried?"

"Yes! So worried she didn't know what to do. What are you accusing her of?"

"Why didn't you go to the police?"

"Because I went to you." Anne drilled him with an accusing look.

"*Touché.*"

In the background, if either of them had been looking, the guard could be seen gesturing at the window of the Impala. Valasco appeared as placid as a jellyfish.

Anne's tone became more conciliatory as she sought Tracer's approval. "I went to you to avoid a scandal. I don't have to explain why I don't want this to blow up and come back at me. If you think that's selfish, that's your problem."

"I didn't say that."

"You don't have to. But as a matter of fact, my marriage would benefit other people. It would have an effect on Mrs. Mendoza for one. Her job would change from being my cleaning lady to becoming the housekeeper of a fairly large estate. Perhaps large enough for her daughter, too. Maybe she and Jenny would never get along to where they could live together. But at least she would be able to give her extra money, presents, things to make Jenny's life a little easier."

Anne's voice took on a righteous tremor. "Mrs. Mendoza didn't go to Mexico because she's heartless and irresponsible. I sent her there, remember? Because *I* know the sacrifices she's making. And, yes, yes! She did answer my wire. Felix is dead as far as she's concerned. She's glad she doesn't know where he is. So you have nothing there, John. Except you were able to dig up a ghost from the past and try to rub it in the face of a woman who doesn't deserve it."

Tracer's shoulders rose and fell in a tired sigh. He nodded, feeling a little like a heel, but not much. "Look, your name hasn't come up in this investigation so far. I don't see any reason why it would have to when I go to the DA's office, either. I'm going to satisfy some questions about the present, not the past. I have an appointment. I could go just out of curiosity. I'd like to be going at your request."

"I'm too rattled to fire you today."

Tracer grinned.

As he turned away from Anne, Valasco shook off his passivity.

"'Casing the joint?' What's that? I'm all lookin' for a job, man!"

"What kind of job?" asked Pop suspiciously.

"Dishwasher. Waiter. Maybe I could show people to their tables."

Pop hooted with relief, "You ignoramus! This ain't a restaurant!"

Valasco heard Anne Walker's voice, in the distance but clear as a bell: "John!"

The guard heard Valasco utter, "Oh-h-h," as benignly as Elliot the pig in *Charlotte's Web*. Pop didn't catch Valasco's eyes tracking Anne Walker.

She was trotting after Tracer, who was heading for the Dart. As Tracer turned to Anne's call, she reached into her purse and held out the envelope from the post office box. She brought her voice back down to conversational level.

"I can understand your frustration. This is what I got in the mail just now."

Valasco watched the man named John take the envelope.

"Hey, I know him. That man is my *amigo*. Johnny, uh . . ."
Valasco snapped his fingers. ". . . it's on the tip of my tongue,
man."

"Tracer?" said Pop.

"Juan Tracer! *Si!*"

Tracer was reading the advertisement with a wry smile.

"Please keep trying," Anne urged. "Believe me, Jenny's
mother is a good person and would want you to keep doing
your best."

Tracer became reconciled to his boss. "You might try
branching out with your classifieds. You've covered the area
where Jenny's come from but not where she might go."

"This is a big state."

"It's a crapshoot. But you haven't hit southern California
yet. A lot of runaways wind up there. Don't put your ads just
in the big dailies. Try the underground papers, too."

"I will." She gave Tracer a quick smile, then hurried back
to her apartment building.

Valasco looked beyond the old fool passing himself off as a
guard, who was saying, "So why don't you try the China-
man's in the Barnyard? I hear they got real good take-out."
Valasco saw Tracer holding the envelope that he had hoped
to take from the Walker bitch himself.

Tracer wondered what he was supposed to do with the
envelope. He tentatively held it in the direction of Anne's
retreat, figured it wasn't worth the trouble of returning and
shoved it into his most convenient pocket. Then he got into
his Dodge and ground it to a start.

The Impala stayed behind the junkheap for a few minutes.
Cesar was in a bad mood. If he was going to rape Anne, he'd
have to break in and do it on his own time. Letting two cars get
between him and his quarry, Valasco wished he was in a
stolen car, so he could just rear end this Tracer son of a bitch

and pound him into the sidewalk when they got out to exchange licenses. As the Dodge moved up to a cross street intersecting Ocean Avenue, Valasco switched on the hydraulics to lift his Impala up to legal clearance. The stream of through traffic sucked in the Dart. The car behind wanted to continue across Ocean, but rather than edge up to the divider and gun on through, spreading cars and pedestrians like Moses splitting the Red Sea, it waited until both crosswalks and all four narrow lanes of the avenue were clear. Valasco laid on his horn, making the driver of the car immediately ahead flip him the finger. Valasco grunted, reaching under the seat for his Glock 9 mm, but as he felt its grip, he sighed with resignation. Too many upstanding witnesses to allow him to get away with a simple drive-by shooting.

Tracer's Dart headed slowly up the hill toward Highway 1.

Carmel Valley and Big Sur lay in one direction; Monterey and the Salinas turnoff in the other. By the time Valasco looked both ways there was no sign of the gringo anywhere.

Letters as blue as the ocean, spelling *Salinas Californian*, were bolted to the newspaper building, two stories of concrete flanked by a municipal parking lot where Tracer's car was doing time at a meter. Its owner, heading toward Alisal Street, quickly jaywalked the four lanes to get to the blocks and columns of Monterey County's judicial and administrative buildings.

In the prosecutor's wing of the courthouse, the corridor was wide and echoing, with wainscoting and a high ceiling built when labor was cheap. Black lettering on thick double doors at the end hall proclaimed entry to the domain of "Simon Bolivar Levin, District Attorney." Tracer felt like he was encroaching on the Wizard of Oz.

Levin looked more impressive in person than he did on television or in the newspapers. He reminded Tracer of a stocky version of Basil Rathbone. The District Attorney's spacious private office felt closed in with memorabilia, including a skeleton missing only the very top of its skull. The room appeared as if it should be overlooking Baker Street, not Alisal, a look that the elected official was only too delighted to perfect.

"Amcheck said you were definitely not a cop."

"That definitely was not a compliment."

"He said I should be nice to you as payback for false arrest. Or allegation thereof. Big difference, you know. Not that I would try to talk you out of going to a lawyer and wasting everyone's time."

"He said you might help me with some information. As a professional courtesy."

"Cops and ex-cops I'm used to. I tell them not to get too zealous with their nightsticks and have *some* probable cause—a complaint, a shriek, I'm not picky—before they raid a party and find a Supervisor's kid with Bolivian marching powder. But outsiders . . . it's hard to know what to expect."

"Sir, I just want a lead on Lloyd French. Maybe he's gotten into trouble or has a record. I haven't had time yet to check DMV, but my man is twenty-three years old. At least that's what a pretty messed-up kid told me."

Levin spread his hands toward a bank of massive wooden filing cabinets. "See those? My case load for twenty years, and ten years as an apprentice to the prosecution. I have 'The Mad Crapper of Pacific Grove' in there. 'The Slut of Soledad Street.' She was giving it away free, but I made the solicitation charge stick because she demanded cab fare home."

Tracer reckoned that the cabinets could have stood behind

Levin's secretaries in the outer office, but the effect would have been less theatrical.

"'The Greatest Alibi in the World.' This fellow robbed a liquor store at eight o'clock in the morning with a sawed-off shotgun and a pair of woman's panties on his head, like a mask. He was picked up ten minutes later, after a high speed chase, with the panties, the shotgun and rolls of nickels, dimes and quarters in the back seat of his car. He refused a court-appointed attorney and represented himself. Do you know what his alibi was?"

"Excuse me, Mr. Levin, but I want to know about Lloyd French."

Levin sounded hurt. "I'm trying to tell you about the vagaries of life, fortune and human nature, but you want to jump right into the real dregs." He spoke as if to himself. "An outsider. No perspective."

"I have a case. What I'm not sure of is how much time I have to solve it."

Sighing and shaking his head, the District Attorney got up and crossed to the cabinets. He opened the drawer of one, rifled the files, chortled at one and pulled out another, which he took back to his desk. All the while he kept up a stream of musings more or less directed at Tracer:

"French, Lloyd. Born in Baltimore, but the most permanent address he ever had was a boys' camp in New Mexico. His rap sheet in California is a Gray Lines Tour of fights, petty theft, drugs. A rubber check charge almost held. I got him for setting fire to a wino. The wino lived, which was too bad because the jury found the old geezer extremely disgusting. I could see it coming, so I dropped the attempted manslaughter and let Mr. French cop a plea for carrying arsonable materials."

Simon Bolivar Levin laughed. "The parole board actually

recommended suspending his sentence. French got the minimum, anyway. A year as a guest of the state."

"At Soledad?"

The prosecutor nodded and gave Tracer a photograph divided into front and back views with prison numbers underneath each. The portraits showed a young male caucasian with long, light-colored hair and a spotty complexion.

"Can I get a copy of this?"

"For the low, low price of just ten dollars."

Tracer flinched.

"Vote Proposition M when it comes up on the ballot." Levin smiled easily. "Sure, I've got a vested interest. But I'm a taxpayer, too. I know how you feel." The smile faded, and his face tensed with sincerity. "The thing is, I've cut so much fat out of the budget, we're down to bone."

"Yeah."

"Enough politicking. To tell you the truth, French is a personable chap. He can make black sound like white while his eyes swim with sincerity. I'll hear from him again. Coyotes will find the remains of some old lady, and guess what? She will have withdrawn all of her savings to give to Mr. French, who told her whatever she needed to hear."

"When did he get out of Soledad?"

Levin gave the file a cursory look. "This says he's still paying his debt to society."

While Tracer grimaced at the thought that he was on a wild goose chase, the District Attorney chuckled.

"It's amusing, isn't it? The notion that a criminal can pay the populace back. With what? Free room and board? The crime is inflicted against a single individual who gets absolutely nothing in return except pain and grief."

Grasping at straws, Tracer asked in a small voice, "Excuse me, sir. Are you sure that data is correct?"

The prosecutor's smile broadened. "That was my first rude awakening. You can't trust official records." Levin tapped his temple. "But the ol' photographic memory hasn't failed me yet." The DA beamed like a lighthouse. "He's been loose for the past month and a half."

"Could I get in touch with his cellmate? Talk to him. Maybe French told him his plans for the outside."

"There's another one of my happy boys. If French is a lady's man, this one's the Cary Grant of psychos. Or was."

"He's dead?"

"Oh, no. No, no. If Mendoza were dead, I wouldn't be an atheist."

"Mendoza?"

"Felix Mendoza. Name mean anything to you?"

The Santa Lucias stood blue-gray against a pale sky. Rows of stately eucalyptus provided windbreaks for the flat patchwork of furrowed fields. In the distance sprinklers threw lacy rooster tails of water. Closer, hunched against the afternoon wind blowing from the north, a crew of laborers worked broccoli, cutting it and loading it into huge wooden bins pulled by tractors. Male and female looked alike; most wore baseball hats with bandannas tucked around the backs of their necks. Their cars and pickups, in many instances their only property, lined a frontage road parallel to US 101.

Tracer took in the Salinas Valley scene, driving southward along the freeway, fifteen miles out of Salinas. His mind was dredging up what DA Levin had said to him:

"The Salinas Valley is the pipeline for most of the heroin coming into the US from Mexico. The small towns in the valley don't have the law enforcement to keep track of illegal aliens moving in and out. The people are easily intimidated, so delivery systems with few traceable ties to the syndicate can be set up. The syndicate in this case is *Nuestra Familia*, Our Family or the so-called 'Mexican Mafia.'"

Tracer's car climbed onto a freeway off ramp marked "Soledad Correctional Facility." The overpass turned east, away from the Santa Lucias. There were more fields and eucalyptus and the brown, low Gabilan Mountains. Also chainlink fences topped with concertina wire. They circled guard towers and cell blocks. A smokestack stood high above Soledad's infamous O Wing, the maximum-security detention center.

Arranging Tracer's entry into the prison, Levin had told him, "Felix Mendoza was—perhaps still is—a lieutenant in *Nuestra Familia*. We picked him up three years ago in a King City fortress with half a million dollars worth of junk."

At general receiving, a metal detector was waved at Tracer like a magic wand. As it beeped, he was forced to remove his watch and his belt because of the buckle, and empty his pockets of change and keys. These were duly catalogued, along with his wallet and identification. He was allowed to keep a photograph, and for being a good boy, he was given a pass to O Wing.

"That's wholesale value," he remembered Levin saying. "Nineteen large bags, one kilo each, nineteen kilos consisting of one part heroin and one part with milk sugar, quinine and a mild laxative called mannite. The adulteration would have increased twenty times as the heroin went through three more major distributors. The profit would have gone up approximately 300 percent, so the street value would have worked out to two million dollars."

Tracer's escort, who didn't pack a gun, left him with two guards who did.

Tracer held up the wall at O Wing receiving, legs spread, arms out and above his head. Obviously not trusting in technological magic, one of the guards performed an old-fashioned pat down while the other examined Tracer's pass. The DA's name didn't seem to impress them although one grumbled that Levin was probably the reason Tracer wasn't being strip searched.

"That's the price we gave to the media," Levin had said. "It made us sound good. War on drugs and all that. But in fact *Nuestra Familia* lost only their initial investment of $500,000."

"Not exactly chicken feed," was Tracer's reply.

The grumbling guard led him into space—a catwalk cantilevered to the highest of three sets of tiered cells. Closeting iron flanked one side of the cell block; echoing vastness yawned open on the other. The guard mumbled that Tracer must really have pull. There was a general lock down in effect because of a rules infraction: prisoners weren't allowed out of their cells, couldn't go the visiting room, and that was the only place visitors were supposed to talk to them, through a phone. But the inmate Tracer wanted to see wouldn't have much use for that, would he?

"Being corrupt," the prosecutor had concluded, "the family suspects everyone else of being the same. They think we played funny with the figures. At least, we think they think that. Maybe there were twenty kilos, not nineteen. Maybe someone made a quick $30,000 profit." There was a chuckle. "I know I bought a new MG that year."

"What about Mendoza?"

"They've been watching him, I'm sure. They're not ones to let something like that go. Maybe he's clean; then again, maybe he'll break. They've got the time, and Soledad is practically their home. But if he can put up with that kind of pressure, he's not going to give you anything. He's probably fathered kids from here to Sacramento and doesn't care

about any of them. I can get you in to see him, but that's all
I can do."

So Tracer didn't expect much when he reached the
promised cell. Felix Mendoza sat in the corner on the floor,
not on the bunk, with his knees hunched to his chest. He was
a fine-featured man, once undoubtedly handsome. Right
now he wasn't clean and he didn't seem to care. Dark circles
hung under his eyes. Something black and sticky rimmed the
inner surfaces of his mouth. Tracer thought Mendoza might
have been sucking licorice, but the man didn't swallow or
move his lips. When Tracer held the snapshot of Jenny
through the bars, Felix Mendoza just sat there like a dumb
animal, not responding.

"This is what Jennifer looks like now. I know you know her
because you saw her just before you were arrested. Your little girl is growing up, Mr. Mendoza, and it's tough, and she
needs your help."

Something glinted in Mendoza's eyes, perhaps tears.

"I don't know her, but I'm starting to think of her as Jenny.
Maybe because I have a daughter of my own. I'm trying to
find Jenny, but I don't know where she is. I think she's in
trouble. You're her father. I know you must care. Please, Mr.
Mendoza, help me find her. Lloyd French has got her."

The name got him.

Mendoza lunged forward, lost his balance and squirmed
on the floor. His hands grasped upward at Tracer. Wounded
animal noises stampeded from Mendoza's mouth, which was
clotted inside with old gore.

The guard and Tracer moved quickly away from the grunts
and groans issuing from the cell.

"Sheeee," griped the guard. "Should of asked me. They
always tell me but never ask me. Tha' sucker just got out of
the infirmary. Fell down in the yard a week ago playin' bas-

ketball. Bit his tongue clean off. Shhheee. Said you wanted to see him, not talk to him. He ain't never gonna talk again. If you ask me, it weren't no accident, neither."

Tracer grabbed the man's arm.

"French. He had a year to talk to French."

"Shee, man, I don't know what they said to each other."

"Where would a drifter like that go?"

"You jes' said it. Driftin'."

"Come on! There had to be someplace special. A pool hall, a chili parlor, I don't know."

The guard jerked his arm free. Rubbing it petulantly, he had a thought. "In the day room he'd root for the Rams."

"Anything else?"

"He liked the Angels."

Tracer nodded. He was getting somewhere.

"Sheee. So do guys from Cleveland."

11

A directory for Monterey and San Benito Counties hung under a pay phone. A huge hand jerked the book onto the shelf and yanked it open to the back. It was as good as any other place for random access to 400,000 entries. "Monterey Peninsula" headlined the first grouping. A thick finger impatiently probed a section of names under the letter "T." Another porcine hand clawed the pages to the next geographical grouping. The Salinas area. Under the "T" listing the finger stopped on the name Tracer, the only one, as in John, in Creekside, off Highway 68. A pen embossed with "Property Of US Government" and a piece of chain dangling from its end flashed onto the page. Cesar Valasco gouged ink around the Tracer entry and ripped the page from the directory for safe keeping. The book was left open on the shelf, not put back where it belonged, and Valasco left the booth, relieved that his boss wouldn't quite kill him for letting the letter almost get lost.

. . .

Its diesel engine crescendoed as the bus from Monterey to Salinas grumbled into higher gear. It had dropped Chris at the Highway 68 turnout for Creekside subdivision, and now she trudged past the fence and bushes skirting the access street to her home. She was irritated that she didn't have the car and took little comfort from John's making as much money in two weeks as she could in three months. His fee had already been spent to make a dent in their debts, and he probably wouldn't get another client any time soon, which meant that Chris was still the main breadwinner, steadily being knocked silly from one temporary job to another. They probably wouldn't be a two-car family again until Congress passed a tax reduction. She figured hell freezing over was more likely. Two years ago the Ford Escort in which John had driven back and forth to Vulcan had gone to one "Happy Hal," a used car dealer recommended by John's Uncle Mike. Chris's parents said that the source of the recommendation should have been enough to warn anyone they wouldn't get a deal. Seven months ago Chris had seen Happy Hal the Price Hacker on TV talking a mile a minute about selling their family wagon, ". . . at two below Book, you crazy campers, and you know what that means!" Thus her beautiful Jeep Cherokee had been replaced by the ugly Dodge Dart, and now she was reduced to taking the bus while John played detective.

A block away in the Tracers' family room, glass doors looked onto a cement patio with old garden furniture and an expanse of high grass. Dog basked in the Indian Summer sun let in by the doors, stupefied by its warmth, probably asleep. Brad lay beside the animal, belly to the floor, chin on forearm, engrossed in a library book festooned with pictures of manacled murderers, grim-faced policemen and shallow graves. Brad heard the front door open and said, "Mom?" but didn't twist around until he heard his mother moving through the kitchen. She emerged through the doorway into the family room, still carrying the mail and glancing at the first couple of past due notices.

"Early start on your homework?"

"I could really help Dad if only he'd let me."

"You could start by getting straight 'A's in school or becoming a superstar in football."

"What good would that do for the case?"

"It would get you into college without our having to pay for it."

Chris sat heavily on the battered Naugahyde couch that ate marbles and pocket change and, she suspected, when no one was looking, probably at midnight, pens and pencils left in other parts of the house. She continued to sort through the mail, but her son was undaunted.

"Remember Dad talking about that tattoo on Jenny's hand?"

"I remember him talking to me very early this morning when you were supposed to be finishing homework that should have been done over the weekend."

"There were three numbers. And the letters 'KC' . . ." The boy took in a deep breath, held it until he needed another, then let it out with a dramatic, ". . . that's a secret code."

"For what, dear?" was the absent reply.

"Buried treasure."

"Do you know what else I remember?"

Brad shook his head from one side to the other, a solemn no.

"Your dad getting very upset." She pointed to the back lawn.

His attention sulked back to the book while hers dutifully

returned to the mail. A government envelope sparked her urgent interest, and she murmured with a pleased start, "The birth certificate."

Brad scrambled to her side as she tore the envelope open, jerked out a photocopy and snapped out the folds. The form indicated that Jennifer Mendoza was born at Sutter Memorial Hospital. A girl child, she was fathered by Felix Mendoza, address not given, and delivered of Annie Mae Walker.

"Annie Walker?" exclaimed Brad. "But that's who we're supposed to be working for!"

At the Pacific Grove Gate of the Del Monte Forest a Chevy, a Buick and a Honda waited for the toll clerk to take five dollars from their respective drivers and allow them entry into the park. Taking advantage of a round-out that skirted the barrier were a Lincoln and a Maserati with resident stickers, followed by a lumbering Gray Lines Tour Bus. The driver addressed his gawking charges through a PA system.

"Scenic 17 Mile Drive takes us into Del Monte Forest, a 4,280-acre private preserve of some of the choicest real estate in America. The Forest is perhaps better known as the home of the famous Crosby Pro-Am Golf Tournament."

Chris tried to look as aloof as possible as she took in a rock wall slipping by, revealing here and there the castle-like battlements of the old Crocker Mansion. She had paid for these views many times before, but only with her husband beside her or driving visitors from outside the area; never in a tour bus behind a man who kept urging his wife to take pictures and look sharp for Bob Hope.

"But that's Palm Springs," the woman whined.

The wall ended at sheer cliffs that plunged into the Pacific. One spectacular promontory was topped by a lone cypress that twisted away from the sea like a crippled sentinel.

"Golfers," said the driver, "from Arnold Palmer to Johnny Miller have found the water hazard particularly difficult." The man in front of Chris guffawed, but his wife only began to snort when she saw other passengers chuckling.

Chris stood up.

Del Monte Lodge loomed ahead of the driver to his left; greens and the Pacific stretched to his right. He had been through his routine a thousand times when Chris came up behind him to give the thousand and first a new wrinkle.

"Within a mile of each other are four of the world's most famous golf courses. And the most famous of all, coming up on our left, is Pebble Beach. That's Del Monte Lodge where you can stay and play . . . and wait two weeks for a tee off time."

"Excuse me. I have to get off here."

The driver put his hand over the goose-necked mike. "Ma'am, there are restroom facilities at the back."

"This is my stop."

"Lady, people on buses don't get off in Del Monte Forest."

Chris reached up and pulled the emergency stop cord. The alarm buzzed on the instrument panel. The driver's automatic reaction was to hit the brakes. Chris reached across him to pull the lever activating the doors. They whipped apart with a whoosh of pent-up air, and Chris bounded down the stairwell and out of the bus before the astonished driver could say anything more.

Chris knew that she was acting mainly on impulse, but since she had seen the birth certificate, she also knew she had to act on something. She had plenty of time to imagine the embarrassing situation she might be getting into, but no time to formulate a plan. Face flushing, she decided this was no time to start thinking rationally.

She asked a question or two of the first people she encoun-

tered and finally found the 19th Hole Clubhouse lying
beyond the Lodge, closer to the water. It overlooked a yacht
anchorage. Chris walked past some tanned golfers and headed for the entrance, where a sign supported by a tripod confirmed that the day's play was in benefit of the Children's
Home Assistance League.

Sporting types mingled around buffet tables and the bar.
From time to time they directed deferential gazes to a line of
four or five personages at the head of the room, paying obei-
sance as to hosts and organizers. A blond so vibrantly beautiful she stopped Chris in her tracks was among the
luminaries. Keeping close to the blond's side was another
magnificent creature—a very tall, very distinguished-looking,
white-haired gentleman. The couple's splendor made the
Anne Walker and Dr. Richard Fencoe of the newspaper photograph look like peasants, and Chris, who had merely
glanced at the newspaper, wasn't sure whether she had
found her mark. Feeling pretty much like a peasant herself,
Chris zigzagged slowly across the room. As she ventured
closer, she passed two old biddies who at least confirmed her
homing instinct. They talked in the voices of dowagers who
had never cared what the servants might think and weren't
about to start now.

"Who is that with Dr. Fencoe?"

"Anne somebody."

"One of his researchers?"

"Oh, no. This one he's going to marry."

"Then who is she?"

"I hear he met her at the Hog's Breath Inn. She probably
wanted to get her hooks into Clint Eastwood. Instead she got
him."

"Well, in my day a man needed to belong to the Bohemian
Club and not have syphilis. But a woman's credentials had

to be impeccable. I don't know what the world's coming to."

Chris made her final approach, speaking breathlessly, "Miss Walker?"

"Dear! How nice to see you. I—" Anne looked more closely and caught herself before faltering completely. "I am sorry. I don't seem to recall your name."

"We've never met. And your picture in the paper didn't do you justice. My name's Christine Tracer."

Anne Walker turned charmingly to the gentleman beside her. "May I introduce you to my fi—" She really faltered now and looked back to Chris. "Christine who?"

"Just call me Chris. My husband works for you."

"Oh!" exclaimed the gentleman, not noticing the color leave his fiancée's face. "And what does he do?" The gentleman suddenly remembered his manners and extended his hand, saying, "My name's Richard Fencoe," then quickly returned his attention to Anne. "I didn't know you had people working for you, my dear." Before she could answer, he was back at Chris: "She's full of surprises. That's why I find her so irresistible."

Anne recovered blithely. "Mr. Tracer is my tax consultant." She leveled an unblinking look at Chris. "And his wife and I are two ladies who need to powder our noses."

The two ladies advanced on the bar, Anne gesturing to the bartender. "Double vodka." She looked at Chris. "You?"

Chris, thinking of the money in her purse, looked momentarily puzzled.

"Your house chablis." Anne smiled at Chris. "Right?"

Chris nodded dumbly.

After Anne paid for the drinks, she lead Chris to a quiet spot on the terrace that overlooked sea and sails.

"I explained to your husband that I really don't want anyone to know that I'm employing a private investigator. I'm therefore assuming that he sent you here on very urgent business. Please make it brief." Anne downed a quarter of her vodka, waiting.

"He doesn't know I'm here."

Anne looked at her steadily, still waiting.

"And he doesn't know that you're Jenny's mother. Not yet."

"What is this? A threat? Blackmail? What is this?"

"I love my husband. I want to know what you've gotten him into."

"Finding a lost girl, but apparently you want to complicate that. Fine. John Tracer's services are no longer required." Anne Walker started to turn away.

"Who are you?"

Anne whirled around, eyes flashing, and in an instant her features wavered between defeat and arrogance. She waited. The past was threatening to break through, but she took control, pushed it back and spoke calmly:

"I'm a woman who's made some mistakes in her life. One of them was acting on impulse in hiring an investigator to find someone who's probably better off forgotten."

She turned again, but Chris grabbed her arm, sloshing some of the liquid out of both their glasses. It was Chris who was not in control, but she didn't care anymore.

"Who are you?"

Miss Walker looked down at the splashes darkening her dress, then lifted her gaze and held it on the woman before her. "Shall I have you thrown out?!"

"You're her mother!"

"Do you need a picture? No one here knows that!"

"What if Jenny told someone?"

Anne glanced about, frustrated by the flutterings of conscience, trying to get some kind of bearing from which to leave doubt behind. "I haven't thought it all out yet. Jenny wouldn't tell on me. She . . . she loves me too much."

"What about your loving her?"

Even if Anne didn't like this woman, perhaps she could get her to understand. Anne did want to be understood, to have people see things her way, so she spoke as candidly as she could.

"Dick wants his own family. Maybe someday he'll be able to accept Jennifer as his step-daughter. I—I don't know. When your husband kept going on and on about unimportant things, I began to see Mrs. Mendoza as another way to bring Jenny into our lives. As a foster child."

"Does Mrs. Mendoza even exist?"

"In a way. She's kind of like the mother I want to be."

"She's the best you could imagine?"

Anne didn't catch the irony of Chris's question. "I haven't talked about it to Dick yet. Maybe I should add some things. It would easier to tell him that Jenny is mine, but I have to make sure of him first. You can see that."

"And what's Jenny supposed to do in the meantime?"

"That's why I'm trying to find her."

"To keep ignoring her again?"

"No! Just until the timing's right."

"So you want to find Jenny to keep your thumb on her. To make sure you know what closet the skeleton is hiding in."

"You don't know what I've been through! Do you know what it's like to have to grow up with an old man who . . . who likes to . . . likes to . . ."

Chris was shocked by the thought that Felix Mendoza might be Anne's father, too. But how could that be? She groped for something to say. "If you were molested, I'm sorry."

"Molested? What are you, a barbie doll? I was fucked, lady.

By my old man, by life, by people like you. I tried to run away at fifteen. Do you know what it's like to drop out of high school? Huh? You talk like shit, you feel like shit and you go out with shits. You gotta work to eat. All kinds of people look good to you when you're in the gutter. Felix was—" She gave a derisive snort. ". . . just a homeboy with pretensions. When he left me and Jenny high and dry, I knew all I had was myself. And when I realized that, I was free, baby, because I knew I had something."

"Yourself? What about Jenny? What about her?"

"Everybody's out for what he can get. So I took what I needed. I'm not ashamed of it. I fought, and I worked, and I learned. And my daughter will benefit someday because I got here."

Anne's eyes jumped wildly, taking in the seascape. "I deserve to be here. I'm not going to be fucked anymore. I have my rights. I did my best. And you could have helped. But no, you're one of those la-dee-da Wonder Bread bitches. Well, you're fired, bitch. Tell that to your husband. I hope you're real proud of yourselves for what you did to Jennifer!"

Burning with indignation, Anne Walker stormed back to the comfort and security of people who understood exactly what she wanted them to.

Chris felt like her psyche had been run over by a Mack truck pulling a couple of Fruehauf trailers loaded with worry. The truck backed up slowly, parked, and Chris felt as if she could scarcely move with the weight of how she was going to tell her husband that they were right back where they had started.

Brad's sister came home from hanging out with a friend in the next block, saw her brother asleep with Dog on the family room floor, made a phone call to the friend, talked about what they had just talked about, then went up to her room to study.

Brad wasn't quite asleep; he was in that weird state between a dream and waking up, and the dream was less of a dream than a wandering memory of those days when no one was worried about everything and his dad used to come home from work and play catch with him. His dad would even take him fishing in Los Padres National Forest where the smell of the sugar pine and redwoods that lined the creeks made you so giddy you could get a headache. Dad was always out of his sleeping bag before dawn, saying that it felt like noon. They would cook bacon, eat it burnt on one end and raw on the other, Dad telling Brad how when he was a kid the best way to catch fish was with something called a Dupont lure. The fingerling rainbows they caught would be rolled in cornmeal and sizzled in the bacon grease. Brad was so hungry he hoped Mom wouldn't feel like cooking and would pick up something at McDonald's. No, that didn't happen very much anymore, but maybe she was picking up frozen french fries at the grocery store. He could hear Shorty outside on the patio talking to somebody. Maybe it was Mom back from Del Monte. It seemed like she had just left. Maybe it was Dad! Brad wanted to be the first one to tell him about the birth certificate. He tried to tell himself to move, but his limbs felt dead and tingly. He was eager to tell Dad about the treasure idea, too. It wasn't fair that Shorty should be the one. Wait a second, he hadn't told her, so he would be the first . . . if he could just move!

Dog made whimpery soft squeaking noises, and when Brad's eyes opened with effort, Dog wasn't there anymore. Brad rolled over, his body coming back to life, as he saw three men peering down at him.

Reuben Bustamonte tapped the glass, then flicked his fingers, gesturing for Brad to trust his easy smile. "Come on, *muchacho*, we don't want to break the door. Open it, please."

Embarrassed, Brad stood and opened the sliding door. The man who spoke looked like he was a television actor or the leader of a salsa band. One of his friends looked like a big playful whale with a pony tail; the other looked sad and hungry.

"Who are those people?" came a shout from over the side fence.

The sad one and the fatty each gave starts, one to the side fence, the other to the back fence perpendicular to it. Bustamonte looked questioningly at Brad.

"That's just Crazy Riley."

"Gardeners," Bustamonte called toward the side fence.

"About time!" replied the disembodied voice.

Bustamonte stepped past Brad into the family room. "You don't mind if we come in, do you?" Following, the whale knocked against Brad and didn't apologize.

"Who are you?"

"I'm Mr. Washington. These are my associates, Mr. Jefferson and Mr. Lincoln."

The fatty seemed to choke, his cheeks rippling.

"Who are you talking to?" came a shout from Shorty upstairs.

The sad one moved quickly toward the living room.

"What are you doing?" demanded Brad.

Bustamonte put a great deal of patience into, "Didn't your parents teach you? Children should be seen and not heard."

Again the fatty's face jiggled with a snorting laugh.

"And where are your parents?"

12

Tracer piloted the car into his driveway, an automatic reflex, and shut down the motor, another reflex. He sat for a while, trying to let the heaviness of the day slip away, but it didn't slip that easily. He got out of the car. He heard the faint clatter and whir of the push mower coming from the back yard, an encouraging sign, and headed for the front door of his shelter, his fortress, his sanctuary.

He let himself in and stopped. An imperceptible something. The sound of the lawn mower was loud, but that only meant the back door in the family room was open.

Dog slunk from hiding in the dining room. He avoided the family room entrance and gave Tracer a cowering glance, then slouched quickly across the living room carpet to curl silently in a corner.

Tracer moved warily for the family room, expecting the linoleum to be dirtied. Nothing could have prepared him.

His wife and daughter sat rigid and white, each giving him

a silent, startled look with fear but no relief in it. Shorty sat close to the open patio doors. Beyond, in the lounge chairs, two strange men were shirtless, taking in the sun.

Hector Montdragon came across as a standard model psychopath with extras including a lizard face and thin, snaky limbs. He turned an unblinking stare in Tracer's direction, a kind of test drive to let Tracer see that his reptilian brain stem was in fine working order.

Brad was struggling to negotiate the mower through a swath of grass. When he spotted his father, he broke for the house with what sounded like a cheer, "Dad!"

But the other man, Cesar Valasco, a great, blubbery fellow, half rose from his chair, which creaked dangerously. "Back to work!" His facial features melted into a jolly smile. "Don't worry. I'll keep on top of him, and this dump will be looking very, very good."

"Who are you?"

There were no introductions forthcoming, but Bustamonte sashayed in from the kitchen with a box of Liquifruit.

"No beer. What kind of hospitality is that?"

"Who are these people?" Tracer demanded of his wife.

The intimidation had been psychological and silent and therefore that much more terrifying. Chris could barely speak.

"Brad tried to warn me when I came in, but . . ."

"They just appeared at the back door," added Shorty.

"Hey," chuckled fat Cesar, "we were just looking."

Bustamonte came forward. "Your son asked us to come in. And, Mrs. Tracer, you have not told us to leave."

"I—I—" she began haplessly, then she tried to explain to John: "They said they had to wait for you. They insisted."

"No force," interjected Bustamonte. "We don't like force."

It made Tracer sound asinine, but it was just one of those

things that came out under pressure: "I'm going to ask to see your identification."

Bustamonte looked hurt. "Identification?"

Cesar's eyes lost definition in a menacing smile. "We don't need no stinking IDs." Then he burst out laughing, jiggling all over.

"We need the letter," explained Bustamonte.

"Letter?" asked Tracer.

"The letter from Jennifer Mendoza. The one that was picked up at the Post Office this morning by *Senorita* Walker, then given to you, Mr. Asshole."

Valasco said, "I'm all followed you from the bitch's apartment, where she gave you the envelope." He glanced for approval at his boss.

"Ah," said Tracer. "That letter."

Lizard face, succumbing to a degree of socialization, tried to match Cesar's broad smile.

"When did you figure that Mendoza didn't have the heroin?"

"Heroin?!" exclaimed Chris.

Tracer glanced at his wife. "They were watching Jenny's father and probably tailed his cellmate when he was released." Tracer looked at Bustamonte. "French's going to Jenny must have made you think you were on to something. But then they gave you the slip."

"We didn't lose nobody."

"Sure. The classifieds were your lucky break. Otherwise, how would you know about the post office? And what are you doing here if you had any idea where to find Jenny and her family?"

"The letter, *pendejo*, or I will give your daughter a taste of what it is to be with a real man."

"Let me," said Valasco.

"John, for God's sake, give them what they want."

Bustamonte held out his hand while Tracer searched his pockets for the letter. When he found the envelope, Bustamonte snatched it. But as Bustamonte studied the advertising, he appeared rapidly disappointed at his chances of winning. Then another one of those things that just happens under pressure took place, this time with force and grace.

Tracer's right fist rammed forward, his shoulder and back solidly behind it. Had his aim been on target with Bustamonte's chin, Bustamonte would have been coldcocked. As it was, Bustamonte's cheek cracked with the blow, and his midsection caved with the quick left that followed.

Brad was never more proud of his father than at that moment. Seizing the opportunity, the boy turned the lawn mower toward the patio and pushed like Hercules. Hector Montdragon was leaping from his chair. Brad yelled, "The door! The door!" As Cesar Valasco flailed like a beached walrus out of his chair, Montdragon rushed the house, all systems go, his brain on full auto troglodyte.

Shorty didn't realize that Brad's shouts were meant for her. With stunned horror she watched Montdragon race past and leap on her father.

Outside, Brad ran the mower onto Valasco's foot and shin. The man wore shoes and pants, but the mower's blades still bruised and cut. Bleeding and yelping, the fat man tumbled to the cement, and Brad backed up to make another run.

Inside, Tracer crashed with Montdragon into the wall. They broke apart and exchanged quick, hard blows.

With a shriek of rage Chris broke a lamp over Bustamonte's back. He stumbled for the back yard.

"The door!" screamed Brad again.

Bustamonte straight-armed the boy just as he was taking chunks out of Cesar's hammy fist and forearm. Brad sprawled to the grass with a wind-jarring *thump*. Bustamonte tried to heave the fat man into a kneeling position.

"*Vamanos! Son locos!*"

Brad lifted his head weakly to see over his chest. He watched his dad take a karate kick to the ribs. His mom went for Montdragon's back but was thrown aside like a rag doll.

"Door," groaned Brad.

Shorty's face finally lit with understanding. She shoved the sliding glass door closed. Montdragon hit it at a full-tilt run. He crashed to the patio in a shower of glass and stumbled onto the lawn, where Brad was gamely staggering toward the mower.

Bustamonte grabbed Cesar's hair, trying to give the man incentive to heave his bulk over the back fence, the one perpendicular to Reily's impenetrable jungle, when Dog made a barking appearance. Cut and bleeding in a hundred places, Montdragon didn't want to take the time to strangle a yapping dog, so he lurched off after his fleeing companions.

Tracer called his son away from the mower with a curt, "Leave him!"

Dog took up the chase but only managed to nip Montdragon's heel as he tumbled over the fence. He and his companions could be heard careening through the adjoining backyard and over its farther fence.

Tracer tasted blood and snot streaming from his nose. His tongue pressed his teeth to test whether they were loose, but what was really shaken were his nerves. He dropped an arm around his son's small shoulders. Tracer squeezed hard to keep himself from trembling.

"Okay?"

There were tears in Brad's eyes, but he kept his lips clamped tight and nodded yes.

They limped back to the house. Their shoes cracked shards

of glass. Tracer looked with concern at Shorty. She gave a little smile, then reached up and wiped the blood from her father's upper lip. He turned to his wife.

There was a goose egg under Chris's eye, but she didn't feel it. She was picking up the bits of the lamp, as if to piece together understanding from the sudden violence that had shattered their lives.

"You all right, honey?"

She shook her head and nodded in the same movement, a kind of twitch.

"Did anybody see a car?"

In answer, Chris flung her hand toward the debris. "It'll take hundreds of dollars to fix this up!"

Tracer got very reasonable, sounding like Bill Cosby restoring order among the Huxtables. "I'm going to call 911. Then I'm going to get some ice cream at the store to celebrate that we're all right."

"We can't afford ice cream. We still have back bills to pay."

Tracer reached out to tenderly touch his wife's bruised cheek. That's when the flood gates opened with an anguised sob:

"And . . . you're fired!"

Tracer sat behind the wheel of his Dodge. He stared at the garish lights of the neighborhood convenience store, vaguely thinking about ice cream. Near the pay phone were two boys with bikes. One wore a flannel shirt, open, the tail flapping over Levis manufactured with rips at the knees; the other a ski parka, gloves and sweat pants. They debated whether to pool their money for Bubble Yumm or a Slurpy. Tracer debated whether to move. When the boys went into the store, he finally dragged himself from the car and walked to the phone.

Tracer punched in Anne Walker's number. Call me a wild optimist, he thought morosely to himself. Maybe they could work out a compromise. Anne's cover hadn't been blown. If he understood what Chris had told him, Anne was still worried about Jenny's whereabouts.

She was worried enough to fear her daughter's voice bleating out of the answering machine and filling her darkened bedroom. Anne was going to take Tracer's advice to extend the reach of her classified ads, but whether Jenny wrote or not, she could still call at the wrong time. Whoever was calling, the ringing interrupted the grunts and groans of Dr. Fencoe making love to Anne. He was unaware that she hadn't inserted her diaphragm. After the run-in with Chris, Anne had decided that from now on she needed to make sure there were no escape routes in their engagement. Dick wasn't thrilled by her unwrapping her heels from behind his neck and rolling out from under, practically breaking off his manhood. He gasped why did she have to answer the bloody phone, but she wasn't about to take a chance on who might be leaving a message. Besides, he was getting the kind of sex he wanted, and whenever other people got what they wanted, Anne didn't much enjoy it.

"Hello?"

"John here."

No response, just breathing. She sounded as if she had run a mile to get the phone.

"Look, I understand you're very upset, but I don't see why your being Jenny's mother changes anything. I still can find her for you. No one has to be the wiser."

She pressed the receiver so hard to her ear it hurt. "Who is this?"

"John. John Tracer. We shouldn't quit on this. I mean, you already paid, and I'm willing to—"

"Listen, you pervert, if you ever use foul language like that again . . . if you ever so much as call this number again . . . I'm going straight to the police!"

Anne slammed the handset down and hugged herself. Fencoe wrapped his arms around her.

"Who was that?"

"An obscene caller." She turned into his arms.

Her phone rang again.

"Don't answer it," Dr. Fencoe said.

"I have to." She picked up the handset, didn't say anything.

"Fine," said Tracer, "I'm fired. But I've racked up expenses. And it's in our contract that—"

Again, she slammed her phone down.

The clerk manning the register bagged Tracer's selection, a half gallon of rocky road. Tracer paid and left.

He was opening the car door when it hit him. He threw the ice cream onto the seat and spun back to the store.

The glass around the entrance was festooned with posters and notices, commercial and public service, both professionally crafted and from the hands of such local artists as Scout Troop 11. But one flyer nearly at ground level had grabbed Tracer's attention—a copy of the one Sergeant Amcheck had given to the soldier, the one about the girl, any girl, missing from Oregon.

The clerk watched with growing amazement as Tracer squeezed past the rack of comic books and dirty magazines. He looked to be reaching for the floor.

"Something I can help you with, Mr. Tracer?"

Mr. Tracer didn't answer. He peeled the flyer from the glass and walked out.

Night students trickled down the main corridor in the Social Sciences Building of Hartnell College. A few were typical teenagers; the rest were adults with circles under their eyes. Inside one of the lecture halls, crabbed handwriting had brightly colored the rules of evidence onto a white display board. Now an eraser soaked in solvent took swipes through them. Prosthesis squeaking, Professor Charley Caputo limped the length of the board to cleanse away the techni-

calities that freed Miranda and other miscreants. The retired
San Francisco police captain grumbled:

"I thought we'd been over this crap."

Tracer sat in the front row of the junior college amphithe-
ater. A huge fan of empty seats engulfed him.

"Yes, sir."

"And you got a 'B' on the test if I recall."

"I was tired, sir."

With a metallic squeal, Caputo pivoted around. "You think
an IRA bomber gives a flying Irish fuck whether you're
tired?"

"No, sir."

Caputo hobbled up to the demonstration bench. He leaned
forward to put body English into a lecture he'd delivered a
hundred times before.

"Missing Persons, Mr. Tracer, have links. Links that con-
nect the past with the present. A habit, a concern, a fetish. A
missing person may often change names but seldom the ini-
tials. If he likes Chinese take-out in Stockton, he'll like it in
Toronto. That's a missing adult. The problem with missing
juveniles is that they have shorter stories."

Caputo turned and began to crab-walk the length of the
board, like a drunk spider. "There's not enough past history
to get them set in their ways; not many credit cards, bounced
checks or irate spouses to hound them. A runaway is headed
more often for a dream than a place on the map. He's willing to hitch rides to nowhere, has few qualms about sleeping
under boardwalks and can look as innocent as Bambi," the
professor picked up a marker from the chalk tray, removed
the cap and began writing, "while filling out a motel registration card with, 'A. Count, Monte Cristo, Nev.' If he has the
money to eat out, Mr. Tracer, it's where eighty billion are
sold." Caputo turned. "Any questions?"

Tracer instinctively glanced over his shoulder for a class-
mate to take him off the hook. "I was hoping—Well, I'm pretty good at interviewing people. I mean, I know how to make
the quiet ones talk their heads off, and I can direct the loud-
mouths into keeping it short and sweet. Generally, I'm just
interested in what people have to say. And I'm not afraid of
the work. But at Vulcan we had forms, references, contacts in
the industry . . ." Tracer shrugged.

"What you're saying is, you want a short cut from walking
endless streets, knocking on a thousand doors, looking at
phone books till you're bug-eyed, and then driving to hell
and gone, and back again."

"I don't know if I'd put it that way. Isn't there some trick
of the trade or something?"

"That's the kind of question I'd expect from a 'B' student."

"Sir, I'm not a starry-eyed undergraduate. I've got a family,
okay? And I told you what happened. My client isn't about to
reinstate me. I'm under no obligation to continue this case.
There might even be a question of professional ethics."

"Oh, professional ethics? That's serious. Like the code of
silence with police officers, so a crooked cop doesn't have to
worry about brother officers turning him in. Or surgeons
turning a blind eye on a guy who can't even quarter a dead
chicken for a barbecue. Or lawyers. Yeah, there you have
professional ethics. Every judge has to have been one of the
gang. A law degree is practically the first requirement to run
for office. A fair price is whatever they can gouge, and thou
shall not give away a photocopy for under a dollar a page.
Unless there are sixteen hundred goddamn television reporters
there for publicity! And you're never gonna see lawyers called
on it because they control everything and protect their own.
Don't talk to me about *professional* ethics. The word is *ethics*,
period, goddamnit."

"Well, I should be looking for another client, not playing the Good Samaritan. So I'm looking for a break, that's all, to see if it's worthwhile to put in a little more."

"When I was on the force," the ex-Captain turned to the board to write a word, "we used to call missing juveniles 'Losers.'" He underlined and repeated the word for emphasis. "*Losers.*"

Caputo turned and arched his eyes with sarcastic sympathy. "What's the matter, Mr. Tracer, I've just given you a great excuse."

Tracer felt like squirming under the man's gaze. "I didn't come here for an excuse."

"Ah. Perhaps the truth then." The professor squeaked to the other side of the demonstration table. "The City of San Francisco was paying me when I got my leg blown off. They didn't pay me enough. But if a man is in this line of work because of the pay, Mr. Tracer, he'd better go back to selling tires."

It was pitch black inside the building. There was a grinding noise. A sliver of dim light sliced across the blackness. With more grinding, the light elongated into a rectangle. The light came from the night sky, and a silhouette in black, the figure of a man, stepped into the rectangle, his head wreathed in smoke.

Tracer stood on the loading dock of Vulcan Tire & Rubber Company. His breath frosted into the building, disappeared. Before him stretched a slab of concrete measured in square acres and sheathed in sheet metal, like a dark abyss from which loomed ghostly shapes—piles of lumber and pipe fittings, fallen ducts, a glistening oil slick, dripping water, and the dismembered hulks of vulcanizers, molds, conveyors, storage racks and compressors, all cannibalized for parts. As

Tracer moved forward, he was quickly swallowed from sight. His footsteps sounded for a while, but soon they too became lost in the vast gloom.

Tracer could feel subtle changes in the air pressure before his eyes, adjusting, made out more human-sized shadows and shapes. His footsteps moved through what had been the plant's clerical area, a warren of offices with ceilings at normal height. Stepping on acoustic tiles which had dropped to the floor, he moved down a hall and put one of his keys into a door. It opened. He walked past empty cubicles, finally entering an office whose door read "Director of Personnel."

A broken window let in the night air. Tracer surveyed the flotsam of his past—a metal desk covered in dust and a swivel chair upended in the corner. Much of the plant's moveable stock had been auctioned; much hadn't. Even in death, the place was badly managed.

Tracer righted the chair, moved it to the desk and sat in it. He wiped some dust away, then laid on the desk the flyer from the convenience store. He looked at the flyer, trying to size up the unknown girl. The examination required time and the utmost concentration. It was as if they were engaged in a serious interview for an important job.

What job?

Maybe it had something to do with humanity. Helping one small part of it, a girl called Jennifer, who didn't have a family killing itself passing out flyers up and down the state.

Who was he kidding?

It was about self-respect.

It had been early August of 1968 when Tracer arrived in Tay Ninh Province to begin duties as a platoon leader for the 1st Brigade, 25th Division. He had missed the enemy's Tet and May general offensives, during which as many as 500 Americans a week were killed throughout the country. He was, however, in time for the year's third assault. Militarily, that boiled down to a relatively minor series of battles and skirmishes launched by the enemy over a ten-day period, for the limited purpose of dislodging the Lancers of Tropic Lightning from Tay Ninh. Eighty-one Americans were killed in action; 400 more were wounded. The enemy suffered an estimated 4,000 casualties before quitting the field to the Americans. The field was about the size of Delaware, and the enemy didn't so much quit as disappear. For the third time in six months they left behind something as tangible as the hooded glares of the civilian population: the sense that they could return in force anytime they wanted. Of course they couldn't, but Tracer slowly realized that the spoor of fear was the psychological equivalent of winning. In the meantime the President, the Congress, the military brass and the American people couldn't agree on what it would take to hold on to tactical victories. Apparently no one wanted to bear the cost of doing whatever was necessary for however long it took; and with that kind of support at home, neither did the soldiers in the field. It was an agonizing lesson for an infantryman with a year left in his tour of duty.

"I got to the war," Tracer told the girl from Oregon, "when we had decided to lose it. And I can't help it, but this country has looked like a loser to me ever since." After a long time he spoke again:

"But I'm not going to go down without a fight. I've been busy looking for this girl, see? I wasn't supposed to find the parents, but I did. Now I just have to finish it."

The sun came up over the Gabilans, its rays slanting over the Vulcan plant and melting the thin frost that crusted the shady areas of the flood plain to Spreckles. The light shone through Chris's kitchen window and danced in the avalanche of for-

gotten goo she was flushing out of the convenience store's
sticky plastic bag. The goose egg from yesterday's fight
throbbed on her cheek. She glanced angrily at her husband,
who was eating cereal at the kitchen table with Shorty and
Brad.

"It's a long shot, okay. But what else is there? It's a pretty
good bet that the tattooed letters 'KC' stand for King City,
where Mendoza got busted. So that's where we'll start putting
up flyers. Before I talked to Matron about selling the sideboard, I called the printer. Five hundred copies for thirty
bucks."

Chris's eyes glistened. "Glass and installation for the door.
$428. Plus tax."

"I think we have to offer a reward, too."

"How about one of the children?"

Tracer gave her a look.

"Or a night with me?"

Tracer glanced at their children. "C'm'on, Chris."

"You promised if there was no case, you'd get a job. A real
one. Now do you want to explain that to us?" She cranked off
the tap.

His children stopped eating and looked at him. Tracer
turned to the friendliest face.

"Do you want me to explain?"

Brad shrugged uncomfortably.

"You?" Tracer asked Shorty in a more defensive tone.

"This is totally barney." She started to get up. "I'm going to
my—"

"Stay right there," ordered her father. He turned to Chris.
"You want an explanation?" He jumped up. "I'll give you an
ex—" He nearly tripped, and Dog yelped from beneath the
table. "I don't have to explain to you! Get out of here!" He
looked at the kids.

"Yeah, I made a promise. Seventeen years ago. To marry your mother. To love, honor and protect her. To forsake all others."

"What others?" asked Chris.

"To go through measles and smallpox with her."

"They had chicken pox."

"We have a family," he shot at Chris; then he appealed again to the gallery: "Do you know how rare that is? Jenny hasn't got a family. She doesn't have people who care. Who take a job," he thumped his belly, "who take it to heart . . . who don't let go!"

"Who are compulsive. Who break promises."

"All right! Fine! You want me to pick lettuce for Bud Antle, I will!"

"You don't have to do stoop labor."

"That's right. Drop the poor little kid down the well. Forget Christian charity."

The kids watched their mother, now on the defense.

"It's a question of priorities. Of survival. If we just had the money . . ."

Brad ventured, "Jesus didn't have money."

"I didn't ask for your opinion," said his mother. "Besides, that's not true. When he had to pay taxes, he paid them."

A honk outside turned Chris's head to the window over the sink. The Heritage Antiques van was parking at the curb. She looked toward her family, a moment of truth.

"Your decision," said her husband.

Sylvester Matron wore a silk jacket and an open-collared shirt. He reluctantly peeled away greenbacks from a silver money clip with a piece of jade as big as an Arizona boulder. As Tracer counted the money, Matron's laborer clanked a handtruck into the back of the van where the sideboard was secured with padded blankets. The man pushed a button to raise the hydraulic lifting platform off the street. It folded back and up, blocking the door.

Tracer looked warily toward the front porch, where his children stood beside their mother and put their arms around her to comfort her.

"You ought to be in sales," Matron said. "You really drive a wicked bargain."

14

The main street of King City was called Broadway because, if nothing else, it was a very wide piece of asphalt. The one- and two-story stores flanking Broadway looked comparatively small and appeared much the same as Steinbeck had seen them as a kid in the 1920s. A billboard and the Southern Pacific depot forced the street to turn sharply to the south. At the turn, a tanker truck with chrome nudes on the mud guards passed Tracer's Dodge Dart.

Tracer's wife sat beside him. His children fidgeted in the back seat. Picked up right after school, they had been cooped up for an hour on a long ride down the valley. Brad was excited to get out, but Shorty was exasperated that her father, as if on a Sunday outing, had taken country roads which he had claimed to know like the back of his hand. They had crossed the Salinas River three times and bounced from the foothills of the Santa Lucias to the foothills of the Gabilans, all at breakneck speed to make up for the time they had lost by not taking the straight shot down US 101.

Shorty screwed her face at a lap full of flyers, fresh from a quick copy shop. Her brother's lap was similarly burdened. The flyers showcased the most recent snapshot of Jenny, with a $500 reward offered for information leading to the whereabouts of. There was a smaller reproduction of Lloyd French's photo, *sans* prison numbers. Shorty decided not to suffer in silence any longer.

"We have to put these up everywhere?"

"Here and there," her father said.

"We don't have a snowball's chance in—" Shorty caught her mother's sharp look.

"You and I will take one side of the street, your father and Brad will do the other."

The wind hit them hard when they got out of car. It started as a light afternoon breeze off the Pacific, funneled through the mountains converging at Monterey Bay, and with the venturi effect increasing its velocity, whipped down the Salinas Valley, driving the heat out of the land.

Brad held flapping flyers and a roll of masking tape while his father used a staple gun to deface one of the sycamore trees fronting King City Joint Union High School. Tracer positioned the flyer next to an index card lamenting a lost cat, then looked long and hard at the school's administrative complex. Brad followed his dad's gaze.

"I know what you're thinking."

"What?"

"The numbers on Jenny's hand."

"And?"

"If you had treasure, you'd stash it in a locker. Shorty says that's lame. But lockers have numbers. Or it could be the combination to a locker."

"It could be a phone number. A room number. Avogadro's Number. The house number of the fortress where Mendoza was arrested. What have we got? Three dozen streets in this town? A number of possibilities for a fat chance."

"Doesn't it need more than three numbers for a phone?"

"'And a child shall lead them.' At least we know where lockers are. Let's go check 'em out."

They crossed a wide lawn, their shoes wading through crumpled papers and soft drink cups that swirled with the dead, wind-driven leaves. In the distance they heard a coach's shrill whistle and the shouts of boys at football practice. Near a concrete block building thrown up during the Sputnik era, father and son found locker #1.

Shorty kept as much distance as possible between herself and her mother, who was taping a flyer to a concrete utility pole.

"What's the matter?"

"People can see."

"That's the idea."

"I mean *us*."

With a wan smile, Chris took a flyer from her daughter and marched toward the closest store, a gift shop whose display window was divided into small panes.

Graffiti—"If you can read this thank a teacher"—marred the wall of a newer concrete building housing social science classrooms. Banked to the side of the building were more lockers, among which Tracer and Brad found #960. Their short walk from one building to the other revealed that many lockers had been vandalized—doors torn off their hinges, books and papers spilled onto the sticky pavement. A few lockers were still secure with combination locks. Brad flicked the open door of one that wasn't.

"If it had a combination lock, it would have been left, right, left. Just three numbers, like on her hand."

Tracer frowned.

"If a kid leaves a lock on at the end of the year, the school cuts it. Every summer they have to hose 'em out and paint 'em."

"So anything stashed by Mendoza would have been found long before now."

"Most schools have given up on lockers."

"But not bus depots."

"Yeah! And bus depots won't have a thousand choices, either."

Shorty watched the proprietor of the gift shop, a balding Latino, diligently tape a flyer to the middle pane of the main window. Then he opened the door for Chris.

Shorty turned away from what she felt was her mother's thunderous thanks. At that moment she was treated to the sight of Brad running, holding out a flyer, flagging down a police car. The car pulled over to a Gulf Station across the street. Her father emerged from the station, which doubled as a Greyhound Bus Terminal, looking a little lost, while her brother thrust his head and a flyer into the squad car. Shorty frowned with embarrassment as Brad hopped and gestured to sell their cause. She turned to her mother.

"You think this is crazy, too! Why are you putting up with it?"

"Remember when you were a Brownie?"

Shorty nodded.

"I hated that crap."

Tracer caught sight of his daughter looking like she had

just stepped on a cockroach. He waved at his wife and yelled, "Are you guys hungry?" He then approached the policeman in the car.

"Know any good places to eat, officer?"

"Keefer's on the highway is real good, but maybe you want Mexican or a salad bar."

"Mexican?" Tracer asked Chris, who approached hesitantly.

"I've heard some of the gals talk about a place here. Not by Bread Alone, I think it's called."

Tracer looked askance at the cop. "Is that the salad bar?"

The officer nodded.

"I don't feel like rabbit food," Tracer said to Chris. "I mean, how's ol' Brad going to grow on crepes and fritata? He needs something that used to walk around the hillsides and weigh half a ton before it was sledgehammered onto his plate."

"Yeah!" agreed Brad.

"Gross," said Shorty.

Chris said, "We want inexpensive."

So as the sun touched the western horizon, the Tracer Family drove south of town, along a frontage road that paralleled the freeway, past fields and farm buildings. A trailer park, motel and restaurant loomed ahead, where the road regained freeway access. Tracer cranked the wheel of his car, and the Dart slowed onto decomposed granite. It passed a row of big trucks. One had chrome nudes on the mud guards. So did another. The Dodge nosed into a space reserved for smaller vehicles that lined the front of the coffee and souvenir shop.

The Tracers got out and headed for food. Shorty hesitated and kept a little behind the rest. As her family entered the Wild Horse Cafe & Truck Stop, she turned back to the car.

She yanked open the back door, reached inside and came out with a fluttering piece of paper, a flyer for Jenny. Then she raced to the building.

The souvenir shop sold key rings, postcards and ice cold beer, and led to the dining area, a lunch counter and booths. A common pay station served both areas. The cashier was a redhead from Oklahoma. Shorty blurted a run-on sentence: "My dad's a private detective and this girl's missing and you have to put this where people can see it and do something about it."

As Shorty took a breath, the woman examined the indicated flyer with a deadpan expression. "I do?"

"Please."

The woman took the flyer. She held it in her fingertips, pinkies curled outward, and draped it in front of the cash register.

"How 'bout there?"

The black-bordered segment of the flyer that read "Call Tracer, Inc. Collect (408) 804-3960" came to Shorty's eye level. She nodded curt approval and thanks, then scurried into the dining area to find her family.

A very big, very sloppy-looking man was unwedging himself from between a swivel seat at the lunch counter. He hitched up his jeans and waddled with his check to the pay area. Behind him, the Tracers made room for Shorty in their booth, and an angular waitress from east Texas descended on the family.

The cashier set aside her Scotch tape dispenser to attend to the next customer. She knew the fat, disheveled truck driver by sight, not by name. He set his bill on top of the flyer, which lay on the counter waiting to be posted. He could have seen the flyer if he had wanted to, but he wanted to load up with potato chips, a Snickers bar and a six-pack of Coors for the road.

The waitress looked with sympathy at the bruise under Chris's eye. Although it was covered with makeup and not as swollen as earlier, it was still noticeable enough to make an observer draw conclusions; so the waitress, who had known man trouble, got real twitchy and turned her glare on the most likely male.

"What you want?"

Tracer was only slightly taken aback. "The steak. Rare. And my wife—"

She cut him short. "Yes, hon?"

"Chef's salad. Do you make your own Thousand Island?"

"We certainly do."

Tracer was studying the menu. "I think I'd like blue cheese on my dinner salad."

The waitress dug her pencil into her pad to note his order. "And my children would like—"

"They can tell me."

Tracer looked up from the menu. If his eyes had been focused for distance, he would have seen the big man leaving the restaurant.

The man circled the **SoCalXpress** rig and made sure the lock on the trailer was secure, a habit he had gotten into lately. Then he started the eighteen-wheeler, rumbled out of the yard and geared up for the freeway approach. The truck rumbled up the highway embankment, passing a sign indicating that US 101 stretched six more miles before it bypassed San Lucas and 289 before it dumped into LA.

Jammed on the big dash, the flyer for Jenny fluttered in the wind from the open window. The driver crammed his face with potato chips and otherwise kept his mind on the road.

When Tracer joined the crush of customers lining up at the cashier's station, Chris waited off to the side, and Shorty bobbed on tiptoes to see whether the flyer was on the register. Her brother heard her mutter, "I knew she wouldn't put it up." Brad was going to ask Shorty what she was talking about, but his father called to him.

"Brad! Something we didn't think of. Warehouses. Private storage rooms. They're like lockers, too."

"Yeah!"

"Go with your mom. Find a phone book. There can't be much around here." Tracer glanced at his watch. "Jeez, nearly six o'clock. Everything's probably closed."

Metz Road swung across the railroad tracks east of town and passed the Cal Spice processing plant. From there a spur road led up the face of the airport mesa. Crop dusters had to dodge the milling tower of a garlic dehydration plant sticking into the air upwind of the mesa. Downwind, the Tracers' car swung onto the airport road and turned into the entrance of a closer hazard, a series of brick buildings, the outermost of which was clearly marked in raised steel letters, "Storage." The office lights were on.

Newt Whaley managed the operation in bib overalls, a wad of Red Man in his cheek and size 13 Red Wings plopped on his desk. He kept his feet up from 7 A.M. to 7 P.M. weekdays, 10 to 5 on Saturdays, and Sundays sat home with the little woman, wondering what to do until he could get back to the yard to rent out spaces and do the little maintenance necessary. If customers needed to get in when he wasn't there, they just had to remember the sequence of six numbers that activated the push button control box of the front gate. And, yeah, if someone wanted to jump the gate or wall, he could do that, too. In fact, that kind of activity had been picking up over the years, not that anyone could lug too many hide-a-beds and what-nots back over the top.

Did he remember a customer named Felix Mendoza?

"'Member? I hope to shout. A man rents a storage room for five years, pays cash up front, you gonna 'member him."

Mr. Whaley spit a gob. It rang in the office wastebasket and impressed Brad enormously.

"Not that it did him any good. Got broke into nearly two weeks ago."

"How do you know?" Tracer asked.

Whaley had to swing his boots to the floor to open a drawer. Then he banged a padlock requiring a key onto the desk top.

"Found this on the ground."

Tracer and son exchanged looks.

"I knew it wasn't a combination," muttered Shorty.

Whaley pulled the locking ring apart where it had been cut. "Hacksaw, I reckon." He spit, and the wastebasket rang again for emphasis.

Dim light enmeshed in wire illuminated a passage that divided a cinderblock building and opened it to the outside. Both sides of the hall were flanked by aluminum roll-up doors. Newt Whaley squatted in front of one of the doors, flipped the latch and stood as the door grated upward. Whaley flicked a wall switch just inside the door, and a low wattage bulb in the ceiling revealed an empty 6' x 6' storage room, the floor covered in dust, the dust tracked by several sets of footprints. Wanting to spit, Whaley turned to what he thought would be clear space in the passage.

Shorty scowled back.

Swallowing, Mr. Whaley swiped the back of his hand across his mouth. "Robbed 'im blind."

Tracer asked, "Did you see what Mendoza put in here?"

"Nope."

Tracer stepped into the storage room. His family stayed back while he took a moment to look around. He pointed to the space where the ceiling joists met the outside wall.

"Brad, I want you to check up there for dust."

He pulled the boy up, and Brad planted his feet on his father's shoulders. Tracer held his son's legs, and Brad made sure of his balance.

Chris squeezed past Whaley, who crammed more tobacco into his mouth and chewed hard with curiosity.

"It's pretty dark," said Brad.

Whaley pulled a flashlight from a baggy back pocket of his overalls. He thumbed the switch; nothing happened. He slapped the barrel against his palm, and a trickle of yellow blinked from the reflector end. He handed the light up to Brad.

Cautiously, Tracer walked with Brad along the wall. After a few moments, Brad said, "Right here, Dad!"

Tracer steadied his son, then the boy hopped to the ground. Brad joined the fingers of his hands to make a circle.

"About that big. No dust."

"What's that mean?" asked Whaley.

"Just a plastic bag worth about thirty thousand," said Tracer.

Very impressed, Whaley spit.

The gob flew past Shorty, splattered into the opposite door and dribbled down the aluminum. She turned her protest on her family.

"But what about the three numbers tattooed on Jenny's hand?"

Her father shrugged.

Brad suddenly pointed.

Above the open storage room a small plate was screwed into the wall. Three digits on it denoted the room's number. Brad looked triumphantly at his sister.

"Told you!"

West of King City, Broadway rose to meet a curve in the freeway. The Dodge passed a sign that said, "US 101 North, Salinas 47, San Francisco 150." The highway spanned the Salinas River, and the Dart sped over a twist of sand braided with water that looked glassy in the moonlight. The Tracers were taking the straight shot home.

Five hours later and 340 miles away, the **SoCalX**press rig stood next to a loading dock that seemed to stretch forever. Security lights made small dents in the post-midnight darkness. Under one light was a pay phone half shell, into which the rig's driver had turned sideways to jam in part of his body. An operator's electronically filtered voice vibrated in his ear.

"Please deposit twenty-five more cents."

"Don't 'spect I got that much." With a grunt, the driver twisted free of the shell.

"Then I can't complete your call, sir."

He squeezed a hand into his pants pocket, then jerked it free, dredging up two cents and a Snickers wrapper.

"Would you like to call collect?"

The driver squirreled his face into the problem. "Dunno."

15

The next morning Chris woke up so excited, she thought about not going to work.

The kids did more than think. Brad said he had a sore throat, to which his father responded, "Look, there's not much we can do now."

"Feel the lumps. I can make up a bed downstairs."

"Near the phone, right?"

"I can study for Friday's math test better down there, and Shorty can talk to my teacher and bring back make-up work."

Tracer narrowed his eyes. "But you're not sick."

"My forehead's all red. It's burning up."

"You're going to school, or your butt's going to be black and blue."

From the bathroom Shorty called out that she thought she was coming down with PMS. Tracer ordered his wife, "You deal with her."

But with household order restored by breakfast time, it was Tracer who seemed the most unsettled.

"What's the matter?" asked Chris.

"Something doesn't add up."

"What do you mean?" said Brad. "I was right about the tattoo. It *was* for treasure. Y'know, bad treasure, but still."

"And when I decided to befriend Tiffany rather than beat her up," said Shorty, "that's when we found out that Jenny had run away with Lloyd French. Who just happened to be in the same cell with Jenny's father for an entire year."

"And," said Chris, "because the children and I were attacked, we now know for sure that Jenny's father did rip off a bag of heroin from *Nuestra Familia*."

"Funny, I thought I was attacked, too."

"And mom and me—"

Chris corrected Brad. "Mom and 'I'."

"Yeah. You and me found out why Anne Walker fooled Dad in the first place. To keep the lid on her past."

Tracer cleared his throat. "Which means Anne Walker probably didn't know about *Nuestra Familia*. Even if she did, with her clawing to the top of the social dung heap, she'd want to steer clear of those boys. There's no reason to suspect that Jenny would have had to know about them, either; she just wants affection."

"How do you know that?" asked Shorty. Her father looked at her until she glanced away.

"So Jenny's wide open when her dad's cellmate rocks up one day, saying how wonderful she is. But all he's really interested in is—"

Brad held up his fist. "The treasure map!"

"But that's just it. We figured it out without ever seeing it."

"Stumbled on to it," corrected Chris.

"Exactly. Two letters for a town. Three numbers for a storage room. There's no combination, no code, no attempt to cover up what a guy could hardly forget no matter how long he was put away."

There was silence for a moment.

"Sometimes," offered Shorty hesitantly, "I know that Brad is hiding something, I just don't know what. French didn't have to know much of anything . . . What I mean is, Jenny's father didn't really have to spill the beans for French to think that Jenny could lead him to something."

"Yes," agreed Chris. "He did take time to sort of court her before they ran away. Why couldn't he have gotten to the storage room the same way we did? More or less. He finds out that Mendoza tattooed Jenny just before he went to prison. He doesn't have to know why. But he hears rumors that his cellmate is being watched for stealing from his bosses. What makes sense is that the tattoo is simple enough to finally figure out."

"But there's no cause and effect. The only one who ever needed to remember where the heroin was, or so we assume, was Jenny's father. Again, unless he has the IQ of an ice cube, how could he forget?"

There was more silence, then Brad said glumly, "But it worked. I mean, I found the hiding place."

"But why a stupid tattoo?"

As silence fell over the table, Chris picked up dishes and took them to the sink. She said, "Maybe it's not cause and effect the way you think. Maybe it's more like in Anthropology 1A."

"Like *what*?"

"Well . . . there are people we've grown up with who can go into the Catholic Church and say a 'Hail Mary,' pray to a Western God, and in the next breath go out and pay some *bruja* to kill a chicken and read its entrails."

"Now Mendoza is into voodoo."

"He doesn't have to be into anything. But why does he have to have a buttoned-down mind? Why does he have to be a way *you* understand? He could just be superstitious. He could be paranoid on top of it because he's a criminal, which in itself says he's not thinking straight. He could have wanted to memorialize the fact that he had double-crossed the big boys. He could have picked a monument they didn't know anything about. He could have marked Jenny because . . . well, because he's a father at best and she's a trophy at worst. He could have been staking his claim to her, or the tattoo could have been his twisted idea of some kind of legacy if anything ever happened to him."

Tracer rubbed his eyes.

"None of the above? Some? All? Why don't you call Mrs. Patronas and see if it'll fly as a theory?"

It flew, in parts, in whole and in combinations. Before hanging up, Mrs. Patronas summarized, "A *chollo* just wants to prove something."

"It still doesn't make sense," said Tracer.

"Only to you," said Chris.

"Because it leads me nowhere."

"It *explains* why we had such a good time with Mr. Whaley last night."

"But it doesn't *do* anything now. So that leaves me to sit around all day, day after day, for God knows how long, waiting for a one-in-a-million phone call from someone who may or may not have thought twice about seeing Jenny and French walking hand-in-hand into the sunset."

"You really think they walked hand-in-hand?"

"No," he said grimly.

"Dear, the flyers were entirely your idea, but I'm sure you'll think of something."

· · ·

Left alone while his children went to school and his wife to
work, Tracer thought of driving a stake into the back yard
and chaining Dog to a three-foot lead. Instead, he played
cheap glazer, ripping up the tool shed's plywood floor, hos-
ing off the sow bugs underneath and fitting it more or less
into the sliding door panel knocked out by Hector Montdragon. Working with a saw gave Tracer another bright idea.

He dropped a plumb line from the top of Riley's peach
tree, just past his side of the fence and to the side flower bed
so darkened by shade that nothing but worms grew in it. He
spent the rest of the afternoon hacking away until the tree
looked like it had been neatly lopped by a huge buzz saw. He
was tying up the limbs and branches into the thirty-pound
bundles required for sanitation pick up when Riley started
screaming.

"What are you doing?! You can't do that!? It's against the
law!"

"It's *not* against the law."

"I'm going to call the cops!"

"Good! They'll put you away."

The shrill voice came closer. "But it's my tree! It grows in
my yard!"

"It throws its branches into *my* yard, onto *my* roof, and I'm
not going to let it be *my* problem anymore! There!" As Tracer gestured defiantly at the wood at his feet, he thought he
caught a glimpse of Riley through cracks in the fence.

Riley's voice was more plaintive, "But they grew off my
tree."

"No, look. They're not growing anymore. They're dead!"
Tracer threw his head back at the slice of blue. "I can see the
sky!" He blinked, then looked down at the debris at his feet.
"My God, that's it."

At that moment Chris arrived from work. "What's going on here?"

"I'm calling the police!" came Riley's voice.

"Let him call the National Guard."

"I will, you, you . . . bully!"

Tracer took Chris's arm and hurried her into the house. "I know what to do now."

"You'll regret this for the rest of your life!"

Pushing through the front door, Tracer kept rolling. "What are the three things we know about Lloyd French?"

"Why'd you cut Mr. Riley's tree?"

"One, he's a junkie. Two, he's got a big bag of heroin."

"Three, it wasn't that bad."

Tracer stopped, confused. "The heroin?"

"No, the *tree*."

"Sweetheart! For crying out loud, I've been thinking about how to narrow this search down. Why don't you give me credit for *something*?!"

They were moving into the family room. Chris looked at the warped, mildew-stained slab of plywood that served as the sliding door. She let out a tired breath of air and sat down.

"Now, what does heroin do to people?"

"I don't know."

"You do, too. Come on."

"I don't know. Makes them feel good, causes addiction, kills them, I don't—"

"Eureka! There you go."

Chris thought that John was grasping at straws, but when Shorty and Brad came home their excitement that the straws might be real, and that they might be floating down to a specific place, finally caught hold of her.

Thus the family was a united front when a Carmel PD

squad car parked in front of the house. The blimpish officer was at the wheel, and the skinny one stayed put for several minutes before hopping out of the passenger's side to greet an MG pulling up. When Tracer responded to the knock at the front door, District Attorney Levin smiled at him.

"You've been a busy boy."

Ten minutes later Chris had made coffee and was offering a sugar bowl to the female officer, who waved it away. The lady and her law enforcement colleagues were engulfed by the big couch in the Tracers' family room. Acting as primary mouthpiece, Detective Sergeant Amcheck explained what brought them:

"A truck driver named Chester A. Montague called the City of Industry Police Department last night."

Simon Bolivar Levin looked at Tracer, whose children had politely jumped out of the couch when he first entered, gesturing that he should take the most comfortable place. "Apparently your flyer inspired him," Levin said.

"Collect," added Amcheck. "A few other jurisdictions had to be notified. Then it all came back to us this morning."

"But why didn't he call here? That's the number on the flyer."

"French had scared the cra—" Amcheck remembered there were children present. He nodded, "Excuse me," to Mrs. Tracer, then continued: "He just wanted to forget all about it. Your flyer pricked his conscience . . ."

Tracer threw a smug smile at Chris.

". . . but it didn't stop him from using his brain. So getting hold of real detectives seemed, uh, more appropriate to Mr.Montague than calling you."

The youngest Tracer asked, "So what are you real detectives going to do about it?"

"Brad!" said Chris.

Amcheck glanced at Levin, who remained stonefaced. The sergeant tried to shrug the question off. "Well, uh, it's hard to do much about a drifter. He probably hitch-hiked to the heroin. He definitely took pot luck with the driver."

"Don't be so definite," argued Tracer. "He has a thing for southern California teams."

"That really narrows it, doesn't it?"

Shorty spoke up. "City of Industry, you said."

Tracer looked with pride at his daughter as Amcheck countered with, "Not exactly a street address."

"No, but it does help. Now Dad doesn't have to start in downtown Los Angeles and work from there."

"Huh?"

"That bag of junk is his security blanket," Tracer said. "Our theory is he'll probably settle down once he makes a few deals."

"Our theory?"

Chris jumped in. "He could slow down long enough to make some deals. After all, that's what this whole thing is about to French—the deal—quick cash."

Levin said, "He's got a record of using drugs himself. Why deal?"

"It's six of one and half dozen of the other," explained Tracer. "He'll hole up in some dive until he runs out of nirvana."

Chris added, "Our hunch is that French doesn't have the class or the clout to score really big. He's like a wino who stumbles across a case of Thunderbird. He thinks he can handle it himself. He's probably out on the street right now, trying to push the stuff to the nearest junkies, real proud that he's cut out the middlemen."

Amcheck raised an eyebrow at Tracer. "You didn't tell me this was a mom and pop outfit."

Brad piped up. "See, you have to start checking hospitals in Southern California."

The sergeant looked at the youngest Tracer, who remained undaunted. "You move in bigger and bigger circles from where he was last spotted."

Amcheck forced a laugh. "Running around in circles. Fun for the whole family, eh?"

It was Shorty who came to the defense of family honor. "It's like any other search. You need a point of reference. Then you fan out to hospitals and emergency centers."

"Until," continued her brother, "you find one that's had an increase of ODs or DOAs in the past couple of weeks. You know why?"

"Because," their mother said, "people on the streets are going to pay the price for the fact that French hasn't done his chemistry homework."

Realizing that his subordinate was hopelessly outnumbered, the District Attorney pulled himself out of the Naugahyde couch with a grunt. "Excuse me, Sergeant." The prosecutor addressed Tracer: "May we have a moment alone?"

"Yes, sir."

As Tracer grunted to pull the plywood door open, Amcheck sidled up to Chris. "Do you have a sweet roll or something? Maybe a sandwich?"

The DA and Tracer strolled across the back lawn.

"Nice family."

"Thanks."

"What's your status on this case?"

"I was given a two-week retainer and asked to find Jenny. A day and a half ago, I was told to back off."

"As in fired?"

"Yes, but I don't want to give up. I—"

"No need to explain yourself. I understand. Who was the client?"

"Jenny's mother."

"And who would that be?"

"Her mother."

"I'm in the process of getting a judge to give me permission to tap Anne Walker's phone. In case Jenny calls."

"Why don't you just talk to—Who'd you say?"

"Your ex-client. Do you think Miss Walker would tell me if Jenny calls or writes?"

"I think she's a dead end. As far as heroin and all that goes, she doesn't know anything. She doesn't know anything about Lloyd French except what I told her, which was nothing. But if she thought her daughter was in trouble . . ." Tracer considered Anne Walker's character. "I don't know what she'd do. But tapping phones, rather than just asking her . . ."

"My philosophy is, why stir up trouble for a woman who's going to marry one of the most famous men in the county? Not including actors, but they're a seedy bunch if you ask me. So I try to keep things quiet if I can, even for doctors who contributed to my rival's campaign in the last election. It's amazing, though, how marriage can soften a man's heart."

"When did you know? Who Anne was. What she was to Felix Mendoza."

"Only after you started stirring up trouble."

"That wouldn't have been a set-up, would it?"

Levin laughed. "Oh, goodness, no. I didn't have time for that when I met you. Not that I wasn't interested. I did send you to the prison, didn't I?"

"Did the ol' photographic memory know Mendoza couldn't talk?"

"I have 503 outstanding cases right now, a good 47 open

from years back. Thousands and thousands of details. Even I can't keep track of them all. When the Sheriff's Department reported the melee here yesterday, I was a little worried that I might have inadvertently baited a hook. Since Mr. Montague's phone call, I'm very worried."

The DA nodded back toward the house. "Is that all of them? Your family, I mean. Do you have brothers and sisters or in-laws?"

"My mom's living with my sister up in Susanville. My older brother's a doctor down in Fullerton. Chris's folks are doing a run through relatives in the Rockies before the snows hit. Why?"

The prosecutor opened the door to the tool shed and glanced inside. "I want to know how far this has gone."

"How far what's gone?"

"No need to get defensive."

"Sorry, sir."

"People who call me 'sir' don't sound like they're going to vote for me."

Tracer grinned warily.

"Relax. We're having a friendly conversation. I just want to know what the rest of your family thinks about what you're doing."

"My mother sometimes thinks I'm the doctor in Fullerton. My sister feels sorry for both of us. Chris's folks . . . what can I tell you? They aren't happy with the way things turned out. They put private investigation in the same league with motorcycle racing. I'm glad they're on vacation, so they don't have to watch my first attempt for a speed record."

Levin nodded toward the house. "Do you take all your work home?"

"We talk."

Levin nodded thoughtfully. After a moment he allowed, "Well, you're talking more or less reasonably. We've already put the word out to the Los Angeles Sheriff's Department and to the police jurisdictions in the eastern basin to be on the alert for French and any new influx of heroin. Baldwin Park, Pico Rivera, places like that. An epicenter of stiffs would help. Better yet, an interview with someone who survives whatever new supply of crap has worked its way into the area."

Tracer put on a self-satisfied smile. "Since French went south, there's been time enough for the crap to have hit the fan. What's the report?"

Levin shifted his gaze and took a while to come back with, "Nothing unusual."

"You're sure?"

"I'm sure that French doesn't have to stay in the southland. He could have passed through and be long gone. Wouldn't you agree?"

"Aren't you gonna arrest him, officer?"

Levin jerked toward the side fence.

"He's the DA, not a cop, you jerk!" shouted Tracer.

Levin looked at his host's red face. Tracer shrugged. "My neighbor, Crazy Riley."

Levin lowered his voice. "What's he know?"

"He's squash rot. Who cares? Hey, I'm not blabbing to everyone in the world about French."

"I didn't say you were. But everyone has a little world. Yours is kind of like the Waltons. Mine is more like *Mean Streets*." Levin looked toward the patio. "Things break when worlds collide."

"Gimme a break."

"Calm down. Maybe you're being interviewed."

"You mean questioned. What for?"

Levin spread his hands noncommittally, as if he hadn't thought that far ahead. "Your own protection?"

"You don't have a family? You don't go home? Your friends don't know when some convicted felon swears he's going to get you?"

"I told you before, it's a matter of perspective."

"Well, my perspective is focused on Jennifer Mendoza."

"Even though you've been fired. That's not perspective: that's a mission."

"I finish what I start. Sir. What do you do?"

The District Attorney smiled. "I watched you prove my hypothesis about Felix Mendoza. Now I'm working on two others. That French is actually in East LA, and like your wife says, he's a bad pharmacist. So I sit back and see what comes up from the sewers. But in fact, we both have only guesses on that score."

"I have to start someplace."

"Uh-uh. You don't have to do anything."

"Look, if you're suggesting I let this thing go . . ."

"I'm not suggesting anything. There's no guessing about French. He's armed and extremely dangerous. There are no gray areas about *Nuestra Familia*'s being on his tail. And they're not the small fry who broke your window. Those punks have bosses who are real slick, real sharp, real deadly."

Levin paused to gain direct eye contact. "This is a law enforcement matter now. So take this as a direct order. You sit tight with your lovely family and from here on let us do our job."

"You mean, finding French?"

"Precisely."

"Thanks a bunch."

"Look. My office gets overloaded with cases. So I have to

go to freelancers from time to time, and from now on you're on the investigators' list."

"Great. Record searches, huh?"

The prosecutor shrugged. "And interviewing witnesses."

When Tracer didn't respond immediately, Levin clapped his back. "Well, Mr. Detective, doesn't that sound good?"

"It's a living."

Levin grinned like a good ol' boy yukking it up when Bubba sets fire to a cat. "Better add a 'sir' to that if you're going to work for me."

Tracer gave him a sideways look and kept his mouth shut.

While Brad and Shorty tore the cushions off the couch and argued over division of a windfall of a quarter, three dimes, a nickel and seven pennies, Tracer dropped a small suitcase open onto the bed and began to pack it with clothes. His wife stood on the other side of the bed with her arms tightly crossed. She didn't want to show her frustration, but trying to reason with him still came out as accusation.

"You said he was very specific. This is a matter for the police."

"He said *French* was a matter for the police. That still leaves Jenny."

"Well, I take his warning seriously, even if you don't."

"Nothing's different from this morning."

"Yes it is! You haven't got a clue where to find her! Not really."

"And if I did?"

"I—" Chris didn't want to strike a bargain. She wanted him to stay home. "So what? How many emergency rooms are there in Pico-Park-bloody-Los Angeles?"

"When French can't use her any longer . . . for sex or drugs or for whatever . . . then he'll get rid of Jenny."

Chris lowered her eyes. Shaking her head, she turned and quietly opened the top bureau drawer. It took time before she could face him again and keep her voice steady. In one hand she held a Colt .45 semi-automatic pistol, military issue; in the other, a clip of jacketed hollow points.

"Maybe you'd better take this. If he's as crazy as everybody says."

She slipped the clip into the magazine and dropped the loaded weapon, which thumped heavily into the soft bed next to the suitcase. Tracer's mouth went dry at the sight of the Colt.

"This is a hell of a goodbye."

Her eyes swept down his body, came back up, lingered on his.

"You're dressed."

At 3:30 Friday morning Tracer left his wife's side and put his suitcase into the trunk of the Dart and the semi-automatic under the front seat. At 4:55 he turned off 101, taking the cut-off for a faster route—east at Paso Robles onto State Highway 46, its two-lane blacktop trafficked by occasional farmers going to work in vineyards and orchards. An hour later he was heading south again, on Interstate 5, two double roadways of concrete cutting through the cotton fields of the San Joaquin Valley. Snow grayed the jagged, pre-dawn outline of the Sierras, but except for some leafless willows, the San Joaquin looked suspended in an endless summer. He gassed up at Buttonwillow, an oasis of motels and fast food franchises for truckers and travelers. The sun was coming up as the Dart's engine lugged through the twisting pass at Grapevine. Levelling off at Fort Tejon, Tracer saw cattle feeding on brown-gold grass on each side of the Interstate. The impression so far was that California was first and fore-

most rural. Suburbs around Magic Mountain hinted that it was also the most populous state in the Union, and I-5 began to clog like a fat man's artery with morning rush-hour traffic. Tracer passed under the Highway 18 overpass which had collapsed during the 6.7 Northridge Earthquake earlier in the year.

The President, Congressmen, Los Angeles County Supervisors, the Mayor and the LA City Council were all congratulating themselves for reconstructing the 18 and the damaged sections of the I-10, the Santa Monica–San Bernardino Freeway, the busiest in the world, within six months of their falling down. But it wasn't all the king's horses and men who had put the roadways together again. The declaration of a Federal Disaster Area allowed Big Government to say no to itself by requiring politicians to step aside, regulatory red tape to be cut and proven contractors to just do the job.

Tracer's feeling about earthquakes in general was the same as most Californians' about rain: it happens, so what? A geological map of the state looked like the broken capillaries in an alcoholic's cheek. But the Northridge quake and the aftershocks that were still going on reminded everyone who lived near the San Andreas Fault—an aorta with huge aneurisms compared to the veins in the drunk's blotchy face—that the Big One could happen any day. Six point seven was big enough, so Tracer had put in one of his infrequent phone calls to his brother Peter, the doctor who lived in Fullerton in Orange County, about forty miles east of the epicenter. It took two days of dialing to get past the recording, "All circuits are busy. Please try again," and the more ominous, "This number is no longer in service. If you need assistance, please call your operator." Swamped with callers, the operator had offered only the short-tempered

advice to watch the news on television. It showed houses off
their foundations, piles of bricks that used to be chimneys,
large apartment complexes condemned, concrete office
blocks cracked like egg shells, storefronts boarded up, fires
burning, people camped out in parks, patients being treated
in the parking lots of hospitals, rescue workers with cranes
and jackhammers trying to get a maintenance man out from
under a fallen parking structure. The ground had heaved at
4:31 A.M. and kept it up for a good thirty seconds; if the
Southland had been awake, residents moving and working,
the twenty-seven fatalities might have been multiplied by a
thousand.

It was Pete who had gotten through first. "Hell, it was just
like I got through telling Sis. You gotta die of something."
There was some plaster cracked in Pete's home, some pictures thrown off the walls and his wife needed Halcion to get
to sleep, but Orange County had been largely spared physical damage. He and John had talked about how they used to
laugh and dance as kids when the ground moved in a low
rumble and dishes in the cupboards rattled. And when their
younger sister came along, how they could make her cry,
demanding that she give them a dime to put in the slot or
they would never have that kind of ride again. A "good"
quake in those happy days usually centered around Hollister
and felt like a freight train was passing right through the
house. A "bad" one, either farther away or from slight slip-
page on one of the minor faults under Salinas, just made
them sway a little or gave a single sharp jolt, then nothing.

Tracer had tried to get through to his brother yesterday
afternoon, hoping that some professional string-pulling
might aid what he was now driving into the Los Angeles
Basin to do, but dialing Pete's office only raised a receptionist who said Dr. Tracer was unavailable, Dr. Wang was in

surgery, Dr. Peacock-Edwards was assisting, but the new man, Dr. Jefferson, didn't happen to have a patient right now, so perhaps he could be of service. John explained that he was Pete's brother. "Oh," the receptionist had said, "he's taken his family to a medical conference in Coronado and won't be in until Monday. I can give you the resort number, and he can call in a prescription from there."

"Just tell him hi when he comes back."

Tracer had to stop and start the Dodge to keep with the jerking flow of morning commuters who must have been late for work already or heading God knows where. They can't all be shoppers, Tracer thought. He passed a sign for Lakeview Terrace, the suburb where Rodney King had been stopped for speeding, and thirty minutes later took the San Bernardino Freeway, skirting the ghostscape of downtown Los Angeles where the *Dragnet* building, otherwise known as City Hall, was barely visible. Ditto for *General Hospital*, a/k/a County-USC Medical Center. No sign of remaining earthquake damage was apparent from the freeway, nor were there signs of the riots and burnings that had raged after the officers accused of beating Rodney King were tried the first time and acquitted.

The mountains all around that on a clear day made Los Angeles look similar to Denver or Seattle, and that had been blackened by wildfires recently, couldn't be seen; and a sky the color of dirty washwater seeped into every nook and cranny of the lower levels. Dingy outlines of houses and buildings stippled the flatlands that went on for mile after endless mile, town after town disappearing in the silty atmosphere. Tracer felt like a bottom-feeding fish.

His eyes smarted and his stomach felt queasy by the time he stopped at 10:30, at a place called Crazy Slade's Cheap Gas in the San Gabriel Valley, to hose down the radiator. He bought a street map index as thick as a dictionary and plotted the rest of his course feeling, like most northern Californians, fully committed to dividing the state in two, with mine fields and concertina wire to define the frontier. But then he heard the sweet, soft *whoosh* of a fuel-injected, double-barrel carb, overhead cam Hemi engine. It powered a metallic purple '54 Ford pickup raked ten degrees that quivered to a stop at the intersection. For Tracer it was like a double-A blast from the past: The Beach Boys, The Ventures, Jan and Dean; bitchin' bikinis on outta sight beaches; "We're out here havin' fun in that warm California sun," meaning anywhere south of Santa Barbara and east of the Whiskey A-Go-Go; a state of mind, teen Mecca. You *ta-rye* to hate it, but you *got to* love it!

The blond gods in the pickup's cab scoped out a bevy of underage cutie-pies pulling up alongside in a Trans Am. The girls appeared indifferent, eyes straight ahead, as the boys whooped like demented gynecologists, proctologists and dentists, screaming how they'd like to fill each and every orifice.

Returning to the nineties, Tracer imagined a nuclear dead zone would work for passport control.

Tracer drove along Proctor Avenue, through the flat, wide spaces of the City of Industry. Here and there were monuments to commerce—factories, warehouses, storage tanks, ventilators letting off steam. He crossed a Union Pacific feeder line, rolled through the nice but smoggy residential neighborhood of La Puente and turned off Bamboo into the Emergency Entrance of Doctors Hospital.

One of its pretty little Vietnamese aides shook her head, no.

• • •

Tracer barreled up Azusa Avenue, turned westbound on
Interstate 10 and stopped dead in another traffic jam. Sweat-
ing, he was finally able to shake free at the off ramp to West
Covina Hospital.

A Filipina aide shook her head, another no.

Afterward, Tracer twisted as he sat in the parking lot,
examining his copy of *Thomas Brothers' Popular Street Atlas
for Los Angeles and Orange Counties*. Map 92 led logically to
Map 48. He turned the thick book and cocked his head, trying to straighten out the kinks in Glendora Avenue which
somehow turned into Hacienda Boulevard, then back into
itself again. One thing for sure: it didn't make a straight
north–south shot.

Tracer pulled into the parking lot of Queen of the Valley Hospital in Orangewood Park. It looked a nice place to languish
in.

He pulled out of Comprehensive Health Care Center Hospital, El Monte, leaving a patch of rubber.

Outside of Community Hospital in South El Monte he
walked past a line of wheelchairs containing very old people
whose heads drooped and listed toward the sun, the bright-
est spot in a sky that was now the color of weak bourbon.

Inside a corridor of Garfield Hospital, Monterey Park, he
passed several pregnant teenagers on their way to a pre-
natal care class. Two of them tittered with delight as they felt
for the baby's kick inside the belly of the third.

At the snack bar in the emergency center of City Terrace he
had lunch sandwiched between a knife victim and her
attacker. Apparently it had just been a family quarrel.

Lunch settled during a traffic jam on the Long Beach Free-way.

He drove through Commerce, Vernon and Bell, and stopped at Doctors Southeast Hospital in Maywood.

He passed streets and street gangs. Huntington Park, Cudahy, South Gate, Lynwood, Downey and Norwalk. The latter had refineries and tanks farms, and an Asian aide at Kaiser Emergency shook her head no.

No at Pico Rivera Hospital.

No at Beverly in Montebello.

No at Whittier Hospital.

Yes at Presbyterian.

Tracer watched a Taiwanese aid talk to her Korean supervisor, a serious-faced woman who quickly disappeared from view. Shortly thereafter, a third-year Hispanic resident emerged to greet Tracer.

"I thought you cops got everything you wanted."

Tracer felt an invisible knife go into his back and twist. He let the wound of Levin's lie go unanswered with a noncommittal shrug.

They walked down a corridor. They entered an elevator. They descended below ground level and walked down another corridor. The resident ushered Tracer into the hospital's morgue and opened a refrigerated body compartment. The corpse inside looked between fifteen and twenty years of age and had the grayish, chalky color that Asians, Caucasians and Mexicans all get when they die.

Yesterday," said the resident.

"More?" asked Tracer.

"Don't you know?"

"I told the lady when I came in. I'm a private investigator."

"But I thought—"

"When were the cops here?"

"I'm not sure I should talk to you."

Tracer gestured at the body. "I bet John Doe's in the back page of the newspaper already, and you don't want to talk to me?"

The resident thought about it.

"My brother's a doctor" opened doors.

Something resembling a young human female lay in bed in intensive care. Plastic bags dangled tubes that fed a needle punched into her arm. Her mouth was half open. So were her eyes, which were glazed. The rest of her was going the color of fine marble.

"About 3:30 this morning," said the resident. "Haven't been able to stabilize her. We've had five in less than two weeks." The young man shrugged.

Tracer moved closer to the bedside. He held the ten-dollar copy of the two-way mug shots of French over the girl's eyes.

"Do you know this man?"

No response.

The resident said, "They already tried that."

"Is he the one who sold you the heroin?"

No response.

"Where did you get it?"

The resident lightly took Tracer's arm. "Junk's everywhere, man. But she comes from West Whittier."

The Nu Haven Motel squatted on Whittier Boulevard between a car lot and a supermarket, offering rooms for $19 a night or a quarter of an hour, whichever came first. Tracer's car was parked where he could make a quick getaway.

He wearily filled out the guest registration card, inking in his name, the company he represented and the make, year and license number of his car. The manager was an Indian immigrant by way of Zambia. He eyed the card as if it were a puff adder. Seldom did he have customers who filled out all the blanks.

"What, please, is Tracer, Inc.?"

"A detective agency."

"Oh, a detective! How exciting!"

Tracer shook his head. "Not really."

"No! Really?"

"You like walking until you get holes in your shoes? Driving to hell and gone?"

"Yes, driving."

"Driving till your car breaks down?"

"Yes, yes. Chases."

"No, no. You just talk to people."

The man nodded his head. "To be solving mysteries."

"To collect information. Lots of information. Most of it doesn't make sense. So you collect lots more. It doesn't have to make sense, either, but maybe there's a pattern."

"A puzzle!"

"More like—" Tracer swiped a drop of perspiration from his forehead to his hairline and briefly itched his scalp. "I don't know. Cooking, maybe. You open the cupboard, thinking you're going to bake bread, but you find the bag of flour has weevils in it."

The manager nodded soberly.

"So you shake it through a sieve until you just have the weevils crawling around by themselves."

"The bad guys, yes?"

"But you were going to bake bread, remember?"

"What do the bugs mean?"

"Maybe nothing. Maybe something. But they're the only pattern you've got."

"And the flour?"

"See? There's another."

"Confusing."

"Tiring."

"Why do you do it?"

Tracer suddenly felt kinship for a man who had left everything and come ten thousand miles to operate what was virtually a whorehouse. "Was it worth it?"

"Excuse please?"

"Coming to America?"

The manager said, "Ohhh," then thought long and hard.

"Did you think the streets would be paved with gold?"

The manager smiled shyly. "Maybe I thought there would be golden streets."

"And?"

"The opportunities here are better than at home. However, it is very tiring, I think, to take advantage of them."

"Want to go back?"

The manager shook his head adamantly.

Tracer said, "To answer your question, I didn't expect this work to be anything like it is. But I love it."

Tracer went for his wallet, but the manager, overcome, waved his hands like hummingbird wings.

"Oh, no. No, no! This is an honor. An honor!"

The small place of honor smelled like mildew, Maalox and old condoms. It was dark . . . well, almost dark if you didn't count the neon and headlights breaking through the window. Night sounds burglarized the thin walls—lots of traffic on one of the state's busiest boulevards, bedsprings creaking as if bearing Thumper in rut and a truck either crashing into the supermarket or making a delivery.

Unfazed, Tracer lay flat on his back on a lumpy mattress. His shoes were untied, his shirt was unbuttoned, and his eyes were at half-mast. He just managed to keep the phone to his ear. "Talk."

"Where are you?" gasped Chris.

He mumbled heavily, "I got a lead."

"What kind of lead?"

"Levin knew yesterday what I found out today."

"Knew what?"

"Whittier. West Whittier is where there's been an influx of bad junk. I guess it captures more votes if our friendly DA corners it without help from," Tracer chuckled, "outsiders with no perspective."

"John, you're not going to do something stupid."

He stretched his free arm, slowing curling his fingers until the knuckles whitened. "I know something he doesn't. Jenny wanted it off." Tracer yawned. "So he can have the mealy worms. I'll stick with the flour."

"What are you talking about?"

"The tattoo. Yeah, I don't understand tattoos, but what else is new?"

"Are you all right?"

"Sure. We're in love, aren't we?" He puckered his lips into a kissing sound that didn't quite come out, then let the phone drop back in the cradle and seconds later was fast asleep.

The next morning Anne Walker took a personal letter out of her post box. A girl's hand, undoubtedly Jenny's, had inscribed the envelope with Anne's address as well as a return. Having gotten what she wanted from the box, Anne abandoned it with the door still open. Ripping the flap off the envelope, she turned toward the post office door.

Preoccupied with reading her daughter's letter, Anne moved down the steps and wandered toward the street. She paused near the flagpole, looking toward her car to orient herself. There were motherly tears in Anne's eyes, a foot or so of space, then Hector Montdragon's cut and bandaged face.

Early that afternoon, the building maid unlocked Anne Walker's door with a passkey and pulled her cart inside. She was glad that the front room looked so tidy and moved to inspect the kitchen.

The refrigerator door was open. Crossing to it, the maid's shoes crunched on glass. She looked down at a broken jar.

Peering cautiously over the counter that separated the kitchen from the dining nook, she saw that the glass doors were open. The glass tabletop was shattered. Blood had congealed on the jagged shards and was splattered in thick brown dollops on the carpet where Anne Walker lay.

The maid screamed loud enough to wake the dead.

People in the neighboring apartment heard and called 911. Pop's contribution was a befuddled, "Hey?" when Fire Department paramedics clattered past his station with a collapsible gurney. By the time he got his glasses on, they had disappeared into the elevator.

None of the hospitals that Tracer had seen in southern California could beat Carmel Community for classiness. The emergency waiting area looked like a cross between a Roman courtyard and the hanging gardens of Babylon. For the convenience of the public, there were many discretely placed phones. Carmel's plainclothes detective was using one while, some distance away, his uniformed colleague hovered like a US Navy sub spotter over Dr. Fencoe. The cardiologist had spent his initial energy as a tightly controlled clinician, consulting with colleagues, acknowledging constrained murmurs of sympathy and assuring the admitting doctor that of course he was really the physician in charge of Miss Walker. Fearing the worst, Fencoe was now as despondent as any layman awaiting news of a loved one.

Glancing at him, Amcheck spoke into the phone. "Sergeant Amcheck here."

"What's up?" said Levin.

"Anne Walker was attacked in her apartment this morning and left for dead."

The prosecutor's jaw muscles constricted. "Suspects?"

"She's in an out of consciousness. Gangbangers is all I can get out of her."

"Motive?"

"She'd just come back from the post office. Something about a letter from her daughter."

"Holy shit."

"We searched the apartment. Nothing."

"I don't care if you have to use sodium pentathol! Find out where that letter came from and meet me at the airport in an hour!"

Simon Bolivar Levin hung up and called the television stations in Salinas and Monterey. Being relatively small, independently owned operations, only one could spare a reporter and camera operator on such short notice. Even though the media's favorite personality was offering a drug bust exclusive that could well be tapped for national attention on the network's news hour, Levin had to promise to cover traveling expenses.

Amcheck hoped Levin was exaggerating about the truth serum. Still, his best hope was a doctor on staff who owed him a big favor. He'd made the doc on a hit and run, then, feeling sorry for a man trying to juggle a wife and a candy striper, dealt with him "administratively." After all, there was only property damage involved and that mostly to the car of the candy striper's steady who may have been the one to ram the doc's Jag in the first place; who could say? No matter how it had happened, the kid needed to wake up to the fact that his girl was a very eager volunteer.

The errant physician, on call in the corridor to the emergency room, furtively patted a pocket of his smock as Amcheck whispered into Anne Walker's ear that he was a priest come to hear her last confession. As her eyes fluttered,

Amcheck pulled the curtain of her cubicle wider and nodded toward the doorway. His female colleague tenderly ushered Dr. Fencoe within earshot.

Lying in the narrow bed, Anne looked as pale as a snow fairy. Paper surgical tape covered a plastic surgeon's hairline stitches that neatly closed several facial lacerations. As Fencoe looked at her, tears streamed from his eyes.

"Oh, my angel, I've been so worried about you."

Anne blubbered softly about trying to hide something from him, a darling little girl, and how if her knight in shinning armor left her now, she'd understand; but only death itself would separate her from that little girl again.

"Where is she?" broke in Amcheck as Anne weakly stroked Fencoe's wet, white cheek.

Amcheck made it to the airport in time. Seated next to Levin in the United commuter to LAX, the news team behind them, the uniformed cop taking up two seats across the aisle, he brought the DA up to date.

"He's one of those enlightened guys. Probably got all incensed when Dan Quayle ragged on unwed mothers. You should have seen it. He's falling in love all over again. Christ, he thinks he's marrying Murphy Brown."

And so, somewhat as Tracer had originally hoped, the long arm of the law was reaching out, its protective embrace winging through the darkening sky, just one flight behind Bustamonte and company.

18

Looking through the East LA Yellow Pages, Tracer was surprised by how few tattoo parlors there were, compared to workmen's comp lawyers and pizza parlors. But, he thought philosophically, that's what detective work is all about. Start with A and drag yourself all the way through Z.

Tracer entered Ace Body Art, a walkup squeezed between a pawn shop and a Western Union outlet whose main advertised function appeared to be "Personal Checks Cashed Reasonable Rates."

A rendering of the Aztec myth of the creation of Mexico City lay along the slope of a woman's back. The dip of her waist and the rise of her hip and haunch told the story of Cortez and Montezuma. Long hair and an earring dangled over her rounded calf. They belonged to a tattoo artist whose shirtless and sweaty body favored an Asian motif. He hunched within kissing distance of the woman's dainty foot. Eyes intent, he massaged her calf with one hand, and with the other wielded an electric needle that hissed color into the Virgin of Guadalupe.

Curtain rings swished, and Tracer appeared in the entrance of the cramped studio. The woman smiled prettily and modestly draped an arm. Tracer coughed tightly. The artist didn't look up.

"Excuse me."

"Not so loud. This is very delicate."

Tracer overcompensated to a whisper. "I'm willing to pay for some information."

"I make a living from my talent, not information."

"It's about a friend of mine. I think she may have had a tattoo removed."

The artist concentrated on his work. "I put them on. I wouldn't dream of taking them off."

"I really do need some help."

The artist was forced to look at a ten-dollar bill. Tracer had stretched far forward and delicately draped the money across the woman's leg. The artist sighed and shook his head. But he leaned back from his work.

"Do you know of any parlors that would remove them?"

"Take your money."

Tracer hesitated. The woman's hand closed on the bill, and she slid it up her leg, like a caress.

"Give him his money, Rosita."

"No, please," Tracer insisted.

With a pout, the woman held out the bill. Tracer was forced to take it back.

The artist said, "Tattoo parlors aren't licensed to do that. Only medical doctors who know lasers and skin grafts. Not beauty."

"Doctors, of course." Tracer felt like a fool. The artist watched him rub his forehead.

"What's the matter?"

"There must be thousands of doctors in the phone book."

The artist smiled benignly. "But only one who advertises that he will treat tattoos. See, unlike the new world, the old one thinks of it as a disease. And not a very glamorous one for a dermatologist to specialize in."

The artist shook his head again, but rather than dwell on such a misguided attitude, he got back to work.

Framed medical certificates decorated a gleaming tile wall. Stainless steel instruments lined a counter. The white-coated dermatologist to whom they belonged looked at Tracer as if he were a festering sore.

"I've given you enough of my time."

"Look, my brother's a sawbones. I know the doctor-patient relationship is supposed to be sacred."

"And my time is very valuable."

"Can't you at least tell me whether you've treated a little girl recently?"

In answer, the doctor opened the door of his examining room. "I have patients waiting, Mr. Tracer."

Tracer exited into a hallway. He passed an office that was open to the hall and to a waiting room. He heard a nurse/receptionist sing-song to an old man:

"I keep telling you, Mr. Hernandez, Doctor can't see you if you've used up all your MediCal stamps."

A light bulb went off in Tracer's brain. He wheeled around.

The doctor turned with a start to see Tracer barging through the door. The seasoned detective held out a twenty-dollar bill.

"You think that can bribe me?"

Several minutes later the nurse/receptionist hurried down

the hall with a patient's chart. She knocked on the examining room door.

The doctor opened the door and took the chart. As he turned with it, flipping it open, Tracer came up on his shoulder. The physician snippily body-checked the detective from further curiosity.

"Fifty dollars bought you a 'yes,' but a medical history is extremely confidential."

"Listen, Doc, I don't care if you got your jollies doing a pelvic. I just want her address."

"I don't know what you think I am, but I would never perform an unnecessary procedure like that."

Tracer snapped his fingers. "That darned Hippocratic Oath."

"Yes, as a matter of fact. I have to be convinced you're doing this for Miss Mendoza's good."

Tracer harvested more green from his wallet. "Yeah, yeah, I'm a friggin' saint."

By nightfall Tracer was sitting behind the wheel of his car, observing an apartment house. A railed balcony provided access to a second floor of units. The building had gone through a dozen landlords, none of whom included repairs in the budget. Tracer leaned forward, reached under the seat and pulled out the Colt Commander. He got out of the car and slipped the pistol under the waistband of his trousers, then positioned his jacket to cover the grip.

A crying baby, a television at full volume and the beat of *banda* seeped from the building. As Tracer approached the thin walls, he didn't see a Lincoln Continental with tinted windows slowly cruising the street behind.

Bustamonte drove the Continental. Valasco and Montdragon sat beside him. Gauze swathed Cesar's hand; Band-Aids made Hector's face look like he had suffered an epileptic fit while shaving. They gaped at Tracer while in the back seat a young man kept his dark, designer glasses trained ahead. He wore a lightweight tailored suit, like a broker, but an open-necked shirt indicated that he had to answer to considerably fewer people.

Valasco, chins jiggling, turned to his boss.

"The *vato*! How could he know?" His hammy fist shook a wrinkled, bloodstained envelope at the man in the back seat. "We got the girl's letter to her *mamacita*. No one else did."

"Did anyone follow you?" asked the man softly.

Valasco looked to Montdragon for an answer. Montdragon moved his head from one side to the other.

"What about the airport? Were there extra police?"

"Just the security guards at the gate," said Bustamonte.

"Turn the car around."

Tracer glared at a downstairs apartment. A face peeked back from a parted curtain. After a moment the curtain fell closed. Tracer mounted the stairs.

On the balcony, Tracer walked past six pairs of doors and windows and stopped at the last door, apartment #12. The curtain over the window glowed dimly from the light of a low wattage bulb. Tracer knocked on the door. He waited a while, not long, then knocked again, much harder. The warped door shuddered, then winked open.

A girl's face appeared in the crack. She had heavy eyelids, vacant brown eyes and smeary makeup over smooth, childish features. Tracer had seen her in photographs and in his mind's eye, but he never imagined her loking so young.

"Jennifer Mendoza?"

"Not here."

She tried to push the door shut, but he placed his hand against it and shoved harder.

She had to step aside or get knocked over. Moving into the front room, Tracer saw that she may have looked young, but she was built like a woman and not wearing much to cover it—a Mickey Mouse T-shirt and a pair of panties. Her hand was bandaged. Her feet were dirty.

Ditto for the apartment. A door opened to the bedroom, where Lloyd French sat on the side of a sagging bed, facing him, hunched forward and wearing a pair of cotton briefs. They had been white three days ago and now sagged in the elastic parts. French looked nearly like a prisoner who had been sitting in a cell for a long, long time. The eyes should have been quick and roving, ready for a rapist or an inmate with a shiv. But French's were blank with a thousand-yard stare that wasn't taking much in. A brown cigarette dangled in his hand and gave off a stink that cleared Tracer's sinuses.

Tracer glanced away. An old Formica table in the dining nook, one whose cracks retained bits and pieces of years of meals, supported a scattering of toy balloons, a can of powdered baby formula, a kitchen scale and other implements, including the pot of gold at the end of hell—white powder in a large plastic bag.

Tracer's eyes flicked back to the girl.

"Get your stuff together, Jenny. I'm getting you out of here."

"Who the fuck are you?"

"What difference does it make? You got a junkie pusher who's using you, and that's putting it mildly. When he's through, he's gonna drop you like a bad habit. Maybe worse."

Her voice slurred and slipped; her face tried to pout. "We don't do heroin. We just get high sometimes. Everybody does. Some booze. Some grass. Some dust. Dope's for losers, man."

Tracer opened his hand toward French. "And that's the jackpot?"

"He loves me. He's just ozoned."

"Angel dust, huh? That's why this place smells like a burning garbage heap?"

"Who are you? Who said you can tell me what to do?"

"Your lover boy has already killed at least one person, and a couple more have OD'd on the crap you're selling."

"I didn't sell—" Her eyes smarted with tears, her mind with frustration. "I don't even know who you are. Why should I go with you? No one ever took me nowhere good."

A shrill, unearthly shriek killed any answer Tracer might have come up with. French leapt to his feet, ripping bedding up with him and stomping the floor at the same time.

"IT BURNED ME!"

He upended the bed looking for the cigarette. Then he turned toward the demons in the front room, his eyes in pinpoint focus.

"YOU BURNED ME!"

He charged Tracer with an intense, horrifying energy that belied his scrawny proportions and tackled him, throwing him to the floor. Clawing hands gripped Tracer's neck, and French slammed his head against Tracer's face, once, twice.

Tracer hammered his attacker's ears with his fists. French tried to bite. Tracer wedged a knee under French, jerked hard and rolled. French pitched into Jenny's legs. She tried to help him up, squealing with despair.

"Are you okay? Did he hurt you?"

As Jenny stumbled to get French to his feet, he punched her. Her scream drew more violence out of him, like squeezing a boil draws pus.

Dazed, Tracer jerked the Colt from his trousers. French slammed Jenny into a wall. Tracer cracked the gun butt against the back of French's head.

French turned slowly, his eyes glinting with fury. Tracer pistol-whipped his face.

French whirled in the direction of the blow, crashing
through the apartment's half open door, and sprawled out of
sight, his body thudding to the balcony.

Tracer turned to Jenny. Blubbering, she squatted against
the wall. Her legs gave way slowly, and she sank lower. Tracer was reaching to help her stand when he heard shuffling in
the doorway.

He turned to French, who was glowering at him. Tracer
instinctively slid back the action of the automatic, chamber-
ing the first round. He leveled the Colt at French, who didn't
move.

"I don't want to shoot."

French tottered into the room.

"Don't make me kill you."

French toppled forward. His face bounced off the floor.
His back sprouted a switchblade buried to the hilt.

Rueben Bustamonte stepped through the doorway, smiling like a Welcome Wagon Hostess.

"*Pendejo*! There is no need."

Bustamonte casually stepped over the body, closing in on
Tracer, and was followed into the apartment by Hector
Montdragon and Cesar Valasco.

Valasco eased closer to Jenny while Montdragon dropped
to one knee and prodded French's lifeless ribs with his finger. Montdragon slipped the knife out of French's back. His
eyes lit up at the soft sucking sound.

Jenny threw her hands to her face and began to sob hys-
terically.

Tracer had the firepower. He waved it from Bustamonte to
Montdragon and Valasco, then back again.

"Up against—" The words were barely audible, and Tracer
swallowed hard to irrigate the numbing dryness in his
throat. "Up against the wall!"

Valasco yanked Jenny into a smothering embrace. In an instant he had slammed the slabs of his arms under her slender limbs, cupped his hands around the back of her neck and shoved her head into her chest, a full Nelson that threatened in the next instant to snap her spinal cord. At least she stopped crying.

"No, *cabron*, I think not."

Bustamonte held out his hand for the gun, but Tracer kept it leveled on Bustamonte's midsection and bargained in desperation.

"I'll kill you first." He glanced to Montdragon and Valasco. "And you two, you'll get it next no matter what happens. Think about that."

Because Montdragon was in full auto trog mode, thought consisted of putting his back to Tracer and his knife to Jenny's chin. He lightly ran the blade to her pubis, hissing into Jenny's ear:

"I want to rearrange your mouth so that it goes all the way down to your belly button. Then you can smile so big and pretty."

Bustamonte looked over his shoulder like a doting mother to a naughty child, then sighed to Tracer, "The mind, it is a terrible thing to waste. He should have been a surgeon." The fingers of Bustamonte's upturned hand wriggled beseechingly. "The gun. Pleeeze, *chingaso*. And then we forget all the trouble you have caused us."

Tracer almost lowered the Colt, but from within someplace he heard a deadly calm voice that sounded like his:

"I told you to think. You get it first."

"But then the girl, she dies, too."

"You came for the heroin."

Bustamonte's eyes scanned the room and fell greedily on the kitchen table. He looked back at Tracer, sizing him up.

"No need for so many good people to die." He nodded to Montdragon.

Montdragon snatched the bag from the table. He jammed it under his shirt, then looked at Tracer, an idea festering in his cortex while his fist milked the handle of the knife.

"No," said Bustamonte. "You've had plenty of fun today."

Montdragon hurried out of the apartment.

If Bustamonte was afraid of the gun, he didn't show it. He put his back to Tracer and eased close to Jenny.

"We know who you are. But we got what we want. It is not good business to take more revenge than necessary, so you just forget all about this, hey, little one?"

The girl's breath rasped through her lips. Valasco tightened his grip, so she nodded.

Bustamonte stepped past her. Valasco followed him outside, first shoving Jenny hard forward, then lightly closing the door.

Jenny's stared wildly at French's body. Her breathing threatened to break with renewed sobs. Tracer felt like crying, too—with relief, utter and complete. His shirt was sopped with sweat and stuck to his torso. He breathed deeply and was reasonably calm when the girl's eyes dumbly rose to his.

"I don't know what happens to you next, Jenny. I just set out to find you. You got free will. It's not my job to change it."

"I—I—I don't even know you. I'm scared." She looked down at herself, a minor in a woman's body standing in her underwear with dirty feet.

"I'm going downstairs. There's a real ugly Dodge Dart parked down there. I'll give you ten minutes to decide. Then I'm going to the police. I'd like you to come with me, but that's up to you. Maybe you'd rather just wait here for the cops."

"I don't want to go to jail."

"They probably won't do anything to you. They may put you in protective custody for a while. Not long."

"I wrote to my mother. She—she put an ad in the *Free Press*. She loves me and wants me to come home."

Her eyes were full of pathetic hope. Tracer looked away to steel his mind with the truth, and when he looked back, he tried to make it as gentle as he could.

"She wanted to know where you were. I can't guarantee you anything about whether she'll want to see you or what after she finds out."

Tears welled over Jenny's eyes. No sound. Just the silent hurt of many years when there was no one to hear.

"But if she doesn't, there's still Mrs. Patronas. She's crazy about you. She'd probably take you back in a minute. But what I know for sure is, if you keep on the run, it won't be good. It's time to face up to life no matter what hand has been dealt. I don't know all the moves myself. I just know you've got those ten minutes. That's time enough to decide the next step." He turned to leave her to her decision.

"Who are you?"

"Just a private eye, honey. That's all."

He shut the door.

She looked from the door to the man on the floor, Lloyd French, a pusher of junk, her father's cellmate, a lover who beat her and made her do things she didn't want to do, but someone who had been there and had made her feel so very, very good.

Tracer walked down the stairway to ground level, where he stopped and looked toward the street.

A Lincoln Continental idled next to his Dodge. The back window was down, and an aristocratic face framed in Daniel Ortega glasses stared back at Tracer. The door opened.

Suddenly, Valasco plowed out of the shrubbery. He grabbed Tracer's arms and jerked them behind his back. Montdragon moved in to drive a fist into Tracer's gut, winding him, and Bustamonte stepped up to jerk the semi-auto from Tracer's pants.

A match flared, and the man in dark glasses caressed the flame against the end of his cigar. Puffing contentedly, he crossed the grass to Tracer.

"For us, it would be very bad for business if anyone—even the lowest slime on earth—ever thought that we were . . . easy." The dark glasses turned to Valasco, "Let him go." To Bustamonte, the man said, "Remind him."

Bustamonte backhanded Tracer with his own weapon.

Tracer dropped, not unconscious, but definitely out of action. He lay still, not daring to move.

The men nonchalantly return to the Continental. It glided away from the curb.

Tracer waited another moment before trying to bring his knees up under his body. What moved was a groan that started in his bowels and came out, "Jesus H. Christ . . ." His hand encircled a rotting garden hose. ". . . how 'bout a little protection next time?" Crawling, Tracer followed the hose to a faucet. He cranked on the tap, and a hammering pipe spit a rusty stream through the hose. Tracer pushed his bruised face into the cold water.

Feeling a little better, Tracer staggered to his feet. He stumbled to his car and flopped against the front fender. After a moment he turned and faced the apartment house, dropping his head back to drink in the air. When another moment passed, he glanced at his watch, looked toward the balcony again, then down at the ground. He closed his eyes, and he prayed for Jenny, realizing there was nothing else to offer her. He asked that Jenny be set free.

A siren wailing in the distance broke Tracer's concentra-

tion and his thoughts turned to his own next step. He faced
the fact that on his first case he'd had the wool pulled over
his eyes from the very beginning. Then he had gone deeper
into debt, endangered his entire family, blundered onto a girl
who didn't want to be rescued and nearly gotten killed twice
in the past fifteen minutes for his trouble. Funny how the
prospect of getting killed at the age of forty-five had a lot
more impact than it did at twenty-two, backed by artillery
and surrounded by young men who thought they were
immortal.

Tracer had withheld his best hunch from the authorities.
Not that he gave a good goddamn about them, but he tried to
imagine himself explaining to Amcheck and Simon Bolivar
Levin why French was dead. No great loss, except the murderers had heroin that would cause a lot more people a lot
more grief, and the DA could very well call Tracer's involve-
ment in that chain of events obstruction of justice.

Oh. And he had lost his gun. Great. That was like Lash
Laroux losing his whip.

As the siren warbled closer, Tracer tried to look on the
bright side. He did have his family. That was something in
today's world. And his health. The broken bicuspid . . . well,
there was at least one dentist back home who could take a
vacation on that. There would be a newspaper in the waiting
room. Maybe he'd see a good job listed in the classifieds.

Rubbing his jaw, Tracer looked up again.

Jenny walked down the stairs. She was dressed in the
clothes she ran away in. She paused, looking furtively as if
for an escape route, but finally she turned hesitantly in his
direction.

"Amen," Tracer said.

20

When Tracer first heard of Jennifer Mendoza, the cool, moldy leaf smell of fall in the air had been overtaken by warm, summer-like scents, and the approach of winter seemed to have been ransomed away. But early Sunday morning, when he returned from Los Angeles, the day dawned damp and chilly.

When Chris heard water running in the bathroom, she flew out of bed and threw open the door to the shower.

"John! Why didn't you wake me?"

He was shaving under the hot water, gingerly scraping the razor around a nasty-looking welt across his jaw. He felt miserable and looked at Chris in a way that reminded her of Brad reporting that he had been sent to the principal's office or Shorty running home in tears after a friend had scorned her. Without hesitation, Chris pulled off her nightgown and stepped into the shower to hug him.

Well, come to think of it, he didn't feel that bad.

But making love didn't turn out so great, either. It was mixed up with the all-night drive to get home, his aching tooth and Chris wanting him to hurry, so they could talk about what happened, which was the last thing he wanted to do.

"But you found Jenny! That's great."

"For who?"

"For her. For you."

"I was a sucker for the DA. Mark my words, Levin's going to try to make it look like *he* found her. He comes in with a whole army of cops and a signal corps of reporters right behind, and I get arrested in the stampede."

"Arrested?!"

"Aw, some storm trooper who thought it was a big drug raid slapped cuffs on me."

"Handcuffs?"

"And they hurt. They don't put 'em on loose, you know."

"Why were you handcuffed?"

"At first it was just the madcap whirl of the festivities. Then the body in the apartment had to be accounted for."

"Body!?"

"Chris, why are you repeating me?"

"Because I don't get it!"

"Get the kids. I don't want to re-live last night again."

Seated on the bed with their folks, Shorty and Brad treated Dad like a conquering hero, which so far was the best part of Tracer's day, especially since they hung on his every word, looking more and more like congenital mouth-breathers, while their mother interrupted with questions.

". . . so Jenny's upstairs crying her heart out over French. I'm downstairs trying to come to my senses. The bad guys have cleared out."

"Where?"

"How would I know that?"

"Go on."

"I'm trying."

"I thought Jenny was downstairs."

"Yeah, that's when Levin comes in like the 7th Cavalry. He's got cops armed to the teeth, and I don't know how many TV people shooting away with their video cameras."

"You're going to be on TV?!"

"No way. They can't use any of what I saw. This was supposed to be a big publicity stunt for the DA, but there was no big raid—just a little girl and little ol' me. Jenny looks like she's going to run for the hills when this 4 x 4 screeches to a halt. It belongs to the LA Sheriff's Department. The doors pop open all at once, and Jenny starts yelling that I betrayed her. Meanwhile, I'm trying to tell the Keystone Cops to go after the Continental. Red and blue lights are flashing, and there's . . . It's like a miniature sun coming at us from some kind of crazy galaxy. Turns out to be the light for the camcorder. And silhouetted in front is this reporter who's babbling about being on the spot when *Nuestra Familia* goes down. Levin had to be pumping her full of hot air. No telling what she thinks now."

"What did you say to her?"

"*Say* to her? I'm trying to figure out why she's all crouched down. Major cringe, y'know. Well, it's because she's in the line of fire of Amcheck and that Navy blimp he keeps making excuses for, the lady cop who hates my guts. Nothing personal. Just me."

"She had her gun out?"

"She's nothing compared to the LA deputy who picked them up at the airport and dropped 'em all in my lap."

"How did they know where you were? Come to think of it, how did those awful men know where Jenny was?"

"Mom, let him just tell the story!"

"The return address on a letter Jenny sent to her mom. But I'll get to that. Right now I'm looking at a deputy who doesn't know who's friend or foe. Probably thinks he's gonna get promoted if Levin's scheme pans out. And this reporter is babbling on about gangsters, remember? You talk about a conditioned reflex, the deputy looks like Pavlov's dog with rabies. So Levin has to jump in."

"To keep him from shooting you?"

"Chris, if he'd shot me, would I be here now, humiliated? The reporter is starting to shove her mike into my face. Levin looks like he's reaching out to strangle me because I'm the last person in the world he wants her to talk to, but he probably doesn't want to get shot in the back, either, so he just tackles her."

"He actually threw her to the ground?!"

"He kind of wrestled her aside. 'Don't get hurt,' he was yelling."

"What did you say?"

"I said, 'Simon, please, tell everyone to take a giant step back, or you'll scare Jenny away.'"

"You had time to say all that?"

"I used the 'A' word and the 'F' word. I think they got the point."

Brad dropped his head, thinking how the combination worked. Shorty whispered, "You have to say 'you' first, then 'F,' then 'A'."

Their mother asked, "What happened to the deputy?"

"Okay. Levin's waltzing with the reporter, telling her he doesn't want her to get hurt. Her cameraman is in the same dance because they're attached by an umbilical cord. The blimp—I have to give her credit for compassion: she makes a beeline to Jenny. 'You're safe! He can't hurt you any more!'"

"'He'! Who's 'he'?"

"At first I thought she was talking about French. I yell, 'He's dead!' Someone says, 'Who's dead?' I don't know who's shouting at me. Everyone, I guess. I don't have eyes in the back of my head, so I can't see what exactly happens next, but I can hear the blimp and Jenny for the next three hours or so, moaning and groaning to each other."

"Three hours!"

"It felt that way because the dep took it into his head to arrest me."

"Didn't you tell him who you were?"

"Yes, of course. I said, 'Sir, I'm a private investigator. You shouldn't do this. There are some bad guys in a Continental, and it would be more intelligent if you radioed for a road-block instead of trying to prove your manhood with me.' Or words to that effect."

"I see. So he arrested you?"

"No one got around to reading my rights until four hours later."

"*Four hours*?!"

"When you're face down on the ground with your hands behind your back, and your shoulders are getting wrenched out of the sockets, it feels like a long time."

"What happened to Amcheck?"

"My last good view of him, he was jumping around like a frog. Left, right, front, back. As far as he knows, we're the Marines at Chosin Reservoir, surrounded by the 200,000 Chinese volunteers. I'm trying to tell him, 'They're gone. Check upstairs. Please get this gentleman off my back.'

"Now I got this dep's knee in my back. He twists on the manacles, stops the blood flow to my hands, but I can distinctly hear Amcheck say, 'He's with the girl.' So I'm thinking, Hey, that's cool, it's over. But nothing happens. The dep radios for backup. Amcheck and Levin clomp upstairs, and they're up there for six hours."

"Six hours? *How* fast did you drive home?"

"I have a toothache from where I got clobbered. I got the other side of my face chewing dirt. It *feels* like a lifetime. Then there's the mini-Andromeda blinding me again, with the reporter, who's been yak-yak-yak with the blimp, asking me how long I've known Jenny. You know, just how friendly are we?"

"'Friendly'?"

"Like in 'Salinas Man Found with Teen in LA Love Nest.'"

"Things just happen to you, don't they?"

"Are you kidding? It's what saved me. 'Cause by then, Levin's back. He can see that the 'Story of the Century' and five round-trip tickets to cover it are going to make him look like a bigger fool than I feel. We start swapping accusations about who screwed whose case. The news team has a pretty good idea by now that the major drug bust and their ticket to a bigger media market are going south. But there's still a body upstairs, so maybe they haven't lost everything. The reporter starts asking Levin if I killed Jenny's lover in a jealous rage.

"And wham, bam, thank-you, ma'am, Levin is suddenly congratulating me for saving a runaway from dope crazed gang members. He's got to bend down because I'm still on the ground; then he's up and moving off to exercise media control. Any day now, I'll be free. I can hear Levin lament the lack of funding that forced his office to use freelance investigators; then he adds a hearty, 'Now if you promise not to touch anything, let's go up and see the good work I asked this citizen to do.'

"They taped the body?"

"Or Amcheck going through the ice box for something to

eat to tide him over. Lloyd French's dead body isn't gonna make this one look any better. Believe me, the only good feeling I have about this is that son of a bitch can't—Sorry."

"That's okay," Brad said. Shorty took hold of her father's hand.

"Levin can't get any publicity. The tape the cameraman took would have to be cut to shreds to make any sense. Ha! Sense?"

"Anyway, you were let out the handcuffs after Levin congratulated you."

"Yeah, like twelve hours later."

"No, tell us really."

"Half an hour maybe. The dep has canceled back up, but he's radioed in forensic. The blimp calls him over, and they take their sweet time, going blah, blah, blah with Jenny for her statement."

"Couldn't you just explain to him?"

"I already did. I explained that if he were in my platoon I'd encourage the men to frag him."

"Well, John, if you act difficult, what do you expect?"

"Oh, I don't know. 'Thank you for helping us. Thank you for putting your life on the line. Sorry about the SS treatment.'"

"He just left you on the ground?"

"Well, it was a little more complicated than that. By now, most of the neighborhood was out to see what the second set of sirens meant. There had been no gunfire. No one they know was dead. To them it was like a big party. I could hear some of them whispering about the Zodiac Killer. How folks from the 'hood were the ones who ran Ramirez down and held him until police arrived. I'm not sure what it meant, but it didn't sound good for me. Then Levin came back and put his face close to mine.

"He said that we were out of his jurisdiction. And when he first saw French—because there was no one else around, just Jenny and me—he thought, well, I must have killed him in self-defense. But French had been stabbed in the back, see? So Levin began wondering whether I'd have to cop to involuntary manslaughter. 'John, I told the press that it's only two to our, and I'm sure the sentence will be suspended in your case.'"

"He seriously thought you could be charged with a crime? But he must have known you couldn't have done it!"

"'Just give me a good story,' he says. 'The kid claims you broke in with your gun drawn and provoked a fight, so just give us something slightly reasonable. I'm not picky.'"

"Jenny said that about you?"

"Hurts, doesn't it?"

"That . . . scamp."

"Maybe, maybe not. I couldn't see where she was. I could barely hear her voice. From her point of view, everything must have seemed very confusing. I can't prove it, but there's another possibility, too: Levin was trying to set me up. Like, 'Your buddy in the next room says you robbed the liquor store while he just waited in the car; what do you say?'"

"What did you say?"

"Not much. I was experiencing a major attitude adjustment. What if Anne Walker was right about Jenny being wild and ungrateful? Her boyfriend was dead, and I seemed to have set off that chain of events. She didn't know the three nasty boys had been looking for her before I ever came along. What if she was worried that it didn't look good that she's associated with those types, her jailbird boyfriend and drug dealing? What if she had some crazy notion about protecting her old man? Her mother? Her sweet little self?

"Anyway, forensic arrives, and Levin gets the deputy back

over to talk to me. Finally, he's going to listen to reason. Oh, sure. He reads me my rights, and Levin says, 'Let's go some- place private.' The crazy sun's out again, see? So we sit in the 4 x 4."

"*Then* did the deputy take the handcuffs off?"

"Yeah, because Levin has promised to vouch for me. Well, I tell the dep the whole story—name, where I live, what I'm doing in his stomping ground. I tell him about French. I tell him that I'm not very good with a knife. I open my mouth and wriggle my tooth and show him where one of the goons had hit me with something."

"Your own gun?"

"I wasn't born yesterday, Chris. I knew that Jenny had said something about my .45, and there was a distinct possibility that she hadn't said anything nice about it or me. And so when the deputy got around to the gun, I said, 'Gun? What gun? You patted me down. Did I have a gun?'"

"You mean, you didn't tell the whole truth?"

"The whole truth is that carrying a concealed weapon without a permit is generally considered a crime. Even if you're trying to save your life with it or protect someone else. I didn't want to become part of some show trial for the gun control nuts, just so that a sensible jury could let me off."

"Dad's right," said Shorty.

"And he only asked a question," said Brad. "He didn't have the gun anymore."

"Okay," sighed Chris, "okay."

"I just wanted to get the whole thing over with, so I could get home quickly. Anyway, I got real nice and cooperative, and mentioned 'false arrest' and 'police brutality' only a cou- ple of times."

Chris shook her head.

"The dep gets that kind of down-his-nose look, like I'm the

scum of the earth, and he wants to make sure I'm available for further questioning if necessary. Levin, who's been acting like my defense attorney, swears that I'll be available any time, and he'll personally make sure I don't leave the state. Then the dep leaves us, and Levin suggests that maybe it would be best if I just said *adios* to the crime scene.

"And I say, 'Thank you very much, and what are you going to do besides make sure I don't talk to the press?'"

"It sounds like he was trying to help you."

"Maybe. I wasn't in the best of moods. But I wanted to know what he was going to do with Jenny."

"But why?" asked Shorty. "Dad, after everything that happened, she doesn't sound like she cared about you at all."

"That's her problem. Curiosity's mine. So Mr. Levin gave me the order of battle. He wanted to fly Jenny out of there as fast as he could. He wanted to get her cleaned up. He wanted to take her to her mother."

Chris asked, "He took her to Anne Walker? Would Anne even want to see her?"

"I suggested that he take her to Mrs. Patronas in Salinas. I told him she was the foster mother who really cared about Jenny."

"That's a great idea."

Tracer stretched and yawned.

"Oh, honey, do you want to get some sleep?"

"I can't sleep." Instead, he explained what Simon Bolivar Levin had told him about Annie Mae Walker, how she had finally received a letter from Jenny and how the men who had broken into their home hadn't given up on following Anne, whose run-in with them was nearly fatal. While they set out for the return address, Anne told the police where her daughter was, Dr. Richard Fencoe standing manfully at her bedside, apparently ready to marry an instant family. Tracer

couldn't guess how the reunion orchestrated by Levin had
gone, but he intended to drop by Carmel Community Hospital and present his out-of-pocket expenses for affecting such
a warm and fuzzy moment.

Chris said she was going to make breakfast. She left the
bedroom, looking back as she turned into the hall. What she
saw was her husband with his shirt off, propped up in bed,
one arm around their daughter, who snuggled into his shoulder, and the other arm around their son, whose head was tilted back to ask, "Do you think it was worth it?"

"When you do the right thing, it doesn't matter."

What Tracer saw was an anxious look in his wife's face. It
wasn't supposed to matter, but it did. Very much. The one
she held most dear had come very close to dying.

The sun couldn't break the overcast that hung over Carmel
Community Hospital. Tracer drove into the lot, left his car
dripping brake fluid and hunched into the wind that had
come up.

The door of Anne's suite was ajar, and Tracer could smell
the room before he got there. There appeared to be more cut
flowers than at a funeral. Helium-filled balloons with bright
"Get Well"s bobbed from the furniture. Soothing sounds
wafted from the TV's closed-circuit music channel. The head
of Anne's bed was cranked up, and she rested with her eyes
closed, her face serene and extremely beautiful without
makeup.

Tracer coughed.

She opened her eyes. "John." The tone was soft, not
unfriendly, but there was always that guarded look.

"May I come in?"

"How can I stop you?"

He heard someone move behind the closed bathroom door as he came closer to the bed.

"I'm embarrassed. I must look a mess."

"Can we talk?"

"About what?"

"First . . ." From his jacket pocket he took out the photo of Jenny that Anne had given him. ". . . this is yours."

"Thank you for remembering." She lifted a weak hand to take the photo, then turned it face down on her bosom. "Dick! Mr. Tracer's here."

A voice came from behind the bathroom door. "Be right out."

"My fiancé knows all about you. What he needs to know, anyway."

Neither Tracer nor Anne had been open books to each other, but of what he had revealed, Tracer wondered what there was left to conceal.

Off his look, she said, "I don't know want him to know I that I fired you."

The toilet could be heard flushing.

"That brings me to another reason I'm here." From his inside pocket Tracer produced an invoice that he had asked Chris to type. "These are my expenses." He began to read, "Twenty dollars for birth certificate. Thirty dollars flyers for missing person. Fifty dollars for a bribe. One thousand, two hundred and seventy car miles times thirty-five cents a mile."

"That pile of rust you drive," she teased, "it should be more like twenty cents a mile."

"Glass and installation at $428." He looked up. "I got three estimates. That's the best."

"Who broke the windshield?"

"Sliding door in my house. Friends of Felix."

The playful mood left. "Don't mention that name again. No need to irritate Dick more than he has been."

"$200 to cap my tooth."

"Mr. Levin mentioned you were hurt. Was personal injury covered by our contract?"

"No."

"I should have taken the daily rate." Anne nodded to the wheeled tray that could slide over her bed at meal times. It held a single rose in a small vase, a box of tissues and a teddy bear with "I love you" on its T-shirt. Tracer put the invoice next to the teddy bear.

"Anything else?"

"Yeah. Jenny."

Dr. Fencoe appeared from the bathroom. His ruddy face was pulled into a professional smile. Right hand out, he walked straight up to Tracer.

"Mr. Tracer?"

"John, this is Dr. Fencoe."

Fencoe pumped Tracer's hand. Fencoe's was damp and pink from scrubbing. "We have so much to thank you for. Words can't express it."

"We were just talking about whether dollars could," said Anne.

"Oh," said Fencoe, "I'll take care of the bill."

"Just expenses," said Tracer.

"Look what else he brought." Anne turned the picture of Jenny over.

"We'll have it framed. What a sweet face. Just like her mother's."

Anne smiled. Tracer still couldn't see the resemblance.

Fencoe was getting into home and hearth. "We'll have to have one of the three of us taken all together."

"That will be so nice."

"When did you see her?" asked Tracer.

"It was very late," Anne said.

"Two a.m.," Fencoe said.

"Dick's been staying in the hospital," Anne said. "The District Attorney brought her in, so Dick had the thrill of meeting her."

"Mr. Levin is a fine, fine man to go to so much trouble on our behalf," Fencoe added.

Anne raised her hand, pointing. "Because there were so many people, Jenny kind of hung back against that wall. She had her hands folded in front of her frock."

"She looked like a little girl at a recital."

"Yes! So beautiful, so shy. I really couldn't see, there were so many tears in my eyes."

"There you go again." Fencoe pulled a tissue from the box on the wheeled tray. It made the "I love you" bear fall over. Fencoe dabbed his fiancee's eyes. She touched his hand.

"I diagnosed immediately that the poor kid was frightened," Fencoe continued. "When's the last time she saw you, darling?"

"Oh," Anne lied, "several times last month."

"But not in the hospital, right?" Fencoe looked at Tracer. "I reached out for her. I said, 'Jennifer, your Mom's going to be back to normal in no time.'

"And I said, 'Jenny, please meet my dear, sweet Dick.' Jenny's eyes lit up like Christmas trees, and she smiled right at him."

"Well, I thought she was a little nervous."

"Oh, no, she warmed right up to you."

"First, though, she came to the bed, and she said . . ." Fencoe looked at Anne to allow her to complete the magic moment.

"She put her hand on my shoulder. She must have known

that a hug would have hurt me. 'Hi, Anne,' she said." Anne sniffed and smiled. "She's always called me by my first name. It's kind of cute, don't you think?"

Tracer suppressed a shudder. "Where is she now?"

"And I must say," Dr. Fencoe was saying, "she had very good things to say about you, Mr. Tracer."

Tracer didn't know if that was true. He didn't know whether to feel good about it if it was.

"Because Dick's staying here until I can leave, Mr. Levin thought that Jenny should spend a few days with Mrs. Patronas."

"I'm really looking forward to getting to know Jennifer," said Fencoe.

"She's a wonderful girl," Anne said. "You'll love her."

Fencoe kissed his fiancé's forehead. "If it's half as much as I love you, darling, we'll be the happiest family on earth."

She gave him a sly smile. "And we're going to give her a brother and a sister, aren't we?"

He smiled back, then turned to Tracer. "Anne needs her rest. May I walk you to your car?"

On the way through the hospital and into the lot, Dr. Fencoe said that he wished Anne had told him about her daughter from the beginning.

"Like on the first date?"

Fencoe said that Anne's past was so horrendous that it had really taken courage to hire Tracer.

"If I only knew sooner how horrendous, I might have been more helpful."

Fencoe said that he and Anne had great hopes for Jennifer's future. There was a finishing school in Switzerland that could open a whole new world for her.

"Well, that sure beats the hell out of hanging around the house, doesn't it?"

Fencoe gave him a curious look, then said that he knew Tracer had been paid off, but if there was anything he could do, anything at all, just let him know.

"Doctor, if I ever need my heart cut out, I'm going to let you do it."

Dr. Fencoe said that he was a cardiologist, not a cardiac surgeon, and as he tried to explain the difference, Tracer slapped him on one shoulder as if to build his confidence.

"Aw, Doc, you'll learn to be good at it."

Driving off, Tracer thought about heading straight for the Patronas'. He had a photograph to return there. Maybe there would be a chance to take Jenny aside and tell her . . .

Tell her what, he wondered as he accelerated into the final stretch home. To never go home? To stay where she was? They didn't know each other; he didn't have the right to say. Maybe if he knew her, he wouldn't like her. Maybe he wouldn't have been so certain that he needed to set out to find her.

He decided to mail the photograph to Mrs. Patronas. He could see it enshrined on the woman's television set, reminding her to at least call from time to time. Maybe with nothing to hide, Jenny would let Mrs. Patronas keep track of her life. Maybe Jenny would even come back.

A light on the dashboard blinked that the engine was overheating.

The gathering wind broke yellowed leaves from the trees, set them rattling down the streets at Creekside to gather in bunches that boys like Brad would have to rake, fruitlessly, because they would only blow back in their faces. For Brad, though, it wasn't so bad because his dad was working alongside, swearing under his breath at the dark clouds rolling over the hills. The clouds piled up on each other all after-

noon, promising needed rain to farmers and threatening
Tracer with having to climb up to the roof and check all the
gutters for another year. A steady drizzle set in at dusk, as
unabated as the ringing in Tracer's ears from all the aspirin
he was taking to ease his aching jaw. He was sure he would
topple from the roof if he went up.

Upon returning from the hospital, Tracer had announced
that he intended to look for normal work. Chris had acted as
if that didn't matter anymore. For his sake. For hers, she had
proved gratitude and devotion by attacking the dentist's
answering service until the dentist himself phoned back to
reiterate that the very earliest he could see her husband was
Monday afternoon.

Tracer held the ladder steady as his son clambered down
from cleaning the gutters. Tracer was so tired he felt he could
sleep forever, but the pain in his mouth and his general
restiveness made him think he'd go crazy if he didn't keep occupied. Last night's end in Los Angeles had been so humiliating
that his first impulse on returning to the bosom of his family
was to kick Dog. Instinctively, the animal didn't even bark.
Then Tracer remembered he hadn't seen it all day today.

"Where's Dog?"

"Hiding."

"Good."

Realizing sea changes were afoot, a somber and solicitous
Shorty had brought extra pillows and a blanket downstairs,
and made a nest for her father on the family room couch. She
now sat on the floor, scrunched under his arm to watch the
Sunday evening news from New York City. He'd missed the
local news lead-in, knowing for an embarrassed certainty
that any story about last night would be a freak show and
probably wouldn't even make the broadcast. Tracer wanted
to watch the national news only to confirm his general feel-

ing that the whole world was racing downhill in a luge with brakes out and steering gone. When Brad asked whether he could change channels during a commercial, Shorty told him to crawl off and die. Instead, her brother went to see what kind of vegetable their mother would be forcing on them at dinner.

The television anchor announced that the network's broadcast would end with a heartwarming human interest story from California.

Shorty gasped, "Oh, my God," as tape of her father flashed on screen. "Daddy's on *Cops!*" she screamed toward the kitchen.

Indeed, the six edited seconds of Tracer's appearance looked as it had been taken from the Fox Television reality series. It also looked as if he were working with the police, directing traffic in some kind of weird dumbshow. He criss-crossed his arms in front of his face. Holding a forearm to his eyes, he gestured wildly to the apartment and seemed to be barking orders at the deputy, whose weapon was strangely angled at his midsection. There was no sound, just narration that identified him as "John Tracer, a private investigator from Los Angeles."

Chris and Brad dashed into the room.

"Who's from Los Angeles?"

"You're not from Los Angeles!"

They briefly saw Jenny being held by the shoulders by Amcheck—just the back of the plainclothes sergeant could be seen—who was identified as Jenny's "step-father."

Tracer was sitting up, mouth open, face red with the embarrassment that comes from basking in glory, no matter how brief or incorrect. Dog jumped into his lap. His wife, his daughter and his son talked all at once, shushed each other, then squealed in overlapping voices:

"What was that?"

"But you said this would never be on the air!"

"What was that? Will we see you again?"

"What did you say?"

"Shh! I can't hear!"

"What was that?"

"You didn't tell us *that!* Why didn't you tell us that?!"

"Because the whole thing's been staged!"

The scene had shifted to Levin kicking in the door of the French apartment, then to French's body being gurneyed onto the balcony by paramedics. Intercut were scenes of Levin issuing sound bites, casually seated in front of the skeleton in his Salinas office. Apparently he had been close to cracking an international drug ring when the opportunity to rescue one of its victims presented itself.

"Gosh," Chris gasped, "we sound like we're with Elliot Ness and *The Untouchables!*"

The story's narrator then became visible as the on-site reporter witnessed the tearful reunion of "Jennifer Walker" and her mother, who looked radiant in a flower-bedecked hospital room.

Then, against the hospital's hanging gardens, the reporter held her mike to Dr. Fencoe, who from the front looked less wrinkled than from the back. "What can a fellow say? I love her like my very own."

Thunder boomed outside as the end credits of the newscast rolled. The phone began ringing. The family rushed toward it, hoping to save Tracer the trouble, who got stiffly to his feet and wanted to be bothered.

Eddie Durand made it a quick proud-to-know-you. Other people wanted to know why the news had mixed up where John lived. All the while, Tracer secretly wondered whether a potential client would try to contact him, maybe via the network or even Levin's office after the prospect got tired of wild goose chases through LA Information. Fat chance he'd ever get through when Chris's mother, calling from an RV park in Spanish Fork, Utah, needed fifteen minutes of assurance that Chris and the children were just fine and that, no, her son-in-law wasn't completely out of his mind. Then the phone fell silent.

Tracer grew morose, aspiring only for congratulations from his own family. If Uncle Mike were holding up his usual bar, he wouldn't have known. Brother Pete was cavorting in San Diego. Midway through dinner, Tracer got up to call his mother and sister in Susanville. Like a lot of people, they claimed to never watch television. For once Tracer believed it. But they could at least talk.

Eerily, a caller was already on the line when he picked up the handset, an instance of the delay between a transmitter's ring and the receiver's impulse.

"Short Dogs," the voice rasped.

"What?"

"Should of told me you were undercover."

"Riley?"

"She couldn't leave 'em alone."

"What are you talking about?"

"I'll bury the hatchet about my peach tree if you can find that she-devil."

Tracer glanced at Chris, who was turned to him with a questioning look. "Who is it?" He put his hand over the mouthpiece.

"Client."

Acknowledgments

Tracer, Inc. really goes back to a mother who read to us and a dad who preferred telling his own stories about Rocky Marciano. Apparently the Champ palled around with Little Red Goofnut, a kid who was younger than my older brother Dan but not as young as I. Then one day Dan, who would rather have been going to Fenway Park to see the Red Sox play, escorted me on the bus for my first look at a public library, where he helped me pick out *The Burnt Hill Mystery*, whose author, I'm sorry to say, I no longer remember.

Years later in Los Angeles it was Jean McEvoy, a friend and fellow screenwriter, who first listened to my thoughts about Tracer and a plot corner I had shoved him into. Mac put up an imaginary flyer—"This child is missing . . . a kid, any kid"—and that's how Tracer got back into the fray.

I still had to produce a manuscript, so I completed the first draft while eating my mother out of house and home. While she pointed out spelling and grammatical errors another long-time friend, Sid Iwanter of Fox Children's Network, read the draft, insisting that I do it again.

My wife and two children put up with six more "again"s. With this novel, as with my other writing, they kept my feet on the ground when my mind was spinning off in all directions.

Robert Hatton, a fraternity brother who became an assistant DA in Monterey County, actually prosecuted the cases mentioned by my fictional Simon Bolivar Levin. Hence rose a merry fight between art, such as it is, and life. On the one hand, Bob is a fine raconteur whose tales bear repeating. On the other, Levin and Tracer aren't remotely like anyone either of us knows; the story herein is not dinner conversation; and so Tracer, being in hot pursuit, just didn't care to hear "The Greatest Alibi in the World" or how ingesting evidence weighed heavily in the insanity defence of "The Mad Crapper of Pacific Grove." If success smiles and there are subsequent novels, perhaps the patient reader will find Tracer taking a little more time to listen.

Bob also referred me to a Carmel police detective, whose name I can no longer find in my notes, who patiently offered data about runaways.

Major Geoff Blanchard, US Army, provided source material on the 25th Infantry Division's Tay Ninh campaign in the form of a book written by Colonel Duke Wolf, a friend of Geoff's father, another soldier. Being polite, Geoff didn't comment after he read the draft on which I was then working.

Robert Boock, an ex-Marine, a family man, and a private investigator in the Sacramento area specializing in missing children, put up with a couple of hours of phone calls for the sake of a mutual friend, Marty Conn, who kept saying,

"Boock really *does* this stuff." Which is probably why I never offered to let him read what I was really writing.

Happily unconcerned with how I might twist what he gave me, Paul Jenkins turned over his study materials from an investigators' school he was attending in Orange County, commenting only that tailing someone in a car "is not easy."

That was also the gist of what Doug, a young man who had been reared in the foster care system, had to say about his experiences. However, I met unflagging volunteers and compasionate foster parents as well who gave me the good side of the system. They are too numerous to mention.

Michael Gama, a bilingual advertiser out of Portland, checked the Spanish and the English and didn't stop there. He offered special insights into characterizations, descriptions, action and politics.

During the final re-write I enjoyed two neighbors, Cissy and Jim Kime, who, like many people before them, offered advice, prayers, encouragement and a shot or two of good whiskey. Through Cissy and her mother, Frances Charles Nelson, the manuscript arrived on the desk of Suzanne Kirk Tomlinson, the executive editor of Scribner's. Suzanne graciously read the manuscript and said that she would take a chance on this Hollywood scriptwriter turned novelist. Then she went to work to make sure *Tracer, Inc.* didn't read so much as if it had been written by a dyslexic whose spelling is as skewed as his thoughts.

The finished product, then, was built on a lot of good backs, none of which should be held responsible for my weaknesses. All agencies, officials and other characters in the book were first cut from imagination, with the facts, such as I understood them, then molded to fit or discarded entirely. There are large parts of Tracer's world that you can't get to with any known map. As for the places that do exist in the here and now, I apologize to residents and passers-by, owners and patrons, if my subjective impressions, colored for the sake of entertainment, have in any way offended the views of those who know better.